# SKY CHILD

T. M. BRENNER

Copyright T. M. Brenner 2014, 2016

Cover Illustration by T. M. Brenner

ISBN: 069231007X

ISBN-13: 978-0692310076

Third Printing

Also by T. M. Brenner

*Luminaries*

*Clandestined*

*Clandestined: Dark Times*

Books in the Sky Child series

*Sky Child*

*Sky Machine*

*Sky War*

SKY CHILD

For Riley and Jordan

# 1

I can hear water dripping, which tells me that the rains have set in, and they may not end for a few days. I push myself upright, out from under the tattered blanket I use to fight off the cold of the Crag. The branches I've tied together into a makeshift bed creak beneath my weight. Off in the distance I can hear the howling of the wind, blowing across the face of the cave that is both my home, and my prison.

Sleeping next to me are my brothers, Jet and Flot. They aren't really my brothers, but I call them that because I look after them as if they were. I watch their blankets move as they breathe. It amazes me how young they look when they are asleep, but how old they seem when they are awake. Flot still sucks his thumb while he's asleep, which is something the new ones stop doing when they are smaller.

I fold up my blanket and set it down on the bed. It takes a moment to change into my clothes. I try my best to be quiet, so that I don't wake up the twins. I grab a glowing stick to carry with me, since parts of the Crag can be very dark. After passing by some of the smaller rooms inside the Crag, I reach the Great Fire.

Moss is there, one of the gray ones, making sure that the Great Fire never goes out. He takes turns with a few of the other gray ones, watching it, keeping it alive. We are taught that if the Great Fire dies, so do we. No way to cook food, or to heat water, or to protect ourselves from the black flyers that live above us in the Crag.

Moss nods his head. His long, stringy gray hair falls off his shoulders. I put the tip of my glowing stick into the Great Fire, stealing some of its life. It never seems to mind that I take from it, but give nothing back in return. Maybe the Great Fire is just happy to have people to watch over it, so it doesn't mind sharing. I smile at Moss, thanking him for the light and warmth then make my way to the entrance of the Crag.

It takes a few moments of creeping past those who are still asleep to get to the mouth of the cave. I look up and see an endless cloud-filled sky. That's how most of my days are; full of darkness and rain. Thankfully, the ground outside the Crag is more interesting to look at. Rocks covered in shades of green. Fields of grass and clover. It would be beautiful, if it wasn't so dangerous.

The sound of footsteps echo behind me. I can tell by the shuffling of his feet that it's Flot. I turn to look at him. The dim light of the hallway's glowing sticks makes him seem smaller than he really is. His sun-colored face and dark brown hair make it difficult to see him in the shadows.

"Over here," I say.

"Sam, what are you doing?" asks Flot.

"I'm just watching the rain. It's going to make the hunt more difficult today."

"You've hunted in the rain before, and you've always come back with something," says Flot.

"That's true, but do you see those dark gray clouds there?"

"Yes."

"Those are the type of clouds that bring sky fire."

"I don't like sky fire," says Flot.

"I don't either. But without it, we wouldn't have the Great Fire."

"Is that where it came from? The gray ones say that it was a gift from the Sky Gods."

"It was, but that's how they gave it to us."

"Oh," says Flot. "So when are we going to hunt?"

"After breakfast, just like always," I say.

"Can't we go now?"

"Don't you want to wait for Jet?" I ask.

"No, not really."

I laugh.

"Well, we're going to wait for him, and the rest of the people going out for the hunt."

"But I'm ready now," says Flot.

"We have to wait for everyone else, because it's dangerous outside. You know that. There are wolves with big sharp teeth, and dragons that will burn your skin right off!"

"I don't believe in dragons."

"That's just because you haven't seen one yet," I say. "You've only been hunting for a few snows."

"Have you ever seen one?" asks Flot.

I worry that if I tell Flot the truth, it might scare him. But I know that I should, because it might keep him safe.

"Yes, I've seen one."

"What was it like?"

I think back to all the people that died that day. The blood covered grass. The smell of burnt flesh. The screams of panic as people ran, trying to find somewhere to hide.

There was a large group of us, and we were out in the fields hunting deer. I had reached enough snows that I was finally able to go hunting with the group, but I was still very new to it. My sling was ready, aimed at a deer, when the dragon came.

Fire rained down from the sky, burning some of our people. One of the gray ones, Lagan, ordered us to scatter. Running as fast as I could, I hid between a pair of large rocks, out of sight of the dragon.

"I can still remember what its roar sounded like: deep and booming, like sky fire. I only saw it for a moment. Its scales were shiny, just like in the legends, and its wings were massive. The dragon had a pair of glowing eyes that still haunt me in my nightmares. It was terrible," I say. "It burned half of us with its fire. I hit it with a rock from my sling, and it

3

bounced off like it was nothing."

"I thought you were good with your sling," says Flot.

"I am good, but the dragon was very strong. There was no way to fight it. Many of us hid. Once the dragon flew off, those of us that survived buried what was left of the bodies."

"What did the dragon want? Why did it attack you?" asks Flot.

"We don't know for sure. Legends tell us that dragons steal great treasures, and keep them hidden and protected. The dragon that attacked us didn't seem to want anything from us. It didn't take our food, or our clothes, or our weapons. It only took our lives. Some believe that it was just protecting its territory, because we were hunting in an area we'd never hunted in before. We don't go to that place anymore, even to see where our people were killed."

"Why don't we figure out a way to kill the dragons?" asks Flot.

"Well, we haven't seen any since. If we hunt in the same fields, they don't bother us," I say.

"Maybe someday you'll find a way. Maybe someday you'll catch a dragon, and then we can eat dragon meat forever!"

"I don't think it would taste very good, but maybe we could find the cave it lives in, and keep the treasures it's stolen," I say, smiling.

"Maybe we could live there. Maybe it's better than the Crag!"

"The Crag isn't too bad," I lie. "It's kept us alive."

"But some of the gray ones are bad. They hurt us, and threaten us, and sometimes one of the new ones disappears. I think some of the gray ones kill them."

"Not all gray ones are bad," I say.

"I like Moss, and Lagan, and Charm, but I hate Chaff. His sons, Sickle and Scythe, both hurt me. Sometimes they knock me over and laugh. Sometimes they kick at me, and sometimes they even take my food."

Surprise becomes anger, and I realize that I've curled my hands into fists.

"I... I'm sorry. I didn't know that. I will talk with them," I say.

"No! That will make it worse! Promise me Sam that you won't talk to them!"

I don't know what to say. Threatening Sickle and Scythe might stop them from bullying Flot, but I've seen murder in both, and I worry that if they find out that Flot told me, they might kill him instead.

When I was a new one, Sickle and Scythe would beat me. Sometimes they would take me into one of the long caves that make up the Crag, tie me to a rock then punch my face or my stomach. Sometimes they would just yell at me, or try to scare me until I cried. I was so small then compared to how I am now. I've seen many more snows since then, and Sickle and Scythe know that if they tried to hurt me now, I could protect myself.

Decisions like this are impossible, because both choices are bad. The most important thing though is to stay alive, so I must continue letting Sickle and Scythe think that no one knows they've been torturing my brother. I will get revenge for Flot though, and until I do, I will keep a closer eye on him. I will make sure that I protect him as much as possible without him knowing. Although he is still young and soft-hearted, he is proud, and would hate to feel like he needed my help.

"What are you doing?" asks a familiar voice.

"We're just talking, Jet. What are you doing?" asks Flot.

"Looking for you. When is breakfast? I'm hungry."

"We can have breakfast right now," I say, as I turn to look into the darkening sky.

2

I hand the glowing stick to Jet, and tell them that I'll bring breakfast back to our room. Jet heads down the tunnel with Flot close behind. I turn and brave the rain, leaving the Crag behind me.

The meat we get from hunting isn't our only source of food. Some of us tend fields of wheat, barley and vegetables, and others take care of chickens, goats and sheep. There is some danger to it, but not like the hunt. Most predators stay away from our fields. We've built walls of stone to protect our animals. During the hunt, we have no walls to protect us. We only have our weapons, and our armor.

It takes me a while to reach the chickens, because I try not to slip on wet rocks. I let myself in through a wooden door, making sure to tie it up behind me so that wolves can't get in and the chickens can't get out. I pick many eggs off the ground, check for cracks, and then place them in different pockets that I've sewn into my clothing.

When I was young, I stitched secret pockets into my clothes. That way, when someone bigger tried to take something, it kept the things I needed hidden. Food, tools, weapons; the things I needed to survive. When I was a new one, I had no parents or older brothers or sisters to protect me, which is why I protect Flot and Jet now. Soon they will be able to look out for themselves, but for now they still need my protection. I have a feeling that if it weren't for me watching over him, things would be much worse for Flot.

I check that the wooden door is tied up good and tight so that the chickens will stay safe. As I leave, I see a flash of light, and with it the familiar boom of sky fire. This time is different. This time, the flash and the boom happen at the same time. I'm surrounded by bright white light. The force of the strike knocks me back, and I can hear the chickens scream out in panic. As I stand back up I check my pockets, and I'm glad to find that the eggs aren't broken.

I run as fast as I can back to the Crag. Looking over my shoulder, I make sure that I'm not being followed by wolves or other dangerous animals. When I get to the mouth of the cave, I jump over a puddle and nearly slip on the wet, moss-covered stone. Knowing that I've reached safety, I turn back to look out at the sky, defying it to try and hurt me while I'm inside the cave.

A streak of sky fire booms right in front of the Crag, charring a large patch of clover. I leap back in surprise, take a moment to catch my breath, and then make my way deeper into the cave.

I decide to burn a tribute just in case I have somehow angered the Sky Gods. Standing by the Great Fire, I take some small twigs from a pile then twist them into what looks like a person. I go back to the entrance of the cave and collect some moss to add as hair. Even though it's hard to tell at first, it is supposed to be me.

Once I'm certain that the Sky Gods will know that it's me by looking at it, I walk back to the Great Fire. I close my eyes, raise up the tribute to the sky then drop it in the fire. It burns quickly, until all the wrong things I have done are burnt up with my stick person.

Hopefully the Sky Gods will forgive me for whatever wrongs I have done. I can't think of anyone or anything that I have harmed, but there must be a reason why they brought sky fire down at me.

It takes me a moment to remove the eggs from my pockets and set them down on the cold stone ground. I grab a pan from a stack next to the Great Fire.

When I was still a new one, I asked Charm how pans were made. She told me never to ask where things come from. Questions like that are forbidden. Charm told me that the pans were gifts from the Sky Gods, like the Great Fire, but I think she just didn't know.

I remember looking up the word 'pan' in our Book of Knowledge. Our Book of Knowledge is good if you want to look up what a word means, but it doesn't tell you how to do things. Some of it I think is pretend. Things like aardvarks, and automobiles, and avocados don't make any sense, and I doubt they really exist. We have a few other books, and you may learn what the books teach you, but you must never question them. You must never disagree with them, for they are sacred.

I crack the eggs I have laid out against the side of the pan, and with each egg I crack, I throw its shell into the Great Fire. I dig into one of my many pockets and pull out a metal scoop. I use it to break up the yolks, and mix them in the pan until they are all the same color. Once they are mixed together, I hold the pan in the flames of the fire. The heat makes my hand and arm warm, but I stay far enough away that I don't get burned.

After a long while, the eggs are firm. I take the pan back to the mouth of the Crag and carefully place the bottom of the pan in the large puddle. It hisses and makes water-smoke float into the air. Once I think the pan has cooled enough, I find my way back to our room.

I notice that Flot had already visited the Great Fire, heating some water in a pot while I was out gathering eggs. He pours some into cups for each of us, and carefully sets them on the ground in the middle of the room. As we sit down in a circle around our feast, we close our eyes and raise our hands up to the Sky Gods as a sign of thanks for our meal. We eat, and we drink, and we talk about the hunt.

"Sam, what are we hunting today?" asks Jet.

"Probably the same things that we always hunt."

"Flot says that you might try to hunt a dragon," says

Jet.

"No, dragons are too dangerous to hunt. You know that we try to stay away from them," I reply.

"But there has to be some way to kill a dragon. What about attacking their eyes?"

"Almost everyone that has ever tried to fight a dragon has died. I only survived because I found a safe place to hide."

"Maybe if the entire Crag went out to fight one, maybe then we could kill it," says Jet.

"I don't think so," I say.

"Are you saying that because you're afraid?"

He's challenging me, waiting to see if I am as tough as I act.

"Yes, I'm afraid. You should be too. You can't kill a dragon."

Jet looks at me and realizes that what I'm saying must be true. I never lie to them, and I never admit to being afraid of anything. He knows that I don't let much scare me. I can't be scared, because no one will ever save me. I've always had to save myself.

"Sam?" says Flot.

"Yes?"

"Can we play jump stones today?"

"Sure, we can play jump stones."

"Will you go easy on me?"

"Never!" I say.

The twins giggle. I just smile at them.

We finish our meal, and I send Jet off to wash the pan that we used.

"Remember to scrub it, and dry it off really well after you wash it," I say.

"I know, I know. This isn't my first time washing pans," says Jet.

"Yes, but for some reason, when I don't remind you, people complain to me about there being dirty pans. Why is that?" I ask.

"Ungh," grunts Jet as he leaves.

I look over at Flot.

"Jump stones?" asks Flot.

Sigh.

"Sure, we can play jump stones now."

Flot pulls out the piece of wood we play jump stones on, with its many squares, and sets up the stones. He keeps the lighter stones, and I play the dark. Flot, for the small number of snows he's seen, is very good at jump stones. He can beat almost everyone in the Crag, except for me. Because of that, and because people that are too smart end up dead, I make sure that Flot only plays with people who aren't a danger to him.

My thoughts drift away from the game to Sickle and Scythe. I need to come up with a plan to protect Flot, and keep him safe. The hard part is being smart about it, so that they won't come after either of us. I don't want to kill them, even though that would fix the problem. I don't want to kill anybody. I just need them to stop hurting Flot.

"Rock!" says Flot.

I look down and realize I haven't been paying attention to the game at all. I watch as Flot replaces his stone with a much larger rock. Now he can move it forward or backward. He's also captured a few more pieces than me. Flot has never beaten me, and I won't let him beat me now.

I stare at the board for a moment, thinking about what it will take to win. I make my move. He moves his rock. I keep my stones in a tight group, making sure there is no way he can jump them with his rock. I keep moving, and he keeps following. Eventually, I'm able to move a stone into his back row, turning it into a rock, but I lose a pair of pieces in the process. I use my rock to jump his. Although I'm down a hands worth of pieces, he only has stones, and I have a rock.

I use my rock to protect another stone, and as he finally turns one of his stones into a rock, I gain another rock. I use my pair of rocks to take apart his army of stones, and finally corner his rock. He moves his last piece out, and I jump over it to win the game. Flot looks unhappy.

"So what did we learn?" I ask.

"Don't play jump stones with you," says Flot.

"No. What you learned is that you should protect what is important to you. I protected my pieces with my rock, to make sure that later in the game I could turn them into rocks and win."

"But you lost a pair of stones to get your first rock," says Flot.

"That is true, but sometimes you have to make your enemy think they are winning to beat them. You thought it was smart to lose your rock just so you could take out a pair of my stones. But then you didn't realize that all I needed to beat you was a rock. That was what you should have stopped. Do whatever you can to keep me from getting rocks. Don't worry so much about losing pieces. You're going to lose pieces. Just make sure that when you do lose pieces, it matters. That they aren't mistakes. That they make you stronger, and closer to winning by losing them."

Flot stares at me for a while, thinking about what I've just told him.

"Okay," says Flot.

I can tell that he gets it. Hopefully, some of what I am teaching him with jump stones will make him better at the hunt, and keep him safe.

"We should get ready for training," I say.

3

Each day we train before the hunt. Both hunters and those that want to become hunters learn how to use weapons. We are also trained how to be quiet, and stay hidden from our prey. We are taught how to think, how to see, and hear, and smell. That way, when the time comes, we might take our prey by surprise.

The hunt is important, not only because it brings food to the Crag for everyone to share, but it also scares away predators. Spreading our scent wherever we go warns the wolves that they are in our territory.

Jet, Flot and I stand outside the mouth of the Crag. The air is crisp and clean smelling. The rain has died down, and it has been a while since anyone has heard sky fire booming across the land. Others start to show up, ready to learn how to be better at the hunt. Eventually Lagan appears. His short, graying beard stands out against his tanned, weather-damaged skin. I notice that he is holding a spear that is thinner and shorter than our normal spears.

Lagan is the Leader of the Hunt, and also our trainer. He earned that right the day we lost our old leader, Hammer, when a dragon attacked. It was Lagan's quick thinking that spared the rest of us.

Lagan is not the best hunter in our group. He is not the strongest, or bravest, but he is the most fair. He is also the person that people come to when there is a problem in the

Crag. He acts as a judge, and does his best to hear both sides of every argument. That is why his decisions are respected, and why he has survived for so long.

Lagan is not the only leader in the Crag. There is also Chaff, the leader of the harvest, Crook, the keeper of animals, and Vault, the protector of the Crag. Vault is a good man, and Crook is a very strong and courageous woman. Chaff though is a monster.

Chaff, in many ways, is worse than his sons. He keeps the secret of growing food to himself, so that he can't be removed as leader of the harvest. He has help from many others with preparing the fields, and with picking what comes from the ground. But no one is sure what he does to make the plants start growing.

Chaff is hungry for power, and if you get on his bad side, he will starve you. He'll do the same to anyone trying to help those on his bad side.

Chaff's fields give us more food than we could ever gather from hunting or taking care of animals. When we hunt, we are lucky to bring back enough meat to share with the others. Everyone gets a taste, but it is not enough to feed everyone. Raising animals requires food to feed them. Grains and vegetables, and things that must be grown and harvested. Without the harvest, the people of the Crag would quickly die. That is why people do not challenge Chaff.

A few people have tried to steal food to survive, but when they are caught, they are sent away from the Crag to die. You are allowed eggs in the morning, before the animal keepers arrive, but they are not enough to survive on alone. Some people have been so desperate to get food that they leave the safety of the Crag on their own. Sometimes they go and never come back. I pray to the Sky Gods for them, hoping that they find a better place to live.

Chaff is the reason why Flot and Jet came to be my brothers. Flot's and Jet's father was part of the harvest, and their mother was a hunter. Barrow, their father, never got along with Chaff. I remember hearing he'd tried to find the secret of the harvest, so that Chaff would no longer have control over our people. But Chaff caught Barrow sneaking into his room. Chaff told the other harvesters that Barrow had been stealing from the garden, the one law that could not be broken. Barrow was sent out into the fields where the dragons live without food or water, and we never saw him again.

Barrow would have put up a fight, would have tried to kill Chaff, but Chaff vowed that if he did, he would have Flot and Jet killed. A day after Barrow's death, his wife, Shoal, died while eating dinner. The whispers said it was poison, but no one knows for sure. That's how Chaff kept control of people; making them fear being poisoned, or being kicked out of the Crag to starve to death.

It is that constant fear that makes me want to leave this place. I hope that somewhere outside of the Crag there are more people. Honest, and hard-working, and good. I also hope that Flot, Jet and I can live there. Maybe another cave where the people aren't as dangerous. Where everyone gets along, and shares, and protects each other. Where Flot won't be bullied anymore. But I don't know if there's a place like that. We've never met people from outside the Crag. For all I know, we could be the only people left in the world. We could be the only survivors of the End War.

We don't know much about the End War, other than it happened a very long time ago. Some of the gray ones tell stories that they remember hearing when they were just new ones. Stories of brave heroes fighting, bright lights of destruction, and the death of almost everything. Animals, people; all gone and burned up. But I think those are just stories told to warn us about fighting with each other. They teach us that if you try to become too powerful, someone else will want to take that power, and war will happen. I just wish people like Chaff would learn from the stories, so that they wouldn't be so evil.

I am lost in my thoughts, and I finally realize that Lagan is showing us how to use the new spear that he has created. It looks like he's taken a thin piece of wood and made points on both ends. It is different from our regular spears, which are thicker, heavier, longer, and only have a point at one end.

Lagan grips the spear one-handed, gets a running start then throws it as far as he can. It doesn't go as far as I can throw a rock with my sling, but it goes far enough that it could take an animal by surprise. It lands in the soft grass, and sticks straight out of the ground.

I am impressed. Our spears do not go very far, and they are not meant to be thrown. They are made to stab, and to keep predators at bay. This new spear could probably kill a deer that was so far away it couldn't smell you.

I want to learn how to use this new weapon very badly, so I walk over to Lagan as soon as he is done talking.

"Lagan, what do you call it?" I ask.

"A sky spear, because it falls from the sky like sky fire," says Lagan in his deep voice.

"Can I try?"

"Yes. I've made a few of them. Try to stand away from the others when you do, because we don't want to hurt anyone," says Lagan.

I pick up one of the sky spears from the pile and walk far away from everyone. Resting one end on the ground, the other end comes to the middle of my chest. I hold onto the front end of the stick, trying to keep it off the ground. I get low, and start running as fast as I can. I throw the spear with all my strength, but it lands on the ground right in front of me. I realize that there must be a trick to throwing them.

I look over at Lagan, who is holding the sky spear loosely, and near the middle. I watch as he gets a running start then doesn't throw it like I had. Instead, he spins his arm in a circle, keeping his arm almost straight. He also lets go of the spear earlier in his throw than I did. It's amazing how far this new spear can go.

I pick my spear up. I hold it in the same place that Lagan did, get my running start then throw it. This time it goes almost as far as Lagan's throw. It ends up right next to his spear. Lagan looks over at me and nods. I see a few other hunters have realized that I picked this up more quickly than them. Most of them are people that I know and do not fear. A few of them are people that I know and do not trust.

I walk over and pick up my sky spear. This time when I throw it, I make sure that everyone sees that my other throw was just luck. It lands right in front of me. I look around, and the few people I was worried about look away.

I hate having to hide my abilities just to stay alive. I could help the Crag if the others would listen to my advice. But if I seem too smart, someone will kill me in my sleep.

Frustration builds inside me as I think about how much I hate hiding my abilities from the others. I throw the sky spear with all my strength. It flies further than anyone else has thrown it, including Lagan. Everyone turns to look at me, and I can tell that I won't be able to sleep safely tonight. Maybe I really am as dumb as I pretend to be.

My next few throws don't go very far, but it's too late. I can tell a few of them are still watching me. Now I can only hope and pray, and ask the Sky Gods to protect me from the other hunters. Maybe the hunt will distract them and make them forget. Maybe I am worrying about it too much, but I know that I'm not, because I've seen people murdered for less. There is no rule against murder in the Crag, because they will kill anyone that tries to stop it.

Still angry with myself for the mistake, I look over at Flot and Jet. Both seem to be having a hard time throwing their sky spears. Flot holds the spear right, but his arms aren't very strong yet, so it doesn't fly very far. Jet is much stronger, but he hasn't figured out the right way to hold it. I see Flot look over at Jet then walk over to him. He says something I can't hear, but I watch as Jet changes where he holds onto the sky spear.

Jet takes a few steps then throws the spear as hard as he can. It flies as far as Lagan's throw. I smile, because I have hope that if something were to happen to me, Flot and Jet would be able to work together to survive. Maybe I've been wrong about them. Maybe they can survive without someone watching over them.

Lagan blows a horn to let us know that our training is over. We all walk back to the Crag to prepare for the hunt.

4

"Sam," says Lagan.

I wait for Flot, Jet, and the rest of the hunters to pass by me. Lagan looks at me like he's worried about something.

"Sam, I'll ask a pair of hunters to take turns standing outside your room tonight," says Lagan.

"I don't think I need protection," I say, lying.

"The others noticed how quickly you picked up the sky spear. You and I both know how dangerous something like that can be."

"People get killed. What does it matter? Why protect me?" I ask.

"Because you are the one who will replace me when I'm too old."

"Me? Why?" I ask.

"You might be able to fool other people, but I've watched you. I know that you're faster and smarter than the others."

My stomach starts to hurt.

"I don't want to lead. I just want to be left alone," I say.

"That's why you would be a good leader. You aren't interested in power. You care about people. I've seen how you take care of your brothers," says Lagan.

"They aren't really my brothers," I say.

"And yet you still protect them. That says even more

about you than if they were your own blood."

"Every other hunter wants to lead," I say. "Find someone else."

"No, the decision has already been made. Your future is to lead the hunt," says Lagan.

I don't know what to say to Lagan. I feel proud that he wants me to lead the hunters once he is too old, but I'm afraid that someone might try to kill me. That it will only make things worse for Flot, too. My instincts tell me to say 'no', to fight him and refuse, but I know he'll never agree.

"Sam, you might be safer as Leader of the Hunt than you are now," says Lagan.

"Somehow I doubt that," I say.

"I have made friends among the hunters, and those friends protect me."

"Yes, but they are your friends, not mine. I don't have any friends, just my brothers."

"My friends can become your friends," says Lagan.

"But I don't know them at all," I reply.

"When you are born, you don't know anybody, either. Everyone you know is someone you met for the first time."

"Yes, but there is a big difference between meeting someone, and trusting them with your life."

"That is true," says Lagan.

"And there are hunters that have seen many more snows than me. They will hate me for this."

"That is also true."

"Do you want me dead?" I ask.

"No, Sam. I want you to finally be alive. All you do, all you have ever done is survive. There is more to life than just seeing your next sunrise. You need to stop hiding, and do what you were meant to do."

I don't know what to say. He's right; I've never done anything more than stay alive. Every day I struggle to eat, to sleep, to be safe. Maybe if I had help, if Lagan's people can be trusted, maybe I can be more than just a simple hunter. But the danger is too much.

"I'm sorry, but I won't," I say.

Lagan just stares at me with his gray eyes. He doesn't react to what I have said.

"No," I say.

"We will see," says Lagan.

With that, Lagan turns from me and keeps walking toward the Crag.

5

When I get back to the room, I see that Flot and Jet are almost ready. They both have their leather armor on. Lagan was the one that discovered that a cow's skin makes good armor. That was when I realized just how smart Lagan is. I've never really thought of him that way, but a lot of what we do as hunters is because of him.

Lagan and a few of the other hunters know how to make leather armor. They won't share how they make it with anyone outside of the hunt though. I think it's because Lagan realizes that if other groups can make their own armor, they will start a war in the Crag.

The armor works well if you fall, or if someone tries to hit or kick you, but it will not stop a spear, and it will not save you from a rock thrown from a sling. It will protect you some from a wolf bite, but you will bleed. Still, it is better than nothing.

I help Flot tie together the last pieces of his armor. He has already helped Jet with his, but I make sure that he has done a good job. It all looks right, and I check it by pulling at the different pieces, making sure they won't fall off.

While I help them, I look at the carvings on the chest pieces. Both have the symbol of the Crag: connected rings, with shapes that look like curved squares outside of the rings. Charm told me that the rings form a clover leaf. One ring for the harvest, one for the animal keepers, and one for the hunt.

The squares are the protectors, standing guard over the other groups.

When I am sure that both Flot and Jet are ready for the hunt, I put on my own hunting armor. My armor is different in a few ways. It is longer, because I am taller than both Flot and Jet. Lagan also made it so that I can move my arms more easily than the hunters who use spears. That is what both Flot and Jet use, and will keep using for a few more snows. My armor makes it easy to use my sling, and should also help when I use the new sky spears.

Flot and Jet both help me get into my armor, not because I need help, but because it's faster. After I'm finished with my arms, legs and chest, I put on my helmet. It covers most of my face, but I can still see. Picking up my sling and bag of rocks, I tie them to the side of my armor.

Whenever I hunt, I carry a bag of rocks that are just the right size and shape for my sling. I know they will fly true, and will hit their mark. Because there are rocks everywhere, I've never run out of them.

Although I have always been good at using a sling, it's only been since the last snow that I could take down the black fliers in the Crag. Sometimes I find a group of them hanging upside down from the ceiling. I can use my sling to hit them with rocks as they sleep. I am good enough now that I can knock down a black flier, and be so quiet that it doesn't wake the other fliers.

It is a good thing too, because fliers have a mean bite. There have been a few times when a black flier's bite has caused a person to... change. They become dangerous, and not like themselves, so we try to stay away from the black fliers as much as possible.

I finally leave our room, with Jet and Flot following behind me. As we pass by the Great Fire, I notice that a small group of gray ones have gathered in front of it. They are there to worship, to ask for happiness and health, and to bless the hunt. Charm is among them. She usually prays before the hunt, praying for Flot's, Jet's and my safety. I go over to her and put a hand on her shoulder, letting her know that we appreciate it. She smiles then turns back to the fire.

Flot and Jet do the same, both placing their hands on her shoulders. This time she is deep in prayer and does not react to their touch. We leave Charm to her prayers and head to the mouth of the Crag.

The weather has decided to hold, which is good news. There is a slow wind blowing across the field. No rain, and no sky fire. The sky is still dark gray, which makes me wonder if the weather will turn bad again. I can hear the sound of grass moving, and in the distance our fields of wheat and barley. It is a beautiful sound, one that calms me and makes me feel alive.

It doesn't take long for the other hunters to appear. Like usual, Lagan is one of the last to arrive. I don't know if he purposely does it, but it gives us a chance to talk to each other before we must focus.

"Sam, do you know where we're hunting today?" asks Jet.

"We will head for where the sun rises," I reply.

"Didn't we do that yesterday? Why do we only hunt in that direction? Why don't we ever go toward the sunset?" asks Jet.

"You know why. It's because dragons are there."

"Why don't we hunt dragons?"

"Because we have nothing to kill them with," I say.

"We could try out Lagan's new spear. I bet it could take one down," says Jet.

"I don't think you could kill a dragon with a sky spear if it was tied up and sleeping."

"But you don't know that for sure."

"Yes, I do. Remember, I tried fighting a dragon before. It was only by the will of the Sky Gods that I'm still alive. I used to think like you, before I met one. That maybe there's a way to kill a dragon. And I tell you, Jet, that it's impossible."

"Maybe someday I will prove you wrong," says Jet.

"I pray to the Sky Gods every day that you never meet

a dragon," I reply.

"Maybe someday I will go off on my own and hunt a dragon."

I turn, grab Jet by the collar of his armor, and bring his face close to mine.

"You better hope that dragon kills you when you find it," I say.

"Why?"

"Because if it doesn't kill you, I will."

I push Jet backward, hard, to get my point through his stubborn head.

"Do you understand?" I ask.

Jet looks back at me with anger.

"Do you understand?" I yell.

The other hunters have turned to look at us. Jet looks around like a sheep, not knowing what to say or do. Finally, he speaks.

"Yes, Sam. I understand."

"Good. And Jet, don't ever look at me like that again. I will end you if I have to."

"Yes, Sam."

Because of the argument, Jet has lost some status with the other hunters. They realize he was acting like a child, and that I treated him like a child. There was no other way to keep him from going after a dragon, though. He has a hard time listening, and you must be strong when telling him what he shouldn't do.

Jet isn't very good about staying safe. I try my best to keep him and Flot from getting hurt. At some point I will let them live their own lives, and hope and pray for the best. But for right now it's my duty to protect him from himself.

6

"I need a few volunteers to carry sky spears during the hunt," says Lagan.

Everyone's arm goes up, even Jet's and Flot's. Even mine is in the air, and I hope that Lagan lets me use one of the new weapons. But Lagan doesn't pick me. He picks a few of the gray ones, and a few of the others; mostly people I don't talk to and don't know very well. Lagan hands out the sky spears to them. He looks over at me, and can tell by the look on my face that I'm not very happy about it.

"Those of you with sky spears have earned it. I've seen with my own eyes that you are the best at throwing them. If you did not get one, try harder next time. Until then, I will not hear any complaining. Not everyone can carry a sky spear. We still need hunters to carry slings, and hunters to protect us with big spears," says Lagan.

I notice a few of the people with murder in their eyes during training look back at me. My stomach turns when I see the vicious smiles on their faces. They think that they are better than me now. That is fine. Now I might be able to sleep in peace tonight, without having to worry about dying at the hands of jealous hunters.

Lagan is very wise to do what he did. He protected me without being obvious about it. I realized it, but the same people that would have killed me don't seem to understand that they are being fooled.

The other smart decision that Lagan made was to call the old spears 'big spears'. The word 'big' in the Crag is very important. If you are called 'big' in the Crag, it means that you are strong and can protect yourself. People won't try to kill you if you are big, because they are afraid that you will kill them first. It makes using an old spear still seem honorable.

I don't know that I could be as wise as Lagan if I replaced him. He always seems to know how to keep people from fighting and killing each other. I'm good at keeping people from killing me, but I don't know if I'd be able to keep things peaceful between the others.

Distracted by my own thoughts, I finally look up and notice Lagan staring at me. I give him a nod of thanks to let him know I realized he's saved my life. He doesn't react to my nod. Instead he looks away. He picks up the last sky spear and carries it in the direction that the sun rises from. The rest of the hunters pick up their weapons then turn and follow behind Lagan.

When we hunt, we form a square made up of rows of people, with big spears at the front and rock throwers like me in the back. This protects us from a direct attack, but it isn't very good when we're attacked from the sides.

One time a pack of wild wolves came at us from the side. A lot of good people died that didn't need to. If the hunters were smarter, more people might have survived.

But the hunters are likely to kill anyone that has too many good ideas. To keep fights from starting, Lagan has been forced to keep things the same way they have always been. It surprises me that he took the risk of showing the hunters the sky spears. Someone might try to take his life tonight because of it.

Our square of hunters moves slowly for a few reasons. The first is to stay quiet. If animals hear us they will run away. The other is to keep hunters from accidentally hurting each other. If you walk too fast with a sharp spear then trip, you might accidentally kill the person in front of you. And if you do, you'll never be allowed to hunt again.

We walk for a long while, searching for animals to hunt. Off in the distance I can see a few wolves attacking a deer. I ready my sling and wait. Wolf meat is filling, but it doesn't taste very good. Deer tastes very good, which is why we keep hunting them. It is disappointing that the wolves will have eaten most of the deer by the time we get to them.

Lagan also notices the wolves and puts his arms out to stop us from walking further. He points to the hunters that carry sky spears, and has them move away from the group. He also makes sure that they are all side-by-side, where none of them are closer to the wolves than the rest.

Lagan holds up his own spear, like he is ready to attack, and the sky spear hunters do the same. Once he is ready, he gets a running start then throws his sky spear toward the wolves. The other hunters do the same.

I can only imagine the fear that the wolves must have felt just before the sky spears came raining down on them. The group of wolves are all struck by the spears. Some of them die instantly, while others will soon die from blood loss. Lagan waves everyone to move closer to the wolves.

We only make it part of the way to the pack before Lagan orders the rock throwers to hit the wolves with our slings. I load up a stone from my bag, spin my sling a few times then launch the stone. It comes down from the sky, crashing into the head of an injured wolf. The good thing is that it isn't awake anymore, and will hopefully be with the Sky Gods soon.

Once all the throwers have had a chance to hit the wolves with their rocks, Lagan brings us even closer. He tells the people with big spears to stab the wolves that are still moving. The big spear hunters do their jobs, and then all is quiet.

There are as many wolves in the pack as there are fingers on both of my hands. It should be enough food for the Crag for a few days if we clean and cook our kill quickly. We also want to leave the killing field before other predators arrive, because we are at our most vulnerable when we are collecting our kill.

When we hunt, we each bring a bag along to carry the meat we have gathered. As I fill mine, I look across the field. I can feel the wind pressing on my face as I see a thick fog coming toward us. It moves like a frightening blanket of hands; fingers of white crawling across the grass.

"Lagan," I yell.

Lagan looks up, turns his head and sees what I see.

"Everyone, quickly, we must get back to the Crag," says Lagan.

I pull the strap of my wolf-filled sack over my head, so that if I fall, I won't lose my kill bag. I'm worried, because in a thick fog it is easy to lose what direction you're walking in. I go over to Flot and Jet, and help them put their kill bags over their heads, too. I push them ahead of me, making sure they move in the right direction so I don't lose them in the mist.

We take a few steps forward before we're swallowed by the fog. The air turns white around us. I can still see Flot and Jet, but it is hard to make out any of the other hunters. I hear Lagan yell out to us.

"Everyone, stay calm and follow my voice. I will talk so that no one is lost."

I am glad that Lagan is thinking well. He seems to be at his best when things are at their worst. He continues talking, giving us a way to keep the hunters together.

I notice that Jet can't seem to walk in the right direction, so I grab him and push him toward Lagan's voice every few steps. I can tell that he hates me doing it, but I don't care, because I'm not going to lose one of my brothers to the fog.

It seems like I am always trying to push Jet in the right direction, like all he ever wants to do is walk toward danger. He just doesn't understand what will happen if he does. That he could end up dead, or maybe even worse. This time though, I think he just can't hear Lagan. It makes me wonder if his ears don't work well. It would make sense, since he doesn't seem to hear my warnings, either.

We continue walking. Things seem to be getting

worse. It doesn't feel like we're walking in a straight line. The sky is so dark with clouds, and the air so thick with fog that I cannot tell if we are heading toward the Crag. I don't say anything to Lagan because I trust him, and I know that he would never lead us in the wrong direction.

But as we walk more, I worry more. It seems like we should have reached the Crag by now. I hear people talking to each other; whispers in the fog. I think that they are worried too. Both Jet and Flot look back at me, trying to see if I'm as worried as they are. I turn them back around toward Lagan's voice.

I can hear the worry in his words. He doesn't sound brave and strong like he normally does; he sounds like he is lost. I think he's still trying to act brave so that the other hunters will stay together and continue following him.

I speak to Flot and Jet through the fog.

"Ready yourselves," I say.

They both look back at me. Flot nods his head, but Jet just turns away. He does listen to me though and raises his spear as well. I place a rock in my sling, just in case we run into predators.

After many more steps, Lagan finally speaks.

"Everyone, ready your weapons. We do not know what we will meet in the fog."

The fog has only grown thicker since it met us, and I reach out to Jet and Flot to make sure they are still ahead of me.

I stop walking. Off in the distance I hear a familiar sound. It is the sound that has haunted my nightmares. It is a sound I haven't heard for many snows, but I will always remember. It is the sound of a dragon.

7

"Lagan, stop!" I yell as loud as I can.

I don't mean to scare the other hunters, but they need to know what they are up against.

"Hunters, do not move," yells out Lagan. "Sam, is that you?"

"Yes."

"Come to me, quickly. Follow my voice."

Lagan continues talking as I bring Flot and Jet with me. The fog is clearing some, which makes things more dangerous. We could have hidden, buried deep within the fog. But now we will be out in the open, and the dragon will see us. There are no rocks to hide behind, no caves to run to, for we are in the middle of a grassy field.

We reach Lagan as the sound of the dragon gets louder.

"What is it, Sam?"

"Can't you hear it?" I ask.

Lagan stops talking. I can see fear on his face as he listens. "We're losing the safety of the fog," he says. "And there's nowhere to hide."

It takes him a moment to think of what to do. Finally, after what feels like too long, he speaks.

"Everyone, I need you ready to face what comes. We have no choice but to fight. You need to move away from each other, and set down your kill bags. Those that sling rocks, as soon as you see our enemy, I want you to try and hit it. Do not stop throwing rocks. Those with sky spears, as soon as you think you can hit the enemy, throw your spear. Pick it back up then throw it again. Do not hit the other hunters. Those of you with big spears, I want you to form a circle outside of the rock throwers and spear throwers. Make sure that no other predators break the circle while we fight our enemy."

"What is our enemy?" yells one of Lagan's protectors.

"A dragon," he growls.

Most of the hunters follow his orders. A few panic and stay exactly where they are.

"Now, hunters; you must move now!" he barks.

The hunters that were frozen now move, as does Lagan. I look at our circle, and I see that both Jet and Flot have their spears ready. Lagan did not send the hunters that carry big spears to the edges of our group to protect us. He spread them out so that the dragon won't kill them as easily. They will be useless in this fight, for the dragon moves swiftly, and will rain fire down on us from above. The hunters with big spears will not be able to throw them high enough to hit the dragon.

Those of us that carry stones will not do much better. We will be able to hit the dragon, but its skin will protect it from our rocks. The only chance we have is with the sky spears. I hope that some of the hunters that Lagan gave sky spears to can hurt the dragon. The decision that Lagan made, to give the sky spears to people who are dangerous, was done to protect me. I pray to the Sky Gods that Lagan's good deed does not cost us.

8

The ground shakes beneath us as the dragon approaches, as if it were living sky fire. I can make out its glowing eyes, casting light through the thinning fog. My breath catches, and my knees weaken. The rock I have resting in my sling falls out, and I hurry to put it back in place.

"When the dragon gets close enough to breathe its fire, I want everyone to run away from the path it's flying in. Dragons move fast, but cannot turn well," shouts Lagan.

As the dragon draws nearer, one of the rock throwers launches a stone from their sling. The rock flies straight at our enemy, but misses because it's still too far away. Thankfully, there are many good stones under foot that can be used to battle the dragon.

Its eyes grow bigger, searching the ground for something to kill. That's when it sees us. I spin my sling, while a few more hunters fire rocks at the dragon. One rock sails way below it, another strikes it in the chin and bounces off. Knowing that it's now close enough to hit, the other rock throwers launch their stones at the dragon.

It is breath-stealing to watch; seeing so many rocks flying together. The rocks land against the face of the dragon and bounce off. Now I fire, hoping that my shot will count. I aim, and it hits one of the dragon's eyes, blinding it. The eye no longer glows, but more fear enters me as I realize that the dragon seems unhurt by it.

I start to move out of the path of the dragon, as do the other rock throwers, and the hunters that carry big spears. The hunters that carry sky spears throw them at the dragon, and I hold my breath, hoping that one of them is lucky and finds a weakness. I watch in disappointment as they just bounce off the dragon's tough skin.

The dragon flies upward, avoiding the few sky spears that haven't been thrown. As it passes overhead, I can feel the heat pouring from its massive body, and feel the ground shake from its roar. We watch as the dragon dives deep into the fog. It becomes harder to hear the dragon, as if it's flying away.

"Quickly" yells Lagan. "Find your sky spears if you have thrown them. I want everyone ready for when it comes back!"

The hunters hurry to gather and ready their weapons. We look around, but the fog still makes it impossible to see very far. Half of our people are still hidden from me. But we can hear. Thankfully, that frightening sound has all but disappeared.

I look around in every direction, trying to see through the fog, but find nothing. Holding my breath, I listen, waiting for the rumble that will mean our deaths. We wait. Silence. None of the hunters speak. Finally, once everything seems calm again, one breaks the silence. A young man named Beacon yells out.

"Maybe it's gone!"

I hear it before I'm able to see it. It is the dragon, and it's now very close. It had dropped through the fog from high above, its roar almost silent as it cuts through the sky. It pulls up at the last moment, just before it would have crashed into the ground, and flies into the middle of our group. Its roar hurts my ears, and makes everyone panic and run.

Some of the sky spear throwers try to run away from the dragon but aren't quick enough. It flies through a group of them, burning them to the ground. I wait to hear Lagan's voice, giving us our next command, but it never comes. I have to do something.

"Regroup around the fallen!" I yell.

The giant circle reforms as the dragon passes overhead. I run as fast as I can to the dead and wounded. That is when I see Lagan's lifeless body on the ground, along with more hunters than I have fingers on one hand. Tears start to form in my eyes, but I can't cry now. I need to be strong, and brave, and lead these people. With Lagan's death, I am now the Leader of the Hunt. I would give anything to have Lagan back.

I realize that Lagan's sky spear is on the ground, outside of the circle. He'd managed to throw it during the dragon's first pass, but he did not injure the dragon.

"Hunters that carry big spears, can you see any sky spears around you? If you find one, bring it to me," I yell.

They hesitate for a moment, unsure of whether to listen to my commands. But without anyone challenging my words, a few hunters break the circle and then come back carrying sky spears with them. I send a hunter back to the circle, keep his sky spear, and have the other big spear throwers ready the sky spears instead.

"This time, try to stay away from where it breathes fire. Aim for a place you think is weak on the dragon. And if you find a weakness, yell it out so that the rest of us can aim for it next time," I say.

The dragon approaches again. A few rocks fly, then more. None of them do any damage. It is now our turn, only I decide to do something different. As the dragon flies over our heads, the hunters throw their sky spears. I wait until the dragon has passed all the way over us then throw my sky spear.

It hits the dragon from behind, near a place that shoots fire. I hear a strange noise as the spear gets pulled inside the dragon. Smoke comes out of the back of it, and I watch as the dragon flies off into the distance and crashes to the ground. We can feel the ground shake as it hits, throwing up dirt and clover into the air.

I look around for Flot and Jet. I start to panic because I don't see them.

"Flot! Jet! Are you still alive?" I yell.

"Sam! I'm alright!" comes a voice from the circle.

I watch as Flot comes running up to me.

"Where is Jet?" I ask, worried that he might be among the dead.

"I am here," comes another familiar voice.

Thank the Sky Gods, they are both alive! I cannot show my happiness, because many of our people have died. All hunters are my brothers and sisters now, and their loss is my loss.

I speak to the group.

"Hunters, you have fought bravely. We have done the impossible, and killed a dragon. We have lost many, but many more of us still live. Let us honor our dead, and the Sky Gods, by covering them in a blanket of grass and clover, so that they may sleep well forever."

Everyone comes to help bury the bodies. There are tears, because brothers, fathers, sons, sisters, mothers and daughters were lost. Though they fought bravely, and they are now with the Sky Gods, we feel the pain of their loss, because we have lost something by not knowing them better.

I look out at the hunters who survived and speak.

"Everyone, pick up your kill bags and weapons. We will go back to where we started the hunt, and find our way home from there."

"How do we get back to the killing place?" asks a hunter.

I look around and notice that the fog has almost disappeared. The sky is still gray, but it is easier to tell where the sun is. I stare for a moment at the ground that covers our dead, and realize we can never return to this place. There might be other dragons here, and they are still too dangerous to fight, even after killing one.

"Follow the blood trail that has dripped from our kill bags. That will lead us back," I say.

Everyone listens to my commands. I am surprised that none of the hunters has tried to kill me yet. It would be bold to attack the Leader of the Hunt with other hunters around, but it has happened before. That is why Lagan used his friends. They were people he could trust to protect him. Now those same people are sworn to protect me too. I should find them.

"Mast, Port and Helm, I would like to speak with you," I yell into the moving crowd.

It is a bad thing that I don't know many people's names, and that I could not easily tell who had died in the dragon's fire. I do not know if any of Lagan's protectors have survived the attack.

I see a pair of hunters break away from the rest of the group. They are Mast and Helm, our biggest hunters. I am glad to see that they are alive, but I do not see Port anywhere.

"What has happened to Port?" I ask.

"She died trying to protect Lagan. As he threw his sky spear, she saw that the dragon was coming right at him. She knocked him down, trying to cover his body with her own. The dragon's fire was too much for them. She gave her life, hoping that he would survive. Remember that, young hunter. A leader that treats their people well and does right by them will have their loyalty," says Mast.

"I will pray to the Sky Gods that I am as good of a person as Lagan, as honorable and as just. Lagan was the best of us, and I will spend every day trying to be more like him. Had he told you he meant for me to be the next Leader of the Hunt?" I ask.

"Yes," replies Helm. "He was very certain of it, even if we did not agree with his decision."

His words sting, but are understandable. There are many here who have been hunters longer than I have, and are loyal and deserving of it. I do not agree with Lagan's decision either.

"I will work hard to earn your trust and respect," I say.

I can tell they worry if I will be a good leader. Whether I'm telling them the truth, and that they can trust me. Even though they don't know me well, Mast and Helm stay by my side, making sure that no one tries to hurt me.

We eventually make it back to the grounds where we killed the wolves. The blood there is sticky but not yet dry. I look around for signs that another predator has been there, but can't find any.

I stare at the drying blood, and think back to when we were attacked. In my head, I can see people dying, killed by the dragon. I feel dizzy and my knees bend. I fight the images, pushing them out of me. I do not want to let fear rule me.

I look up and point in the direction of the Crag. It's much easier to tell where it is, now that we are somewhere familiar. I want to get home so I can pull my blanket over my head and pretend that today never happened.

Our army of hunters moves in the direction I point. They are an army now, for instead of hunting we fought, and we fought bravely. There is no telling what will happen when we return to the Crag, nor how the battle has changed us.

9

$A$s we walk together, I look to the edges of our group and see Flot and Jet. Both seem tired but unhurt. It's amazing that neither of them were injured fighting the dragon. Especially Jet, since he's a risk taker. The Sky Gods are looking down on them, protecting them.

It is not long before we find the Crag. When we arrive, a few families have gathered to greet us at the mouth of the cave. Men, women, and children all wait for their loved ones to return. My heart is broken, because I realize that I will need to talk to the families of the dead, and tell them the horrible news. I ask Helm and Mast for the names of those that fell while battling the dragon.

Not all of the hunters have found their families yet, but I decide to tell the group that has gathered. That way, they will hear it from my mouth first.

"Families of the hunt, I bring news that will be difficult to hear, and that cuts my heart to say. During the hunt we became lost. We battled a dragon. Brave hunters were killed during the fight. They gave their lives so that the rest of us could live. We have buried them as the Sky Gods have asked us to, in blankets of grass and clover, to honor their sacrifice. May they be with the Sky Gods now, looking down upon us, protecting us and loving us. Among the dead was Lagan, our leader. He fought bravely, and died with honor. The others that died are Port, Compass, Flagg, Knot, Mooring, Buoy,

Cannon and Pier."

Families cry over the loss of the people they loved. One family, Cannon's, does not. They looked surprised, but not sad. I make a point of speaking to his wife, Bay, and their children.

"I'm sorry that you lost your husband."

She stares at me for a moment, deciding what to say.

"Cannon was horrible to us. He would steal more than his share of beer, and he would beat us while he was full of drink. It is sad, but I feel safer now that he's gone. I don't know why I ever joined with him. I only wish he'd died sooner."

Her words are like a punch to my stomach. I want to say something, but sometimes there isn't a way to make things better. I can only hope that Bay and her children will be able to move on.

"Bay, I will make sure that your family is taken care of. That you receive the food and protection that you need."

"Thank you, Sam. I will pray to the Sky Gods for your health and safety."

I watch as families move deeper into the Crag together, until only Jet and Flot are still at the mouth of the cave with me. Now that we are finally alone, they hug me. I'm so glad they are both safe that tears form in the corners of my eyes. Only I can't let them see my tears. I can't let anyone see them anymore, because peoples' lives are now in my hands. I must lead, whether I want to or not.

"Jet, now that you've seen a dragon in real life, do you understand why we should fear them? Why going after one alone would be dangerous, and could get you killed?" I ask.

"Yes, I understand now. I will try to listen better," says Jet.

"Do something for me, Jet. Don't just do what I tell you to do. Make good decisions. Stay away from danger. Be safe," I say.

"Aren't you going to say the same thing to Flot?" asks Jet.

"No, because he already makes good decisions."

Flot stares at me, and gives me a look that says 'Really? As if I don't have enough problems to deal with, now I have to deal with a jealous brother. Thanks a lot!' I just smile at him, because I know that Jet will never be a real danger to him.

For brothers, they are good about letting the other know that they care. That doesn't mean they don't fight, and wrestle, and act like new ones sometimes. I've had to pull one off the other before, and no, I'm not always pulling Jet off Flot. Sometimes it is soft-hearted Flot that I have to pull off Jet.

"Let's go inside. We still need to clean our kill," I say.

I let Flot and Jet walk in front of me, and I stop as we come to the Great Fire. I kneel on the hard stone ground, bow my head and raise my hands up. I say a silent prayer of thanks for protecting Jet, Flot and me, and peaceful sleep for those that we lost to the dragon. I also pray that Cannon's family will be protected and safe, now that they have lost him.

I bring my arms back down to my sides and stand up. I notice Jet and Flot also praying at the Great Fire. I wait for them to stand up before we walk back to our room.

It takes us a while to get out of our armor. I help both of them undo the straps that hold their armor together. Thankfully, none of us were injured. Aside from a small amount of blood from moving the dead, and the grass and clover we dug up, our armor is still mostly clean. It is not easy to get stains out of leather, so most of them stay on your armor until a new stain takes its place.

Once we get out of our armor, we each put on our meat cutting clothes. Cleaning our kill is what I hate most about being a hunter. Taking something that lived and making it food. Most of the other hunters aren't bothered by it, once they have done it for a few snows. It bothers me much less now, but it is still something I dread.

Flot surprises me. He's never had a problem with skinning and preparing meat. It is Jet that seems to hate dealing with dead animals. People are hard to understand sometimes, and I'm constantly surprised by them. No one is exactly what you would expect.

Inside our room we have small tables, one for each of us, that we use for cutting meat. There isn't much meat on a wolf normally, because they are hunters too, and they use their speed to kill other animals. A wolf that becomes fat loses its speed, so it cannot catch as much. It seems that the Sky Gods have made it so that wolves will always stay thin.

The same is true of the hunters of the Crag. We are all lean and strong, for we are constantly moving. Those people that are part of the harvest are generally bigger than us. Especially Chaff. He sometimes has difficulty moving through the narrow tunnels of the Crag.

I think the reason Chaff's so large is that he only works hard once every snow, when he makes the fruits and vegetables come alive. He also takes more than his fair share of food and beer. Much more.

Beer is something that helps keep us alive during the snows. It can stay in barrels and buckets for a long time until we need it. Meat is hard to come by during those times, because the animals hide when the snows come. Vegetables are also a problem, because they rot away if they are not eaten quickly. We can also make bread during those times, but it can be difficult keeping the grains dry, especially inside of a cave that sometimes fills to your ankles with water.

I work on skinning the wolf. We keep the pelts which can be made into clothes or blankets, or other things. We throw the bones into a pile on a blanket then carry them to a place we call the boneyard. The meat we put in baskets, which we give to the cooks in the Crag. They will turn what we've caught into steaks, or they will smoke the meats outside so that they become tough. That way, the meat will last longer.

As I finish, I look down at the bloody cutting table and think back to Lagan dying. I did not see it happen, but for some reason it feels like I did, like the memory of it is somehow in my mind. I start to lose my balance, so I put a hand out, catching myself on the edge of the table.

I look over at Jet and Flot, and thankfully neither of them saw me lose my strength. I don't want them to worry, so I won't tell them I'm seeing the deaths of the hunters in my mind.

I finish cleaning my kill, and use a bucket of water to wash away the blood from my cutting table. You can tell that you're standing in the room of a hunter, for when you look down, the stone is always dark red. I hope that someday, Jet, Flot and I will live where our floors are gray.

# 10

I carry the wolf bones to the boneyard, which is a long walk from the Crag. We keep it far away from the cave because it brings animals. Black birds, wolves and other creatures like to come and pick the bones clean.

I don't like going to the boneyard, because it always reminds me of death. So many skeletons. White pieces of once-living creatures sticking out. And not all the skeletons are from animals. There are bodies there too, hidden in the piles. Sometimes, when a person disappears from the Crag, we look there. Sometimes they are found.

As I approach the boneyard, handfuls of black birds scatter, flying into the air and away from me. The smell of rotting meat turns my stomach. I pick a place to dump the bones, away from any new piles, because flies are also a problem. If you drop your bones into a new pile, you will have flies following you for days. I unroll my blanket and let the bones fall out. They make such a strange noise when they crash on the ground. I shake the blanket to make sure no small bones are stuck to it, roll it up then leave.

Once I get back, we take our meat to the cooks so that they can be made into dinner. The cooks are part of the protectors, and learn how to defend themselves against animals. The reason they are not part of the harvest, hunters or keepers, is that the first group of people who lived in the Crag thought it best to give them some responsibility for the Crag's food. It also takes many people to cook, and clean dishes, and serve food, while it only takes a few to watch over the Crag. It gave the protectors about the same number of people as the other groups.

"Thank you, Sam," says Cleave, the head cook.

"What are you making tonight?" I ask.

"Wolf stew. This pack were a bit thin, so the meat is tough. Cooking it for a while should help make it chew better," says Cleave.

"I like your stew," I say.

"It takes a while to make, but I like it too. It's worth it."

I watch as Cleave cuts a pepper, and pulls out the round pieces of poison from inside. Some of our foods have poison in them, so to be safe, the cooks take out the dangerous parts and throws them in a basket. Each day, a member of the harvest comes for the basket, so that Chaff can get rid of the pieces of poison for us.

I smile at Cleave and leave her to her work. We head back to our room and I strip off my bloody clothes. I carry them and a bar of soap to the loud waters. Flot and Jet follow behind me. They know that they won't get dinner if they don't also clean up.

When we get to the loud waters, there are already a few people there washing up. The loud waters is a stream in the cave that runs by very quickly and makes a lot of noise. At one end, where the water first comes in, people are filling buckets with water for drinking and cooking with. At the other, there are people washing their bodies and clothes.

Soap can be made from the fat of the animals we kill. Only one person in the Crag makes soap, but unlike Chaff he is nice. He will share how to make it with anyone that is interested. His name is Echo, because he always stays in the caves. He has been told not to leave the Crag, because he has a hard time understanding things, and cannot protect himself. Echo always greets me with a smile. Not many people have a reason to smile in the Crag.

I walk into the water holding my blood covered shirt. The water only goes as high as my ankles. New ones must be careful not to fall though, or they can be swept away by it. Kneeling, I put my shirt into the water then rub it with soap. I get as much blood off as I can. After I have rinsed the soap out of my shirt, I do the same with my pants, until I am sure that they are as clean as I can make them. Once I'm finished, I use the soap on my body, trying to get rid of the sweat, and blood, and memories of people dying.

Twisting and squeezing the water out of my clothes, I grab my soap and head back to our room. It takes Jet and Flot longer to finish, and when they finally return I have already hung up my clothes and changed into clean ones.

I lie down on my bed of branches for a moment, trying to give my body some rest. I cannot lay there too long or I will fall asleep and miss dinner. Worrying has been making my stomach hurt, and food is the only thing that I know will help.

At night, almost everyone in the Crag goes to a large chamber and eats together. It's one of the few times where people seem happy. Part of that happiness comes from the beer we drink. Some of us drink too much, though. Sometimes a fight starts, which ends the happiness for everyone.

The new ones are not allowed to drink beer, for it seems to make more problems for them than for the adults. Jet and Flot have not seen enough snows yet to drink beer, but I can. I choose not to, because beer makes you dumb, and dangerous, and I need my mind so that I can protect my brothers.

Sometimes during the snows, when we don't have enough food, I will drink some. But I am very careful to only drink enough to survive, and not enough to be too-full-of-drink. I also hate the taste. It reminds me of the smell of meat when it goes bad.

Flot and Jet finish changing. I get up from my bed. Standing hurts, because I feel pain in my muscles from fighting the dragon and burying the dead. It has been a hard day, and not just for my body, but for my mind and my heart.

I force myself to start walking toward the feast chamber, even though I'm still as tired as the dead. Flot seems just as tired as I am, but for some reason Jet seems to be happy. Why would Jet be happy? People died today. Was the thought of dinner enough for him to be happy? It's not like we haven't had wolf before, and he has helped the hunt many, many times. Nothing has changed. Unless...

I let Flot go ahead while I walk slowly with Jet.

"Jet, I have to ask you something," I say.

"Okay," says Jet, sounding worried.

"Is there a girl you like?" I ask.

His face turns red at the question.

"I have friends that are girls," says Jet.

"No, I mean is there a girl you *like*?"

He looks away from me.

"There is!" I say in surprise.

Jet's face gets even more red.

"Sam, can you not tell anyone about it please?"

I stand there, smiling at him.

"Sure. I can keep a secret. But who is it? Which girl do you like?" I ask.

"Her name is Till. She's part of the harvest."

"What is she like?"

"Her hair is long and dark like the night. Her skin is soft, and her eyes are the color of the sky when there are no clouds," says Jet

"When you speak of her, it sounds like you are in love."

"Don't tease me!" says Jet.

"I'm not, I am serious!" I say. "Does she know that you like her?"

"I think so. I haven't told her, but she notices that I stare at her, and she smiles back."

"That is a good sign," I say. "Do you want to join with her?"

Jet just turns and slugs my arm.

"I'm not ready for that and you know it! I only started liking girls a few snows ago. I want to be more grown up, like you, before I join with anyone," says Jet.

"That sounds like a very wise idea. Until then, you can still get to know her. Maybe she is very nice, but maybe she is not. Make sure that you really know someone before you join with them. Otherwise, your life could be very, very unhappy."

"I know all that. I'm not dumb, you know."

"I know you're not dumb. I didn't mean anything. So, when are you going to talk to her?" I ask.

"I was thinking tonight. I mean, I just helped kill a dragon, and I'm already feeling pretty brave," says Jet.

"Brave men often get the girls they like," I say, smiling.

"When will you join with someone, Sam? You've seen enough snows now."

I can feel my own face turn warm and red.

"I don't know. There isn't really anyone I like, and definitely no one that I would want to join with," I say.

"No one?"

"Not really."

"How come?"

"I don't know. I just don't feel that way about anyone."

"Well, it's probably harder for you to find someone when you don't talk to anyone," says Jet.

"I do talk to people! Like Moss, and Charm, and..."

I was going to say Lagan, but Lagan isn't here anymore. He is up with the Sky Gods now. I swallow hard to keep the tears away from my eyes.

"Yeah, all you do is talk to gray ones. You need to talk to people that have only seen as many snows as you," says Jet.

"They don't seem to like me very much," I say.

"That's just because they don't know you like I know you. Because if they really knew you, they would hate you," says Jet, laughing.

Now it's my turn to punch Jet in the arm.

"Hey, that hurt," says Jet.

"Good, it was supposed to," I say.

"Yeah, well, it did."

"Sorry."

"It's okay."

We are almost to the feast chamber, and I can hear the noise of people talking too loudly.

"Jet, I hope things go well with Till. Just let me know what she says," I say.

"I will. And Sam?"

"Yeah?"

"Thanks," says Jet, hugging me.

We don't hug much, if ever. I hug him back, but I am not very good at it. I hope he knows that I mean it, though.

# 11

When Jet and I finally arrive at the feast, I see Flot sitting with a few of the hunters, eating a bowl of wolf stew and a long piece of corn. I stare up at the ceiling of the feast chamber. It is different from most rooms, because the rock piles that normally grow from the ceiling have been smoothed down. It looks as if someone worked very hard to make it flat.

There are many glowing sticks attached to the walls, making it the brightest room in the Crag, but it is still not as bright as being outside in the sunlight. The tables are old and made of wood, and they are stained with the color of spilled food, beer, and blood.

People begin noticing that I've entered. The noise in the chamber dies down, and the loud talking turns into whispers. I start to worry and look around. My guess is that word has spread about the dragon. I stand in line for food, and the noise of talking starts to grow again. Maybe things won't be so bad. But then I hear someone say the words 'Sky Child.'

The Sky Child is a story that has been passed down from before the gray ones were new ones. It is about the one who would be given as a gift from the Sky Gods. They will come to the Crag and bring peace and health and food. They will change the lives of the people in the Crag forever. But I couldn't be the Sky Child, because I'm just a normal person.

The realization that people might think that I'm the Sky Child makes my stomach hurt. In a place where being different can get you killed, imagine what it would be like to be thought of as a god. I have killed a dragon, and if they think I'm the Sky Child now, I am as good as dead.

I try to forget about it and deal with what I have in front of me, which is waiting for my dinner. I look around and watch people drinking, eating, and talking. I've never liked being in the feast chamber, because it reminds me that I don't fit in.

Anyone can sit where they want. It is a good thing, because it allows people from different groups to talk to each other. You also have a better chance of joining with someone outside of your group.

Long ago, people would only join with people from their own group. That caused bad things to happen. It seemed to make the next group of new ones less smart than their parents. There were also problems with the new ones' bodies. Some new ones would be born without enough fingers, or their mouths would be put together wrong, or they would have problems walking. Once they started mixing the groups, the new ones had less problems with their minds and bodies.

Another good rule is that new ones, when they have seen enough snows, can choose either group that their parents belong to. Many people that want children will pick someone outside of their own group to join with, so that their new ones will have a better chance at finding something they are good at.

Sometimes parents from the same group have a new one that is terrible at what they are both good at. This can make the new ones hate their parents. I know that a new one killed their parents once because they didn't want to work the harvest.

Even though everyone can sit where they want to, if you are a leader, it is expected that you sit at the head table. The head table is different than the others. All the other tables are long, and can seat many people at them. The head table is square. Each leader has a pair of people from their own group sitting with them: one to their right, and one to their left.

The people that sit at a leader's sides are there to

protect them. They also act as advisors, and only pass along important information or questions. There are many times when one leader has a question for another leader, and the information is already known by the advisors. This saves a lot of time, and allows the leaders to eat.

You must pick your advisors carefully though, because they can provide bad information, or form alliances without your knowledge. In the past, there have even been advisors that set up their leaders to fail, so that they could take their place. When that happens, it seems that someone always dies. Whether it is the old leader, or the lying advisor.

I get my stew and take some warm bread to go with it. I walk slowly to the head table and notice that it is full, except for Lagan's old seat, the seat between Helm and Mast. They keep their eyes fixed on me as I walk up and sit down. I grab the cup in front of me and fill it with water from a pitcher. Taking a drink, I look around the table.

The leader to my right is Crook, to my left is Vault, and straight across from me is Chaff. Crook and Vault both smile at me as I look at them, but Chaff completely ignores me. While he picks apart his meal, I stare at Chaff's bald spot. Dark, curly red hair runs from ear-to-ear, around the back of his head. He fills his face with food, acting like nothing has changed. That is fine, let him think that I am beneath him, that I am unimportant.

I decide to do the same to him, show no fear or concern. Pretend that he doesn't even exist. I have found that bullies hate being treated the way that they treat others. It is the surest way to get their attention. To push the point, I raise my cup to Crook, and nod my head, then do the same to Vault. Both return the nod. I have shown both of them respect, and gave no respect to Chaff. It is funny that I work so hard to stay alive, yet I seem to do things that will most definitely get me killed.

It works though. I catch out of the corner of my eye Chaff looking at me, murder in his. I ignore him and start eating my stew. I know that I have just made an enemy. But I would rather have an enemy in front of me than one trying to kill me from behind. He would have been my enemy no matter what, because I despise him.

Sickle and Scythe, his sons, are also his advisors. They look at me with the same disgust I feel for them. I am sure that they are both unhappy that I've become a leader before they have. They are no less dangerous than Chaff himself, but they aren't as smart as Chaff. They will never be as good as their father at manipulation and control.

Sickle is shorter and thin, with stringy black hair. His barely grown moustache makes him look like the rats that sometimes hide in the Crag. Scythe is tall and thick of arms, legs and head. His mouth is always open, and I can only guess how many flies have climbed into it, looking for a home.

I smile at each of them, a fake looking smile so that they know I don't mean it. Sickle's eyes narrow, and Scythe's brow wrinkles in anger.

Halfway through the meal, Helm rises from his seat. He stands very tall. He is a wall of muscle. His skin is very dark compared to mine, as if he had spent his entire life in the sun. It reminds me of the beautiful, deep shades of tree bark. He wears his beard clean on his cheeks, full around his mouth, and a thumb's length down from his chin. There is gray in it, but not much. I would guess that he has seen as many snows as me, and that many more again.

"People of the Crag," he starts, waiting for the chamber to become silent. "As many of you have heard, we have lost our Leader of the Hunt. Lagan died bravely in battle, killed by the fire of a dragon. In that same battle, we lost many others. But many hunters returned. It is because of Sam's quick thinking and leadership that we are still alive. Sam was the one that brought down the dragon and then showed us the way home. The hunters owe their lives and their loyalty to Sam. To Sam!"

The hunters all stand up, place their right fists on their heart, and slide them downward. It is a sign of loyalty and respect, meaning that they would rather cut out their own heart than to dishonor or be disloyal to me.

I stand up, look around at each of the hunters one at a time. I then return the gesture, so that they know I will honor, respect, and be loyal to them. I realize the weight of what it means to lead; that each of their lives are now in my hands, and are my responsibility. I will do what needs to be done to make sure that they are all protected and treated as fair as possible.

"Thank you, but I cannot celebrate this as a victory, for we have still lost many hunters that were good, and loyal, and brave. I will do whatever I can to help the hunters stay safe, so that this never happens again. The Sky Gods were watching us today, protecting us. They are the ones that deserve your thanks," I say.

Everyone sits back down and continues eating. I go back to eating my stew. I tear off pieces of the bread and dip them in the sauce. It is delicious, and when I finish my meal, there aren't any spots of stew left in my bowl. I swallow the last of my water then lean back in my chair.

I look over at Chaff. Even after Helm's speech he continues acting like I'm not there. I try not to let it bother me, but it makes me realize just how powerful he thinks he is. I decide to ignore it for now. At some point he will need to talk to me, which I don't look forward to. Better to wait and see what happens than to anger him. I think there have been enough deaths today. I don't want him to try and kill me, and I don't want to have to kill him.

A woman comes up to Chaff. I think her name is Fallow. I believe that she's part of the harvest. She's very thin and sickly looking. Her skin has no color, and her eyes have no light.

"Chaff, please, I'm begging you! Please let us eat! My children are starving," says Fallow.

Chaff doesn't look at her.

"Please!" she yells, grabbing his shirt sleeve.

Chaff pulls her fingers away from his clothes.

I start to stand up, but I feel Helm's hand on my arm,

holding me down. I quickly turn to look at him, and he looks back. I see both worry and sadness in his eyes. They also tell me not to fight Chaff on this. I turn back to see Fallow crying into her hands. After a moment, she gives up and runs away from Chaff. He looks up at the rest of us.

"I have to keep people motivated somehow. Otherwise they won't work hard. They stand around in the fields all day, talking," said Chaff.

I can feel my face warming, turning red with anger. Chaff looks at me and smiles. I shut my eyes and take in some breaths to calm the rage inside me. Eventually, I'm able to calm down. I stand up, pick up my bowl and add it to the growing stack of used bowls in the corner of the feast chamber. I walk back and sit down at the table. Helm turns to me.

"Sam, I think someone should stand guard for you tonight. In the past, when someone new takes over as a leader, people generally try to kill them. There have been a lot of reasons: jealousy, hatred, fear. One time a new leader for the animals was killed just because the killer was bored. The killer died a day later when his son stabbed him with a spear. People in the Crag are dangerous."

My first instinct is to refuse, and tell him that I can protect myself, but I know better. I know that there's a good chance that someone will try to kill me tonight. If I fall asleep alone, I may never wake up.

"Okay Helm, at least for tonight, you can post a guard in front of my room," I say.

"And they will also follow you the rest of the night," says Helm.

"I wasn't agreeing to that," I say.

"Look Sam, you don't seem stupid. You know that the Crag is dangerous just walking from room to room. There are so many places a person can hide. So many rooms, so many shadows, so many tunnels. You should let someone walk with you, and make sure that no one tries to attack you."

The last thing I want to do is look weak, like I need

54

someone watching over me all the time. But maybe I do. Maybe I need someone to keep me alive. At least for a while. In a few days people might forget what happened. Maybe they won't treat me like an outcast. Someone to be hated, feared, or even worse: worshipped.

"Fine," I say.

Helm stands up and points at one of the hunters. I think her name is Ebb. He waves her to come over. She stands up and makes her way to us.

"Helm, you have need of me?" asks Ebb.

"Yes. Ebb, this is Sam. I don't know if you have met the new Leader of the Hunt yet," says Helm.

"I have not," says Ebb.

I smile and shake hands with her.

"Ebb, we need you to do something for us tonight," says Helm.

"What do you need?"

"We need you to protect Sam. There could be killers hiding in the shadows, and someone needs to act as Sam's guardian. Can you do that?"

"Yes. Yes of course," says Ebb.

Ebb seems genuinely honored to be asked.

"Thank you, Ebb. I owe you a debt for this," I say.

"It is nothing. And you can thank me tomorrow, if we survive."

"Ebb, I am heading to Charm's room first then back to my room. Are you up for that?" I ask.

"I will protect you with my life," says Ebb.

I place a hand on her shoulder and bow my head to her as a sign of thanks.

"Oh, and Sam, may I put my armor on first?" asks Ebb.

"Yes, of course."

I honestly hope she doesn't need the armor, but she will make a much more dangerous looking guard than if she just dressed in her normal clothes. I am glad that I have someone looking out for me, but I also don't want anyone to get hurt. Especially if it's to save my life.

# 12

I walk with Ebb to her room so that she can change into her armor. She decides to go first, checking down side-tunnels, making sure that no one is waiting to attack us. It takes much longer to get to her room, but it's worth it to be safe. I would rather wait than die; it's a simple choice.

Ebb invites me into her room while she changes, just to make sure no one passing by will see me. Her room has the same red floor as ours, which makes me sad. I don't like looking at the red floor in our room. Here it feels so... wrong. Ebb seems strong though, like she can handle it. Maybe it doesn't bother her as much as it bothers me.

Something else I notice about Ebb's room is that it smells like wildflowers. Our room doesn't smell like flowers, and I had never thought to do that. It makes Ebb's room feel less like a place to sleep, and more like a place where you can just... be.

Ebb takes off her shirt and pants then puts on her armor. I help her tie the straps together so that her armor will stay on. It doesn't take very long, and I don't mind helping.

"Thanks, Sam. You know, I can put the armor on myself, but it's nice to have help," says Ebb.

"You're welcome, and I am the same way. I can get my armor on by myself, but with help it goes much faster. Flot and Jet usually help me put it on," I say.

"Those are your brothers, right?" asks Ebb.

"Yes, although I guess they aren't really my brothers. We don't come from the same parents. I just watch over them and make sure that they are safe. But I call them my brothers."

"Well then since I'm watching over you, I guess you have a new big sister," says Ebb.

"I don't know if I would say you were my big sister, because I think we've seen the same amount of snows," I mention.

"It definitely seems like it, or at least close. Fine then, I will just be your sister," says Ebb, smiling.

I smile back, but inside it kind of hurts. I have spent so long trying to survive, that I haven't tried making friends with anyone. I don't know Ebb well enough yet to know if I can trust her, and especially not enough to call her a friend, but I hope that someday I will.

I wonder if I scare people away so that they can't hurt me, whether it's with their fists and weapons, or by hurting me inside, in my heart. I realize that Ebb is looking at me, waiting, while I am lost in my thoughts.

"I don't have any friends," I admit.

"I doubt that's true, Sam. I'm sure you have many friends," says Ebb.

"I am friends with a few gray ones, but no one that was a new one when I was."

Her smile fades.

"I could imagine it would be difficult for you to make friends, Sam, when people think that you are the Sky Child."

"I think that people only started believing that because of what happened today," I say.

"Actually, there are a few of us who have believed it for a long time, or at least thought it might be true," says Ebb.

"So you think I might be the Sky Child?"

"It's possible, but you seem like a normal person to me. I would think that the Sky Child would be covered in flames like a glowing stick, and could fly like a bird, and things like that."

"Yeah, I can't do any of those, but I'm good with my

sling," I say.

"I know. I've seen you use it during the hunt. You have very good aim, when you aren't purposely missing," says Ebb.

"Um, what do you mean?" I ask.

"I know that you miss on purpose, so that the other hunters won't know you're as good as you are," says Ebb.

"Why do you think that?"

"Because I've seen you use your sling, and when it matters you never miss. And some of the rocks that you've thrown with it have struck very small targets. When you hit an animal, you almost always hit them in the head. Why is that?"

It takes me a moment to think.

"Because I don't want them to suffer. If you hit them in the head, it will either kill them or make them go to sleep. They won't feel any pain," I say.

"That is very kind of you, Sam," says Ebb.

"I don't like killing things. I only do it because I must, so that we can all live and have food to eat. I really only think about surviving," I say.

"That's sad. There is more to life than just surviving. But I imagine it would be hard to do more than just survive when you're taking care of a pair of brothers."

I just nod.

"I'm ready to visit Charm now, if you are," says Ebb.

"I'm ready too," I say.

It takes us a while to walk to Charm's room, because it's down some long tunnels that are tucked into the very back of the Crag. Ebb makes sure to check every corner again before I walk past.

I look forward to seeing Charm, because she's the closest thing to a parent I've ever had. I never knew my real parents. I don't know who they were, and no one in the Crag seems to know either. I have asked many, but all that they remember was that I was very young when I was found outside the cave. I was left out in the rain, and several of the women that were unjoined, and women that were gray ones took care of me.

Charm is the one I remember taking care of me more than any of my other mothers. She has always been so good of heart, and has always treated me well. But instead of caring for me until I was no longer a new one, like how I've protected Flot and Jet, after a few snows I was left to grow up on my own. I was still allowed to talk to Charm, but I was given my own room, and told not to see her much.

I still wonder why things changed, if I had done something wrong, or if one of the leaders decided to keep me from her. Maybe I had grown too close to her, or relied on her too much.

Being strong enough to take care of yourself is important, because everyone must help the Crag. How can people help the Crag if they cannot even help themselves? It's possible that someone decided to change my life, so I'd grow up strong, so that I could someday fight and someday lead.

Maybe that's what it was all about. Maybe the leaders had been planning for me to lead the hunt all along. It would explain why Lagan wanted me to replace him. Maybe even as a new one I showed skills that they would want in a leader.

I may never know, because the one man I would ask, Lagan, has been covered in grass and clover. Maybe Charm knows why I was taken from her.

We finally reach her room. I pull Charm's curtain back and put my head inside.

"Charm, it's Sam and Ebb. Can we come in?"

"Yes, of course you can come in," says Charm.

We step inside. There is just enough room for Charm's bed, her clothes, and the stumps that she uses as chairs. Ebb and I both sit down. Charm's long white hair touches the bed that she's sitting on. It's so straight and beautiful that it seems out of place in the Crag. She is knitting something out of yarn.

Charm is one of the best in the Crag at knitting. Each snow she knits me a new shirt or pair of pants. The clothes that she makes are very strong and last a long time.

"So why have you come to visit, Sam? Is it because of

the dragon you fought?" asks Charm.

"You heard about that?"

"Of course I did. What, do you think an old woman like me wouldn't talk to people, wouldn't hear things?" asks Charm, smiling at me.

I can tell that Charm isn't upset at me, that she's just teasing. That has always been Charm's way. Thankfully, she is very good at knowing who is safe to tease, and who is not.

"No, it's not that at all Charm," I say.

"Good. Just because I'm a gray one doesn't mean that I'm useless."

"I know!"

"Yes, well now that I know that you know, what have you come for, if not to tell me about killing a dragon?" asks Charm.

"I have been wondering why I was taken from you when I was still a new one," I say.

Charm's face shows loss and sadness, and I think I even see some anger in it. I feel bad for asking, because it makes her unhappy to think about it.

"I've been wondering when you would get around to asking me that," says Charm. "You see, when you were first found, you couldn't walk or talk, or even eat without help. There were a few of us that hadn't yet had any new ones, so we took turns feeding you, cleaning you and watching over you. As the snows came and left, most of those that helped take care of you found other people to join with, and they started having new ones of their own."

"But you never had any new ones," I say.

"No, I never did. Until I met you, I never wanted to have new ones. But by then, I couldn't have new ones anymore."

"I'm sorry, Charm."

"Oh, don't be. I loved you as if you were my own new one. Once I saw you, something inside me changed. You were so small, and so pink, and your eyes were always wide open, looking at things. I could tell that you would grow up smart.

That someday you would do great things," says Charm.

"I haven't done anything great," I say.

"Yes you have. You saved the hunters today. At least, that is what people are saying."

"Don't believe what people say. They're also saying that I'm the Sky Child."

Charm looks at me for a moment, smiling.

"That's because you are," says Charm.

I look over at Ebb, who seems surprised by Charm's words, but she smiles at me and nods. I turn back to Charm.

"I can't be the Sky Child," I say. "I'm not special."

"You are to me," says Charm.

"Then why was I taken from you? Why did you let that happen?" I ask.

Charm looks very hurt. I know it wasn't her decision, but I have always felt like maybe Charm didn't try very hard to keep me. That's why it's difficult to be around her sometimes. I feel like she gave up on me.

"I did everything I could to keep you, Sam. I pray to the Sky Gods you know that. Chaff was the one that suggested you be on your own. He told Hammer that since you were the Sky Child, that you should be raised to be strong, and not rely on anyone. Hammer wasn't sure that it was a good idea at such a young age. Chaff came to me and said that if I didn't agree to let you go, that he would have you killed."

"Why? Why would Chaff want me dead?" I ask.

"Because, just like everyone else, he believes the stories. He worried that you were the Sky Child."

"I still don't understand why people think I'm the Sky Child."

"Because you weren't born in the Crag. You are the only person we have ever seen from outside the cave. Most people believe we are the only ones that survived the End War. So how else could you be here? Only the Sky Gods could have given you to us."

"Even if I was the Sky Child, why would he want to kill me? The Sky Child is supposed to bring peace, and food, and happiness to everyone."

"Not to Chaff. You see, if everyone has plenty of food, then Chaff has no control anymore. He loses the one thing that makes him powerful and feared in the Crag. Chaff threatened me so that I would agree to give you up. I talked to Hammer and said that I thought it was a good idea for you to be on your own," says Charm.

"But if I were such a threat to Chaff, why didn't he just kill me?" I ask.

"Because he's a coward. If people knew he was behind your death, they would kill him, too. There are people that believe very strongly that you are the Sky Child, Sam, and they would do anything to protect you."

"Why didn't he send someone else to kill me then?"

"Because he didn't trust anyone, and no one trusted him. He knows that everyone hates him. So why would someone want to help Chaff kill the one person that might get rid of him? I think he hoped that someone would do it for him. That someone would get jealous of you and kill you. Maybe even someone who has lived as many snows as you have," says Charm.

I think for a moment. I start to realize that maybe Chaff had told Sickle and Scythe to bully me when I was a new one. He may even send one of them to kill me someday. Knowing that Chaff would use his own sons that way makes me hate him even more.

"I am sorry Charm for hurting you with my questions. I know that you did what you had to. I didn't know why until now, but thank you for telling me the truth," I say.

"The truth, Sam, is that I would do anything for you. Even if that means having you live somewhere else. Even if I miss you every day. Even if I wish things could be different, and that we could be together again. You have no idea how hard it has been for me. I don't get to be there for you, not the way I want to. I see you change, and become older. You are a parent now to your brothers. Can you imagine how hard it would be to have them taken away from you?"

"I can't."

"I did it because I love you, Sam."

I reach out and hug Charm. I wish that I had talked to her about this sooner, instead of letting the questions and doubt make me wonder if she cared about me.

"I love you too, Charm."

I'm surprised that I said it out loud. I know I feel love for Charm, but I never tell anyone that I love them. Not even Flot and Jet.

"Okay, you are going to have to stop all of this," says Ebb. "You're making me cry."

Charm and I both laugh.

"We should probably be letting you sleep now, Charm," I say.

"I hope that you stay safe and happy, Sky Child. I pray to the Sky Gods every day that you are," says Charm.

I smile back at her as Ebb and I stand up to leave.

"Oh, Charm, there is one more thing I was wondering about," I say.

"Yes?"

"How did I get my name?" I ask.

"Sam, your name was stitched into the blanket we found you wrapped in," says Charm.

"I thought that maybe you had named me."

"I wish I had, but no, the Sky Gods had already given you a name."

I nod my head, not really believing that the Sky Gods had named me, but not disagreeing with Charm's memory. Ebb and I leave.

Once we are well away from Charm's room, I turn to Ebb.

"Ebb, please don't tell anyone what Charm and I talked about. If anyone outside of us knew what she said, it could be dangerous. It could be dangerous for a lot of people," I say.

"Sam, I would never betray you like that," says Ebb.

"Thank you, Ebb, for protecting both my life and my

secrets."

"It is an honor."

While checking for danger along the way, Ebb walks me back to my room. As I make my way inside, Ebb smiles then turns and stands guard at the entrance of our room. I smile, because finally I may have made a friend.

# 13

It's not until I wake up that I realize how hard yesterday was on me. I am sore in my entire body. Every time I breathe out, it feels like my life is flowing out of me. When the people that drink too much beer talk about what the next morning is like, I imagine that this is how they feel.

Jet and Flot are busy snoring, which is what they both do best. I poke my head outside our room and see that Ebb is still there. She looks very tired.

"Ebb, I am up now. Thank you for protecting us last night. Please, go get some sleep," I say.

"Are you sure you will be safe?" asks Ebb.

"Yes. I have my brothers with me now, and they are more than enough protection for me," I say.

"I can tell that they are dangerous by how well they snore," says Ebb.

"They are amazing snorers," I admit.

"Well, take care then Sam."

"And you, Ebb."

I watch as Ebb leaves.

After a while I grow bored because I have nothing to do, and Jet and Flot are still asleep. I decide to make breakfast. I realize it may not be safe for me to be on my own right now, but things are most dangerous at night when they think you are asleep. Most killers in the Crag are cowards, and they won't risk attacking someone who can defend themselves.

I make my way to the mouth of the cave. The sun is still rising, and it is low enough that I cannot see it yet. The sky is gray and covered in clouds that cast white light all around me. It is barely raining; just enough to wet your hair, but not soak you. I hurry to where we keep the animals, so that I can stay as dry as possible.

When I reach the chickens, I see one of the hunters, Anchor, collecting his own breakfast. Anchor is tall and thin, and he's so thin that I wonder how he stands without falling into pieces. His arms and legs move in strange ways, like they are not a part of him. His black hair covers his moon-white face when he leans over. I can tell that he must wear his helmet whenever he is outside in the sun.

Anchor catches me out of the corner of his eye and turns to me. I stop quickly, not knowing whether I am in danger or not. I keep my hands at my sides, formed into fists, ready to use them if necessary.

"Sam, you startled me!" says Anchor. "I have news for you."

I have seen him use a big spear, and he is very good with it. He always seems to hit a place on an animal that will make it die quickly. It makes me think that he is like me, and doesn't want to see the animals in pain.

"What is your news, Anchor?" I ask, still tense.

"Oh, good, you know me."

"You're one of Lagan's friends," I say.

"Yes, we are friends. I mean, we were friends."

The smile leaves Anchor's face.

"I am sorry about Lagan," I say.

"Me too. He was the best of us. He always tried to keep peace among the hunters. Oh, but now we have you," says Anchor, trying to smile through his sadness.

"So what is your news?"

"Mast talked to me last night, and he thought we should make you some special armor, since you're our leader now. Something that would be good enough for the Sky Child."

67

"Anchor, I am not the Sky Child."

"That's what Mast said you would say."

"No, really, I'm not the Sky Child. It's just a story," I say.

"You will need to come to my room when you are done with breakfast, so that I can get your outline," says Anchor, ignoring what I said.

"The armor I have is fine," I say.

"Sam, we need to be able to see you when we're hunting, so that we can protect you," says Anchor.

I think about it for a moment. It does make sense for me to look different than everyone else, just so they know who to follow. Lagan had leather armor that was light gray like a cloudy sky. They had used ash from the Great Fire to color it. It made him stand out very well.

"Okay," I finally agree.

"I won't be the only one working on it."

"Who else will?" I ask.

"Jib and Stanchion," says Anchor.

I know that Jib makes armor, but Stanchion is someone that fixes things that are made of metal. We don't have much metal in the Crag. We only have what has been passed down to us from the gray ones many, many snows ago.

When something metal isn't needed any more, or is broken too badly to be fixed, Stanchion makes new things out of it. Sometimes they are useful things, and sometimes they are things to look at. He has made scraps into objects that are given as gifts. They are very beautiful. It is an honor to have him working on my armor.

"Thank you, Anchor. I will try to help however I can," I say.

"See you after breakfast then," says Anchor, walking away with his eggs.

I collect as many eggs as I can carry in my pockets and walk back to the Crag. After cooking breakfast at the Great Fire, I head back to our room. When I get there, Flot and Jet are awake and dressed. Flot has already heated a pot of water, and set out cups for each of us.

"What took so long?" asks Flot.

I give him an angry stare. I set the pan on the red stone floor and all of us wolf down the eggs. About halfway through breakfast, Flot stops eating.

"Seriously Sam, why did it take you so long to get breakfast?" asks Flot.

"Anchor was getting eggs too, and he stopped me," I say.

"Why did he do that?"

"He needed something."

"What did he need?"

"He needed to talk to me," I say.

"Sam, why are you being a stupid butt?" asks Flot.

"Because you smell like one," I say.

Flot rolls his eyes at me.

"Okay, fine. Anchor needs me to go to his room so that he can make new armor for me," I say.

"Really?" says Jet.

"Yes, really," I say.

"Are you going to make it gray like Lagan's armor was?" asks Flot.

"Probably not. But we will need to figure out a color that doesn't look like the armor that the hunters already wear."

"Who is 'we'?" asks Flot.

"Me and Anchor. And Jib. And Stanchion," I say.

"Wait, Stanchion is working on your armor?" asks Flot.

I nod my head. "I don't know what he's making for the armor, but they wouldn't have asked him if they didn't need his help."

"Can we come along?" asks Jet.

"Yes, but all they are doing is getting my outline. They won't have anything for me to try on yet," I say.

"Okay, that does sound kind of boring," says Jet. "Never mind."

We finish up our breakfast and I send Jet off to clean

69

the pan. Once I leave our room, I head to the Great Fire to ask Moss which path leads to Anchor's room. Moss tells me that it is only a few rooms away from Charm's, and to follow that path.

I have a hard time finding it. When I get to Charm's room, I ask her for help. She tells me that you take a narrow side-tunnel to get there, and it is not easy to see. I have to look around for a while before I finally find the tunnel.

Although I can get into the side-tunnel with no problem, I can see how larger people wouldn't be able to. I doubt Chaff could ever fit down this tunnel. I start to wonder if maybe Jet, Flot and I should move into this area just for protection. But I hate small spaces. They make me nervous.

I walk down the tunnel, and I can feel my palms and forehead sweat. Dizziness threatens to make me fall. After closing my eyes and taking a deep breath, I'm finally able to walk down the tunnel and enter Anchor's room.

It is quite large as rooms go. You could probably have a pair of families staying in it and still have room. My guess is that he didn't kill anyone for the room. He probably took it because no one else wanted it, since it is hard to get to. He might be like me, not wanting to be bothered much.

"Ah, Sam, you came. All I need is for you to lie down on the ground over here," says Anchor, pointing to a spot near the wall.

I go over to where he pointed and lie down on the hard stone. I can feel the cold of the floor through my hair and clothes.

"Okay, now I am going to make the outline," says Anchor.

Anchor takes a light-colored rock and scratches the floor all around me. When he is finally done, I stand up and stare at what is left. It looks kind of like me, or at least my shape. But with the white line on the dark red floor, it is very easy to see.

"So what color did you want your armor?" asks Anchor. "I can do yellow, gray, white, green, red or blue. I can also mix some of the colors together, but some of them don't mix well. Also, so that you don't look like the other hunters, you can't pick brown or black."

"I'm not sure," I say.

"What if we made your armor blue, since you are the Sky Child, and the sky is blue?"

I close my eyes and bite down hard, trying not to yell at Anchor for saying I'm the Sky Child.

"I don't think it should be blue. I do like that color, but the sky isn't blue very often," I say.

"How about red, like blood?" asks Anchor.

"I don't know that I would like red either, because I don't want to think about blood every time we go hunting. There is enough real blood when we kill something," I say. "How about green?"

"Yes, we can make it green."

"Can it be a green like clover? Dark, and light, and strong at the same time?"

"I think we can do that," says Anchor.

"Thank you," I say, shaking Anchor's hand.

I leave Anchor's place, and make my way back to our room.

Halfway there, as I turn down a twisting tunnel, I hear a struggle. I move my feet faster, trying to find out who's fighting. I stop where the tunnel either continues toward our room, or splits off toward an even darker side-tunnel. I stand and listen for a moment, trying to decide which pathway to go down. Unable to tell which direction the fight is, I try the darker tunnel.

The sounds of punching and grunts of pain get louder. As I turn the corner, I see Sickle and Scythe standing in front of Flot. Sickle is punching him hard in the stomach.

"Stop!" I yell.

Sickle and Scythe look surprised but don't move. After a tense moment, Sickle takes a step toward me, dropping Flot to the ground. Scythe starts to move forward, following his brother's lead.

"Oh, did you want to get hit too?" asks Sickle. "We can hurt you if you want, just like we used to."

I realize I don't have any weapons on me, nothing I can use to hurt them badly. I'm also not very good with my fists. But I need to do something, to protect Flot.

Before they can say anything else, I jump toward Sickle, and use my fist to hit him in the ear. I'd meant to hit him in the face, maybe blind him, but hitting him in the ear at least made him cover his head.

I look over at Scythe, who is surprised I attacked Sickle. I try to use that to my advantage and punch Scythe in the gut, but he's too big. My punch doesn't seem to do anything. The look of surprise changes to anger as he reaches out and grabs me by the shirt, pulls me hard, and sends me into a wall, knocking me to the ground.

I'm surprised by how quickly Scythe reaches out for me again. He grabs onto my shirt, forcing me up, and as he does I kick out at his legs. I miss, but try again. This time, I kick his leg hard enough that he lets go.

I can tell that Sickle's recovered now, so I try to hit him in the face again. This time I miss, and Sickle hits me in the face instead. My cheek is on fire, and I can tell that I'm bleeding. I swing again, and this time I hit his face, which splits open his lip. Covering his bloody face with his hands, he kicks out at me, tripping me and knocking me to the ground. Before I can get up, he runs off down the tunnel.

Scythe, still holding his leg where I kicked him, looks at me, then looks down the tunnel that Sickle just ran down. It takes him a moment to decide, but thankfully he follows his brother. I wait until the echo of their footsteps disappears then hurry back to Flot.

"Are you okay?" I ask.

"Ungh, just leave me alone, Sam."

"Do you want me to get back at them?"

"No. I don't want you fighting my battles for me. I'll be fine. Go away."

"But Flot... "

"JUST GO!"

Flot yelling in my face startles me, and I back up. I can see in his eyes a deep anger, but I don't know if it's anger at me for trying to help, or if it's anger at Sickle and Scythe for torturing him. He could even be angry at himself. I felt the same way growing up. I hated that I let Sickle and Scythe bully me. There wasn't much I could do, being so small. The few times I did fight back, things were much worse for me. They would hit me even harder, or stomp on me with their feet. And no one ever came to help. I think that was the hardest part; not having someone to protect me, or to patch my wounds.

I feel anger building inside. Not just for Sickle and Scythe being evil, but for failing Flot. He is going through what I went through; what I tried to spare him from. I just hope he knows that he's not alone.

I nod at him, and walk back to our room.

14

When I get back to our room, Jet isn't there, but Mast is waiting inside for me. I start to worry, because I'm surprised Mast would come into our room without being invited. Something serious must have brought him here.

I notice that he's not wearing his armor. I'm not used to seeing him in normal clothes. I don't look at a lot of people. I feel like if I don't notice others, then they won't notice me. It's helped me stay alive. So even if I passed by him in the tunnels, I wouldn't have noticed what he looked like.

He has a beard, though not very long, and it has patches of white in it. He is not a gray one yet, but it probably won't be many snows before he looks like one. His eyes are serious, like he has lived a long and dangerous life, and there is little happiness in them.

Mast's hair is dark brown, like the color of dirt when it rains. His skin is colored red where the sun has done its work. He wears his long hair tied back to keep it out of his face. His body looks like a tree stump, very sturdy and strong, and his arms look like he could move the largest rock in the Crag. I am glad that Chaff is my enemy, and not Mast. As I wipe the blood from my cheek carefully with a towel, I try not to press too hard because of the pain.

"Do you have need of me, Mast?" I ask.

"No, I bring you news. Before you are truly the Leader of the Hunt, you must face the trials. Then, and only then will you be allowed to lead," says Mast.

"Mast, I don't want to lead," I say.

"That makes no difference. You will start tomorrow at sunrise. Be prepared for anything."

Mast walks past me, but I stop him.

"Wait, are the trials dangerous? Could I die?" I ask.

"Yes."

"Then I'm not doing them."

"I am sorry Sam, but you have no choice."

"You always have a choice," I say.

"Then you must choose either to go through the trials, or we will kill you, and someone will take your place," says Mast.

"So I can't make someone else the Leader of the Hunt?"

"No."

"Fine then. Kill me," I say.

Mast stares at me in disbelief.

"I didn't want this," I say. "Why should I bother when I will probably die anyway?"

"Think of Jet and Flot. What will they do without you? Think of the Crag, and of the hunters. We need a leader like you. I know you don't really want to die. It's why you've worked so hard to survive. Why you took control when Lagan died," says Mast.

"Did Lagan and Hammer have to go through the trials?" I ask.

"Yes, but it is different for everyone. What you will face will be meant for you alone."

"How many people have died in the trials?"

"Many," says Mast. "Many more than have succeeded."

I think to myself for a moment.

"Fine, I will do your trials. But once I am leader, I will change the rules so that no one will suffer to become leader ever again," I say.

"You miss the point of why the rule exists. It was put

into place so that only someone brave, and strong, and smart would lead the hunters. It also keeps people from wanting to kill the current leader to take their place. It is meant to protect the hunters from having an evil coward for a leader."

"Like Chaff?"

"I am certain that people like him are the reason the trials exist," says Mast.

I take a moment longer to think.

"I understand," I say.

Mast turns around then leaves.

I wish I could leave everything behind me. Forget being the Leader of the Hunt, or even a hunter at all. I'd never have to kill a living thing again. Just take Jet and Flot and leave the Crag. But there is nowhere to go. We would walk around with no direction, praying to the Sky Gods that we find somewhere new to live.

I can't do that. I can't risk their lives to avoid the trials. Going out on our own would be just as dangerous. So I will go through the trials for them, if for no other reason than to give them the chance to stay here, and stay alive.

I sit on my bed and think for a while, trying to decide how to ready myself for the trials. Eventually Flot returns. I look at him, but he won't look at me. He tries to act like nothing has happened; like he isn't injured. Even though he is not very strong, Flot tries very hard to be tough.

"So what did Mast come to talk about?" asks Flot.

"I have to go through trials so that I can become the Leader of the Hunt. If I refuse, they will put me to death," I say.

Jet walks in right then, having heard what I'd just said. I look at both of their faces, and I see the same fear and worry I feel inside.

"What do you need to do for the trials?" asks Jet.

"I will be tested, but they didn't say how," I say.

"Could you die?" asks Flot.

"Yes, but I'm not going to. I'm going to live for many more snows. I don't want to do this, but I have no choice."

Neither Flot nor Jet say a word.

"Now I need to train," I say.

"How do you train for something, when you don't even know what that something is?" asks Flot.

"I really don't know," I say.

"Well, did Mast say anything? Anything that might help?" asks Flot.

"He said that the trials are meant to test if someone is brave, and strong, and smart."

"At least that's something," says Flot. "But how do you practice being brave? Strong you can practice by lifting heavy things. You aren't very smart, so you should probably play a few games of jump stones with me for practice."

I give Flot a fake look of anger.

"You're right," I say. "It is a good idea to play a few games. And I probably won't get much stronger, even if I worked very hard at it until the sun sets. I also think that I am as brave as I will ever be. Okay Flot, you win. We can play jump stones."

I'm glad to have the game as a distraction, so that I don't worry as much. I do my best to pay attention, but my thoughts keep going back to the trials. Sometimes worrying about something is worse than what actually happens, but sometimes it isn't.

The first game goes by quickly. I beat Flot easily. The next takes much longer. Flot paid attention to the first game and learned from it. I think he is taking it very seriously, because he wants to help me. I know if either Flot or Jet had to go through the trials, I would be working very, very hard to make sure they were ready for it.

I win the next game, but not by much. I only have a few pieces left. Jet has been watching us play, and I think he is starting to pick up some of the tricks that I use. He smiles right before I make an important move, and cringes when I make a mistake. Maybe Jet is better at strategy than I realized.

The last game is the best game of jump stones that I have ever played. It seems to take forever. Flot thinks through every move very, very slowly, making sure he makes the best decision he can.

Normally when I play, I don't have to think about the first few moves because I have done them so many times. There are only so many pieces you can move, and places you can move them to. But even those moves take a while as Flot tries his best to win.

I don't know if it is pride or stubbornness, but I try my hardest too. I don't want Flot to beat me, even if it would mean so much to him. As hard as he is trying, I don't think he wants to beat me either. I think he just wants me doing my best, so that I have a chance at surviving the trials.

I lose pieces, and Flot loses pieces. He gets a rock, and this time he does everything he can to protect it. He remembers to protect what is most important to him. I get a rock, and then another rock. Flot looks worried, until he gets another rock, too.

I can't remember a game we have played where he had a pair of rocks. I can tell that Flot is very happy to get another rock. The question is, will he be able to figure out how to use his pair of rocks together?

Slowly, I pick apart his pieces, until only my pair of rocks remain. Flot looks unhappy, but he still smiles.

"Good game," he says.

"Good game," I reply. "You did very, very well Flot. Once you have more experience with how to use a pair of rocks, I am sure you will soon beat me."

"I don't know, Sam. It seems like every time I get better, you get better."

"I have to. I don't like to lose."

"Sam, have you ever lost at jump stones?" asks Jet.

"Sure, lots of times when I was first learning. The important thing is to learn from your losses. Sometimes you get more out of losing than you do from winning, because sometimes you just get lucky when you beat someone. Maybe they make a mistake, or don't try very hard. There can be things you learn from victories, but it's your losses that make you stronger. Learn from your enemies."

"But you aren't my enemy," says Flot.

"Yes I am, when we play jump stones. That's the point. We play games to war with each other without hurting anyone. They are meant to teach you things more important about yourself, and about others, than what you could learn by talking with them. You learn how they think, and how they see things. You can bet that someone good at jump stones would be good at war," I say.

"But I have always heard that a game is just a game," says Jet.

"Games are never just games. The people that say that usually aren't very good at them. It is a way of saying that the game does not matter to them, so if they lose, it doesn't hurt them inside."

"I try not to let it hurt me inside," says Flot.

"I know, but it's okay to let it hurt a little, so that it makes you want to be better. It should make you want to work harder, and get better, so that you win, and then the pain goes away."

"I never thought of it that way," says Flot.

"Neither had I, until now," I admit.

## 15

I spend the rest of the day trying to stay busy. I clean our room, wash my clothes, and bathe in the loud waters. Flot and Jet both go off and get into whatever kind of trouble they can find. Near the end of the day, Ebb visits me.

"Sam?" I hear her sweet voice say. Then she sees me. "What happened?"

"My face? Sickle and Scythe happened," I reply.

Her face flashes anger, but I shake my head 'no', asking her not to do anything about it. After a tense moment, she calms down, but I can tell she still wants to fight them, so I change the subject. "Did you get some rest?" I ask.

"Yes. It wasn't easy at first, with people walking by my room. But I was so tired from staying up all night that I was able to sleep."

"I'm sorry that you had to stay up all night because of me," I say.

"You don't need to apologize, Sam. Keeping you safe is worth it," she says. "From the look of your face though, I have failed."

"You haven't failed. I ran into a fight, to protect Flot. It isn't your fault." I think for a moment. "Have you heard about the trials?"

"No, I haven't. What are 'the trials'?"

"Before I can become the Leader of the Hunt I must go through trials to see if I am brave enough, strong enough and smart enough to lead."

"Are they dangerous?"

"There's a chance I'll die."

"Can't you refuse?" asks Ebb.

"Mast says that if I do, they will kill me. I have no choice."

"Run away then, Sam."

"To where?" I ask. "There's nowhere to run to."

"But I don't want you to die," says Ebb.

"I don't want to die either, but I don't have a choice. Maybe I'll survive the trials."

"But why take the chance?"

"Because I can't just take my brothers and leave. I need to think about them too. If it was just me, I might risk living outside of the Crag. I know how to hunt, so I could feed myself, and I would have my armor to protect me. But I can't risk Flot's and Jet's lives."

"So you're going through with it?" says Ebb.

"Yes."

Ebb's face is filled with sadness. She stares at the ground, and won't look me in the eyes.

"Is there anything I can do to help you prepare?"

"I can't think of anything. Flot and I played jump stones, but I don't feel any smarter," I say.

"And you can't practice how to be brave," says Ebb. "But it's also supposed to test your strength?"

"Yeah, but you would have to move large stones for many sunrises to really get much stronger. There is no time for that."

"Maybe they don't mean for you to be stronger, like lifting heavy things. Maybe they mean for you to be good at combat."

"I think I will be okay," I say. "I can protect myself with my sling, or use a spear."

"But what if they give you neither of those? What if you have to protect yourself with only your hands?"

"I hadn't thought of that. So how will I get better at

hand combat?" I ask. "I'm not very good at it."

"I could teach you," says Ebb.

"You know how to fight with your fists?"

"Yes, my father showed me how. He used to drink beer and fight people. Sometimes he would fight people to win more food, or blankets. Sometimes he would just fight to show someone he was stronger."

"Did he ever kill anyone?" I ask.

"Not that he ever told me. But I asked him once, and he became very sad. He wouldn't talk to me about it," says Ebb.

"I imagine if I killed someone, that it would be very hard for me. I would hurt inside very much. I would only ever kill someone if I had to. To protect Jet or Flot. People I love," I say. "So how are you going to teach me to hand fight?"

"Well, we'll need to go outside. The sun should still be in the sky, but we won't have very long. Let's hurry."

Ebb and I leave the Crag, and walk for a while so that no one will see us. The ground is soaked from the rains. I can see small patches of blue sky, but the sun has not been able to dry up the land. The clouds keep the ground wet.

For the first time, I realize how beautiful Ebb is, now that I can see her in the white light of a gray sky. Her hair is the color of wheat, which is unlike the hair of most of our people. My hair is deep brown, with parts that are almost a dark red color.

"We should find a place where the dirt is soft, so that if we fall, it will not hurt," says Ebb.

We walk until we find a patch of dirt that has now become mud. I figure that should work, and Ebb agrees.

"Okay, the first thing I will teach you is how to stand," says Ebb. "You want to spread your feet apart, about as wide as your shoulders, then bend your knees."

"Like this?" I ask.

"You are bending your knees too much. Just bend them a little. Yes, that is better. Now put your fists in the air."

I put my fists in the air.

"Not that high," says Ebb. "Here, like this."

Ebb puts her fists up near her face, with her elbows bent.

"Why do you put them near your face?" I ask.

"So you can protect it from punches. Most people swing for the head."

"That makes sense," I say.

"Which hand do you use more?"

"My right."

"Okay, so you want to have your left foot closer to your enemy," says Ebb.

"That doesn't make any sense," I say. "Don't you want the arm you hit harder with closer to your enemy?"

"No, you want it further back, so that when you swing it, it will do more damage."

"Oh. Then what do you do with your other arm?" I ask.

"You can use it to protect yourself, and to make short punches with it just to distract your enemy. Here, watch."

Ebb comes up to me, putting her left foot closer to me than her right. Then she throws a quick punch with her left hand that hits my forehead. Thankfully, she misses where I'd already been punched by Sickle.

"Hey!" I say.

"Hey what? You knew I was going to do it, because I told you. You could have moved out of the way at the last moment. That is another thing you should do. When someone tries to throw a punch, you should move out of the way so that you don't get hit," says Ebb.

"Now you are making sense again," I say.

"I've been making sense since we started," says Ebb. "Do you remember how getting hit in the forehead made you stop thinking, and stop moving?"

"Yes," I say.

"Well, it's good to follow one of those with a punch from your strong hand. Like this," says Ebb.

She hits me in the face with a short punch from her

left hand again, but thankfully it gives me just enough time to move out of the way of her right hand. It comes quickly, and she tries to hit me with all her strength. I bend over out of the way, and I hit her in the stomach with my left hand. Not thinking, just moving.

"Ungh," groans Ebb.

"I'm sorry!" I say, worried I hurt her.

Ebb throws a punch that I never see. Her left fist comes from below, and hits my chin, sending me to the muddy ground. The world goes dark.

* * *

"Sam? Sam? Are you okay?" asks Ebb.

"What happened?" I ask.

"I punched you really hard."

"Ow," I groan. "You really did. You hit me so hard I fell asleep!"

"I don't know if I would call it sleep," says Ebb. "But you definitely weren't awake."

I stand back up, out of the mud, which is now dripping off me.

"Okay, the next thing I'm going to... " starts Ebb.

Before she can finish her sentence, I tackle her around the waist. I knock her into the mud, and we roll around. She seems surprised by the attack. I try to hold her arms down, but she punches me in the stomach. I roll over onto my back, my stomach filled with pain. She uses that against me. Ebb climbs on top of me, holds me around the neck with her left hand and holds her right fist up high.

"Do you want another punch to your head?" says Ebb.

"No, I'll stop. I promise," I say.

"I'm trying to help you," says Ebb.

"I know. I'm sorry."

We both stand back up.

"Just so you know, Sam, that was smart of you. You surprised me. You want to do that in any fight, especially when the person is bigger than you. Hand fighting isn't just about fists, it's also about being smart. Use what you have around you, like this," says Ebb.

Ebb throws a ball of mud at my face. I somehow manage to move out of the way, but it still hits my ear. It is very hard for me not to do the same back.

"What I was trying to do was cover your eyes in mud," says Ebb. "That way you couldn't see me. I would be able to hit you while your eyes didn't work, and it would be harder for you to hit me. Make sense?"

"That seems unfair," I say.

"Yeah, well fights aren't fair, are they?" says Ebb. "Sometimes you are fighting for your life. When you are fighting in the trials, it *will* be for your life. Remember that, Sam."

"I will," I say.

"The last thing I'm going to teach you is how to kick," says Ebb.

"Are you allowed to kick in a hand fight?" I ask.

"Have you ever read a book on hand fighting?" asks Ebb.

"No."

"That's because there isn't one. There are no rules for fighting. Use anything you can. Bite your enemy if you must, or claw at their eyes. All that matters is surviving. If that means you have to kill your enemy, kill your enemy, because they would kill you."

"Okay, so how do I kick then?" I ask.

"You can use a kick like a punch. You know how you use your left hand to throw a short punch? Do the same thing with your left foot," says Ebb.

"You mean like this?" I say.

I use my left foot to stomp the ground.

"Yes, something like that. The best places you can kick at are the inside part of the foot, and at the knee. If you damage your enemy's knee, they will not be able to fight, and they definitely won't be able to run and catch you. The inside of the foot will hurt your enemy, but after a moment they will be able to continue attacking you. Remember that, if you are being attacked."

"Can I kick any higher?" I ask.

"It is not a good idea, but go ahead and try it," says Ebb.

I try kicking her in the stomach and miss. Instead, she catches and holds onto my leg. I lose my balance and fall into the mud.

"Yeah, I can see why I shouldn't do that," I say as I get back up. "Is there anything else I need to learn?" I ask.

"Not that I can think of. But you should probably practice what I have taught you. Go ahead and attack me."

I try hard to attack Ebb without hurting her. I know that when the time comes, I will need to hurt my enemy. But for now, it helps just knowing what attacks I should use.

As we practice fighting, I learn how to use my arms to protect my stomach and face. I also learn how to block kicks with my shins. It hurts, but it is better than having a broken foot or knee. Ebb doesn't hold back much, but I know that she is trying not to hurt me either. For her training to work, and to help me survive, it must be as real as she can make it.

The sun starts to set. We are both very tired. She attacks me one last time, tackling me to the ground. We roll around in the mud a bit, but finally she ends up on top of me, pinning my arms to the ground.

"Do you give up?" asks Ebb.

"Never!" I say.

We both laugh. Ebb rolls off me and onto her back. We just lie in the mud for a moment.

"Thank you, Ebb. What you've taught me may save my life. I will forever owe you a debt," I say.

"Just survive, Sam. I don't want you to die."

"I will do everything I can to live."

There is just enough sun left in the sky that we're able to find our way back to the Crag.

16

When we get back I notice how muddy we are. I suggest to
Ebb that we wash off what we can in the puddle at the mouth
of the Crag. It takes us a few minutes to get the mud off our
feet and legs. I figure it should work until we can make it to the
loud waters. Once we are only half-covered in mud, we walk
back to my room.

Flot and Jet are inside, talking to each other. They
have surprised and guilty looks on their faces, like we walked in
on them planning someone's death.

"Ebb, I would like to introduce you to my brothers," I
say.

Before I can say their names, they both stand up from
the ground. Flot reaches out a hand to Ebb.

"I'm Flot," he says, shaking hands.

"Jet," says Jet, also shaking her hand. "So, you watched
over us last night?"

"Yes, I did," says Ebb.

"So why are you here?" asks Flot.

"We're grabbing some soap," I say.

"Good, because you look horrible. Have you been
rolling around in the mud again?" asks Flot.

"Ebb was teaching me how to hand fight," I say.

Both Flot and Jet smile.

"What kind of evil have you been up to?" I ask.

"Nothing," says Flot. "Nothing we want you to know

about."

I just stare at them.

"Anyway, we're off to the loud waters," I say.

We grab the soap then leave.

"Your brothers seem nice," says Ebb.

"Yes, they do *seem* nice," I say.

"It is also nice to see them when they aren't asleep."

"I'm not sure I agree with that."

We arrive at the loud waters. Ebb and I wade in, close to where the water is leaving the cave. We both lie down, completely covering ourselves in water. I hold my breath and let the water do its job. I can feel the clumps of mud pull away from my face and clothes. It also feels good to have the cool water on my bruises.

After I feel like I'm rinsed, I stand up. Ebb does the same. We both take off our clothes and start washing them with soap. I look over at Ebb then quickly look away. She looks over at me.

"Sam, are you blushing?" asks Ebb.

"Um, what do you mean?" I say.

"Your face is turning red."

"Must be from the mud."

I don't know why I would blush. It's not like I haven't washed my clothes and bathed in front of other people my entire life. I don't blush when I wash around Flot or Jet, or anyone else.

I finish up washing my clothes. I rest near the edge of the loud waters, waiting for Ebb to wash her long hair. It takes her a while to wash hers; much longer than I spend on mine.

We take our clothes to the Great Fire and hang them up. Ebb and I use the warmth of the fire to dry off. Moss is there, and he looks at us both then smiles at me.

Eventually we are both dry.

"I hope you do well in the trials," says Ebb.

"I will do my best to survive, and to remember what you have taught me."

"Just keep inside your mind that the trials aren't a

game. There is more to lose than your life. Do what you must to survive. That is all that matters."

"I will," I say.

Ebb places a small kiss on my cheek then hurries back to her room.

## 17

I head back to our room and put on some clean clothes. Flot and Jet are still there. Flot is reading a book, and Jet is cleaning his armor. Flot finally looks up.

"Wow, she really must have punched you a lot. Your face looks even worse. So are your arms and chest. Are you hurt?" asks Flot.

"I'm fine," I say.

I hurry to put clothes on, so that most of the bruises are covered. It doesn't take me long to change.

"Did you hit her back?" asks Jet.

"A few times, but I was trying not to hurt her."

"Oh, so you got beat up just so you wouldn't hurt her?" asks Flot.

"No, she was better than me," I admit.

"Wait, you're saying that someone was better than you at something?" says Flot.

"... Yes."

"Just what I thought. You aren't the Sky Child," says Flot.

"How did you hear about that?" I ask.

"What, you being the Sky Child? Seems like that's the only thing people are talking about. Though, when everyone hears about how Ebb beat you up, I'm sure they won't think you're the Sky Child anymore," says Flot.

"How will everyone hear that Ebb beat me?" I ask.

"Because I'm going to tell everyone about it!" says Flot.

Jet laughs.

"Do you want me to use what she taught me on your head?" I ask.

Flot covers his face with his book, and Jet goes quiet.

"I'm heading to the feast now. Are you coming?" I ask.

"Yeah," says Jet.

"I will come when I'm done with this chapter," says Flot.

"What are you reading?" I ask.

Flot ignores the question. I look at it, and I remember reading it a few snows ago. The name of it has something to do with the end of a sidewalk, but I have no idea what a sidewalk is. Most of the stories in it are short and strange, and make no sense, but I like them.

Jet follows me out of the room. I turn to him.

"So, what are you and Flot up to?" I ask.

"Oh, nothing," says Jet.

"I'm serious, I need to know," I say.

"We've been talking about girls is all."

"Oh, that's right! You really like that girl, Till," I say.

"Shut up!" says Jet.

"Did you finally talk to her?" I ask.

"Yes."

"And?"

"And it's none of your business," says Jet.

"Must have gone fairly well, or you would be complaining about it."

"She might like me. She says nice things to me, but I can't tell if she just wants to be friends or not."

"Friends isn't what you want to be?" I ask.

"I want to maybe be more than friends."

"That sounds serious," I say.

"I'm too young to be serious with someone."

"Well, friends is a good place to start. I hope it works out, and I hope that she's nice."

"She is," says Jet.

After walking for a while, we finally reach the feast chamber. I get into line so that I can get some food. Jet stays next to me. I look around and I see Ebb. She smiles at me, and I nod back.

"I'm glad that you've finally made a friend," says Jet.

"Me too."

We get our food and it's more wolf stew. I think since we didn't hunt today, Cleave and the other cooks just made what they could out of leftover meat. It's not as good as yesterday's wolf stew.

I sit down at the head table. I watch as Jet finds a seat far away from where I'm sitting. I also see a few girls sit down next to him. The girls seem interested in him, but he either doesn't care, or he just doesn't realize it.

I look across the table, and I catch Chaff staring at me. His mouth is twisted into an evil grin that makes my stomach sick. Helm turns and whispers to me.

"Chaff wanted to wish you good luck on the trials."

"I'm sure he did," I say.

"My guess is he actually wants you to fail," says Helm.

"I'm sure he does."

Chaff is pathetic. It only makes me want to do better in the trials. Maybe I will get lucky, and one of the trials will be fighting my worst enemy. I would very much like to beat Chaff with my fists. He wouldn't be able to smile that evil grin anymore.

"Do you think you are ready for the trials?" asks Helm.

"If I said no, would you give me more time?" I ask.

"No."

"Then what does it matter? I have done what I can. Hopefully this isn't my last meal," I say.

I realize that it could be my last meal. I don't know if I will be able to make breakfast in the morning, before the trials start, so my last meal is old stew. That makes me sad.

I can feel Sickle and Scythe staring at me, and I know that they too hope I die tomorrow. I wish they were the ones going through the trials.

I look up and see that Flot has finally come to eat. I watch as he gets food then sits next to one of his friends.

I wish I could eat with Flot and Jet, but I must do what is expected of me now. I liked things better when people didn't expect anything from me. All I had to do was hunt and stay alive. They let me keep to myself, and they definitely didn't make me go through any trials.

But if I wasn't going through this, if they didn't think I was the Sky Child, I never would have made friends with Ebb. I don't know her very well yet, but I am still glad that she is my friend. I keep that thought in my head, that what I'm going through will all be worth it. Worth it if I survive.

I don't want to talk to Mast or Helm, because I'm angry at them. I know they aren't the ones that created the trials, but they are the people that are making me go through them.

I finish my meal and head toward our room. I decide to take a side-tunnel that is shorter than using the big circle of the Crag. As I pass by rooms I look inside, not paying attention to them. All of them are lit except one. When I reach the dark room, I hear a noise coming from inside. It is very quiet, but I recognize the sound of breathing. I turn and look into the darkness.

That is when it looks back at me. I see a pair of eyes, but they are hard to make out. Without warning, the shadow attacks me. They kick me in the stomach and I fall to the ground. I wait for them to move closer, and I punch the shadow in its groin.

The shadow groans in pain, clutching itself. I get up off the ground and put my fists up, the way that Ebb taught me to. Even in the darkness I can see the sharp metal object that the shadow is holding. The shadow reaches out with its arm and tries to stab me. I step away from the arm and send my right fist flying as hard as I can, right where I can see the shadow's eyes.

I am very lucky, because my punch hits exactly where

I'd hoped. The shadow falls to the ground, and I can tell that they will be asleep for a while. I hear the clank of the knife hitting the ground. I also hear footsteps running up to me. I hold up my hands again, ready to fight my new attacker. Only it isn't a new attacker, it's Ebb.

"Are you okay, Sam?"

"Yes, I am fine," I say.

"Why didn't you wait for me?" asks Ebb.

"I wasn't thinking. I am sorry. I'm just so worried about dying in the trials that I forgot people were still be trying to kill me," I say.

"You will never beat the trials if you don't pay attention to your surroundings," says Ebb.

"At least I heard them and then saw them before they attacked," I say.

"But you could have been killed!" says Ebb.

"I know. I'm sorry," is all I can manage.

I reach down and pick up the knife then drag the attacker into the light. It looks like they have taken a dark shirt and wrapped it around their face to cover it. I remove the shirt and stare at my attacker.

I don't know who this person is.

"Ebb, do you know him?" I ask.

"No."

It is a man who looks closer to being a gray one than a new one. There is nothing different or interesting about his face. He just looks like a person. Someone that maybe wouldn't be noticed. His hair does not cover much of his head, and his stomach sticks out.

"What are you going to do with him, Sam?" asks Ebb.

"He tried to kill me, but I don't know why. I don't think he is a hunter, because I have never seen him, and he doesn't look like he's been outside much. To be safe, I should probably kill him, but I don't think that I can. Not when he can't defend himself. Killing him right now would be something a coward would do," I say.

"I agree. But if you don't kill him, then he might try to

kill you again."

"That is true as well."

I try to think of a different, better way.

"What if we have him thrown out of the Crag?" I ask.

"We might be able to do that."

"Can you help me drag his body?"

"Yes," says Ebb.

I hold the knife between my teeth, with the sharp edge aimed away from my mouth. We each grab an arm and drag his body to the Great Fire.

There are many people there, praying to the Sky Gods for a safe night. Most seem surprised to see us dragging a man's body to the Great Fire.

I take off the man's other shirt and tie his feet together, while Ebb uses the shirt he had on his face to tie his hands together. I pull him into a sitting position and rest him against a large rock.

"Ebb, can you go and get Mast and Helm, and anyone else you think should be here for this decision?" I ask.

"Yes, I will do that," she says.

I watch Ebb run down one of the connecting tunnels. I notice that a pair of the people that were praying have left. I do not worry, for I have a knife in my hand now. I will be safe. I look back at the attacker, and it seems like he is waking up.

"If you try to get up, or attack me again, I will kill you," I say.

The man just stares at me through his evil, dark eyes.

Eventually Ebb shows up with Mast, Helm, Vault and Crook.

"Why is that man tied up?" asks Vault.

"He was hiding in the shadows and tried to kill me," I say.

"Why didn't you kill him back?" asks Crook.

"Because I didn't want to kill him. What I want to do is throw him out of the Crag," I say.

"No!" comes a voice from a side-tunnel.

It is Chaff. One of the people praying must have

found him and brought him here.

"He is of my blood," says Chaff, as he nears the Great Fire. "He is my cousin. A harvester."

"Did you send him to kill me?" I ask.

"I would never do such a thing!" says Chaff, faking disbelief.

I stare into Chaff's eyes, and it takes all my strength not to attack him with the knife.

"This man must leave the Crag forever," I say.

"No, I will talk to him, and make sure that this never happens again," says Chaff. "He really is a good person. This is probably just a misunderstanding."

"How is attacking someone in the dark, with a knife, a misunderstanding?" I ask.

"He isn't very smart. He was probably just confused. Maybe he was at the feast, thought he needed his knife to eat with, and came back for it. Then he accidentally scared you."

"He kicked me in the stomach and tried to cut me with the knife," I say.

"Maybe he was afraid you were going to attack him. It was self-defense. You have killed a dragon, haven't you, so you must be very dangerous," says Chaff. "In fact, did you have any weapons?"

"No."

"Yet you were able to hit him so hard that he was no longer awake."

My grip on the knife tightens. I look over at Vault. He shakes his head 'no', telling me that I shouldn't kill Chaff. Crook stares at Chaff, and looks like she wants to kill him herself. But she doesn't. She knows, just like me, that we can't kill Chaff. It would doom us all.

"If anyone else attacks me, I will kill them," I say. "I will not control my blade the way I am controlling it now. So, for your sake Chaff, make sure that your family does not 'accidentally' attack me again."

"I am sure that no harm will come to you now that this unfortunate situation has been cleared up," says Chaff.

"Oh, and may my cousin have his knife back?"

"Yes," I say.

"Good," says Chaff.

"When he pries it from my cold, dead fingers."

"I hope it does not come to that," says Chaff. "But however you would like things to be."

Chaff helps his cousin up, and unties his hands and feet. They walk off together, down the same tunnel Chaff came from.

"You handled that well," says Vault.

I just shake my head. I toss the knife in the Great Fire and start walking back to my room. I hear Ebb running to catch up to me.

"Vault was right, you did the right thing," says Ebb.

"Did I? Chaff thinks he has even more power now, since I didn't kill his cousin. He thinks he can send people to attack me and I won't fight back. If anything, I showed him I was weak," I say.

"Not weak, smart."

"Sometimes the smart thing is the weak thing. I don't want to be weak."

"You aren't. It would have been easy to kill Chaff, but you didn't. You controlled yourself."

"I wish I hadn't. I wish I'd stabbed him. Made him realize that he's not as powerful as he thinks," I say.

"But then everyone in the Crag would have suffered for it."

"Maybe it would be worth it."

"You know that isn't true."

I don't respond to her. I just keep walking back to my room. I go inside, and both Flot and Jet are already asleep. I put out the glowing stick, curl up with my blanket, and try to forget that when I wake up, it may be to my last sunrise.

18

The next morning, I wake up tired. I had a hard time sleeping, because I was having nightmares about the man who attacked me, and the trials I haven't yet faced.

As I move around, I hear footsteps. They seem to be walking away from our room. I wonder if it's Ebb, who was standing watch over us. She may have left, now that I'm awake. I was not kind to her last night, and I hope I can apologize. If I die today, I don't want my last thought to be sad, because I never told her I was sorry.

I walk to the mouth of the Crag and see that it's still dark out. I head back into the tunnels, until I reach the loud waters. No one else is there. I take off my clothes and leave them in a pile on the ground. The water is colder than normal, and it shocks me awake.

I get out of the water as quickly as I can, pick up my clothes and walk to the Great Fire. I can feel bumps on my skin, telling me that I'm cold.

The warmth of the Great Fire is better. It takes me a while to break the chill. As I dry off, I heat my clothes, which will help keep me warm while I collect breakfast.

I pick up one of the pans and carry it with me. It is not normal to take a pan with you outside the Crag, but I wanted a weapon in case I'm attacked again.

The sun is starting to rise, just enough to turn the sky from black to dark blue. I can barely see, but my eyes adjust as

I make my way to the chickens. I collect some eggs then make my way back to the Crag.

Normally, I make breakfast and eat it with Flot and Jet. Today, though, I make breakfast at the Great Fire, and eat there too. The eggs have little flavor, but with my stomach already aching, it is nice to eat something that won't make it worse.

I take what is left of my breakfast and return to our room. Flot and Jet are both still asleep. All that I care about is that they are safe. I set the pan down on the ground between them. It has cooled enough that I'm not worried they will burn themselves on it.

I leave my sleeping brothers and head toward Ebb's room. I have a hard time remembering where it is, because I have only been there once. It's not far from our room though, which makes it easier.

Some of the rooms I pass by have glowing sticks that are burning brightly. Ebb's room is dark. I stand just outside of it, and I can smell the wildflowers inside. I whisper into the darkness, so that I don't wake Ebb if she is already asleep.

"I'm sorry Ebb. I wish you peace and happiness."

I turn away from her room, and start my walk back to the mouth of the Crag. As I leave, I think I can hear someone whisper back, but I cannot tell what they said. I wait a moment, listening for another sound, but it does not come. I'm sure that if it was important they would have said it louder.

When I get outside, Helm and Mast are already waiting for me. They are both wearing their armor, although I do not see why. They are not the ones who will be fighting for their lives.

I am wearing my normal clothes, and I start to wonder if that was a mistake. I guess it's too late now. If I'm attacked by another hunter, the armor would do little to protect me anyway.

"Follow us," says Helm.

We walk back into the Crag. Helm and Mast bring me down some tunnels I have never seen before. The walls are smooth, and there are no other rooms that connect to it. It looks as if something dug into the walls, carving out this strange tunnel. I can tell from the dust and crawler webs that it was made a long time ago.

At the end of the tunnel is a wooden door. It is odd, because I don't remember seeing any other wooden doors in the Crag. Many people hang cloth across their entrances to prevent people from looking in. This is different, and it worries me. Mast opens the door and waves me inside.

There isn't much in this room, although it appears that another room is connected to it. The walls have been carved, just like the tunnel. There is only one dim torch lighting the room, and it makes it difficult to see.

"What is back there?" I ask, pointing to the other room.

"That is not for you to worry about. Worry about your first trial. It will begin now," says Helm.

A small, very old looking man comes out from the other room carrying a stack of metal buckets. He also carries a pair of glowing sticks that aren't burning, and another stick that is. He sits down on the smooth floor and motions me to sit down too.

The old man sets the glowing sticks apart from each other, with the burning one in the middle. He then places the buckets upside-down, one on top of each of the glowing sticks. Before I realize what he's doing, he moves the buckets around. I get confused, and I cannot remember which one contains the glowing stick that is on fire. The old man stops moving the buckets then looks up at me.

"Choose," says the old man, in a voice that comes from my nightmares.

"Choose what?" I ask.

"CHOOOOOOSE."

"Do you want me to choose which one is still on fire?" I ask.

"Yesssss."

I look at the buckets then I look around. I realize that

Mast is aiming a spear at me. I reach my hand out to touch the buckets. If I can feel which bucket is warm, then I will know which one contains the fire.

"NO," warns the old man.

Mast moves his spear close to my head. I pull my hand away from the buckets. I wish there was some way to tell which bucket had the burning stick inside. I look for smoke, but there is none.

I start to panic. I try to remember how the buckets were moved. No matter how hard I try, I cannot remember. I take in a deep breath and think. How can I figure out which one has the fire inside of it?

"Chooooooooose."

I look at the old man, hoping that I can tell by what he is looking at which bucket has the fire in it. But he is just looking straight at me.

Come on, Sam. Think!

After a long moment, I think I've it figured out.

I smile at the old man.

"Chooooooooose."

I just keep smiling. The old man looks angry.

"CHOOOOOOOOSE."

He startles me, but I won't choose.

"CHOOSE NOOOOOW."

I don't choose.

"CHOOSE NOW OR DIE."

Mast raises the spear until the point just touches my head.

"None of them," I say.

The old man looks puzzled by my response. Then he looks at me and smiles. He lifts the bucket to my right. The glowing stick is not on fire.

The old man grows angry. His thin lips twist into an evil line of rage. He lifts another bucket, and again the glowing stick is not on fire. He throws both buckets away, and lifts the last bucket. No fire.

The old man throws the bucket at me. I put my arms

up and it bounces off.

"You cheated!" growls the old man.

Mast lowers the spear. I look up at him, and he stares back at me. I look over at Helm, and he looks surprised, but relieved. I have passed the first test.

The old man stands up, spits on me, then goes back into the other room.

"How did you do that?" asks Helm. "Can you control fire?"

"No. It is something I figured out on my own. When I put out glowing sticks, instead of smashing them into the floor, or soaking them in a bucket of water, I set a bowl on top of them. After a while they go out on their own. I am not sure why. If I were to guess, I would say that fire is like people. It needs to breathe. If it can't breathe, it dies."

"That was supposed to be a test of your ability to focus," says Mast.

"Well, Sam passed, which is all that matters. Sam, you will be given time to rest outside before we begin the next trial," says Helm.

"Before we go, who is the old man?" I ask.

"It does not matter," says Mast.

"It matters to me," I say.

"Yes, but your knowing does not matter to us," says Mast.

I start to walk toward the other room, but Mast grabs me and pulls me back.

"No," is all he says.

Mast shoves me back toward the tunnel then points the spear at me. I decide to give up for now, but I want to know who he was. I turn around and head back through the long, carved out tunnel. Mast follows me, but Helm stays behind.

I make my way outside, and I'm happy to breathe fresh air again. I feel better now that I have passed my first test. I know that there are still more trials though, and I cannot be overconfident.

I lay down in a dry patch of clover and look up at the sky. Only a few clouds hang in the endless blue above me. I stare at one as it passes slowly overhead. I close my eyes and feel the cool wind move against my skin.

After I have calmed down, I sit up.

"I am ready for the next trial," I say.

"Then run," says Mast. "Before I kill you."

19

I get up from the clover patch and run as fast as I can away from Mast. He waits a moment before chasing after me. I think it's to give me a chance to hide before he hunts me down and kills me.

Mast is bigger and stronger than me, but he has also seen many more snows than me. He is not young like I am, and he may not be able to run as far as me. He is also carrying a spear, and wearing armor, and they are slowing him down.

I head toward the field where we killed the wolves only a few days ago. I look behind me, and Mast is so far back that he's difficult to see. I don't have any weapons, and there's no place to hide. Once I am sure that Mast won't catch me for a long while, I look for the spot where we killed the wolves.

When I finally find the place where we last hunted, I see mostly blood stained grass. The birds and smaller animals have already picked apart most of what was left of the deer. But there may still be something I can use here.

I look at one of the deer skeletons, and find a bone that a wolf bit in half. It has a sharp edge to it. I take the bone and cut what is left of the deer's skin. Very carefully, but very quickly, I cut as long of a strip as I can. The piece is only as long as my arm is, but it will have to do.

I also grab the antlers and try to pry them from the skull, but I'm not strong enough. I stomp on the skull many times until finally the antlers break free. I put the sharp bone in a pocket on my chest, and I twist it to make sure it won't cut me. I also look around for small, loose stones. I find a few and try out my deer-skin sling.

The sling does not work as well as the one I normally use. I can't get the stones to fly as fast or as true as I can with my own, and this one spins much faster. After a few tries, I am used to the sling.

I look up and Mast is getting close. I use the sling to launch a rock at him. The first rock I send misses him by a great distance, but he stops coming after me. I send another rock flying at him, and this one misses as well. I can only guess that he wonders how I found a sling out here.

Mast raises his spear and continues walking toward me. I shoot one more rock at him, and it finds its target, but he deflects it with the spear. He's able to use it almost like a shield, protecting the parts of him that would take the most damage. I send another rock flying toward him, but he blocks that one just as easily.

I drop the sling, because I realize it will not do what I need it to. I pick up the antlers and hold one in each hand, with the branches aiming up and away from me.

Mast starts moving faster toward me, realizing that I have no way to attack him from a distance. I bend my knees, a little more than Ebb taught me, but I want to make myself a small target.

I yell as loud as I can, hoping to scare Mast. Startled, he slows down, but then runs even faster, yelling back at me.

He is now very near. It seems like everything slows down, as my heart beats fiercely inside my chest. The point of the spear cuts through the air, aimed straight at my stomach. I use the antlers to deflect the attack to my side, and the spear passes by me.

I can see Mast's face now, and he seems surprised by my weapons. The antlers won't work very well for stabbing, but they will protect me from the spear.

I kick at Mast with my foot, while holding the point of his spear to the ground. The spear is too long and I miss. Mast pulls the spear back, and easily slides away from the antlers.

Mast attacks again, but this time instead of moving the spear to my side with the antlers, I use them to push it upward into the air. I take a step, then another toward him, until the spear is pointing almost straight up. That is when I knee him in the groin.

The leather protects him some, but not enough. Mast lets go of the spear and bends over in pain. I hold the spear between the antlers then toss the spear away from us.

Mast is still folded over. He sees me move in to attack again, and he puts a hand up, telling me to stop. I ignore it. I knee him in the face as hard as I can. Mast grabs his nose and falls to the ground.

I pull the small bone knife out of my pocket. I move in close to his face, punch it again to get my point across then hold the knife to his throat. He looks at me, wondering what I'm going to do to him.

"Why shouldn't I kill you?" I ask.

He stares at me in silence.

"TELL ME!" I yell.

He doesn't even blink.

I take off his helmet and throw it on the ground. I grab him by the hair then punch his face as hard as I can. It makes him fall asleep.

I pocket the knife and pick up the spear. I realize that if I leave him here alone, the wolves will tear him apart as he sleeps. Instead of going back to the Crag I stand guard, both against the wolves and against him.

It feels like it takes forever for Mast to wake up again. When he finally starts moving around, I tap his chest with the point of the spear.

"Try to attack me again and I will kill you," I say.

Mast nods his head in understanding.

"We are heading back to the Crag now, so get up," I say.

Mast slowly gets up from the ground, picks up his helmet, and puts it back on his head. We walk back together.

He keeps his arms at his sides. I keep the point of the spear pushed against his back.

"Why didn't you kill me?" asks Mast.

"Because I don't want to kill you," I say.

"But I tried to kill you," says Mast.

"And you failed."

"I still tried."

"Did you really think you would be able to kill the Sky Child so easily?" I ask.

"So, you are finally starting to believe that you're the Sky Child?"

"No. I meant it as a joke. I beat you because I outsmarted you, and not because I'm stronger, or faster, or a better fighter."

Mast doesn't respond.

"So why did you try to kill me?" I ask.

"It was part of the trials," says Mast. "If it matters to you, I did not want to kill you. I was hoping that you would kill me."

"Do you want to die?" I ask.

"No, but you were supposed to kill me if you won. It was my duty to attack you, to try and kill you, and I have fulfilled that duty. But I hoped that you would win."

"There is no way for me to 'win' these trials. Only in games are there winners. Trying to kill someone isn't a game. Games are meant to protect us from real war, real death. I either survive the trials, or I do not. But there is no winning. We all lose when someone tries to take a life."

When we get to the mouth of the Crag, Helm is waiting outside for us.

"Mast, I see that Sam has your spear. I knew I shouldn't have worried," says Helm.

"I am done with your trials," I say.

"There is still one more trial left," says Helm.

"Then I give up and you win," I say.

"Sam, you are so close to succeeding. You know we have to kill you if you don't finish the trials," says Helm.

107

"You can try. I am the one with the spear. How much longer will it be before I have the point of a spear in your back?" I ask.

"Sam, you know why we must do this, why you must go through the trials. It is to protect the hunters. We do not want to see you fail. Mast and I have both prayed to the Sky Gods that you succeed. He knew that he might die in that trial. In fact, he prayed to the Sky Gods for just that. He wanted to die, so that you might live and bring peace to the Crag," says Helm.

I don't know how to feel. I start to wonder who has been telling Helm and Mast what their duties are. Are they just doing what has always been done, or is someone telling them what to do here and now? Is it the old man? And who is he?

"Fine. I will do the last trial," I say.

I only agree because I want to know who the old man is. If I am Leader of the Hunt, they will be forced to tell me.

"Then follow me, Sam," says Helm. "And you do not need to hold Mast captive anymore. You have succeeded in the trial, and he means you no more harm."

I look at the end of the spear. I move the point of it away from Mast's back then drop it on the ground. My arms are tired and sore, and I shake them some to get them working again. I may need them soon, because I don't know what I will face next.

## 20

Helm and Mast lead me back down the carved-out tunnel they brought me through in the first trial. Something seems wrong, though. A scent. A familiar scent that I can't place. What is that smell?

Helm opens the wooden door and I enter the room. I realize too late that Mast has the spear against my back again. They have control. I must pass this last trial, or I am dead.

What I see inside the room hurts my stomach. Fear-sweat drips from me, and I feel dizzy for a moment. I fight the urge to vomit. Tied up and on the floor are Flot and Jet.

As quickly as I grew ill, I grow angry. I can feel my skin turn red, and my fists clench. I will make them pay for putting my brothers in danger.

"Let them go, NOW!" I yell.

The old man comes walking out from the other room.

"No," he says, in his evil voice.

I feel the point of the spear dig into my back. It does not pierce the skin, but it is meant to remind me that if I fight them, they will kill us.

"Untie them now, or I will kill you," I say.

The old man ignores me. He raises an old crooked finger toward me, but I see that he is also pointing downward. I hadn't noticed that there is a cup sitting on a small wooden table between us.

"Poison," says the old man.

"What do you want me to do with it?" I ask.

"Choose."

"Choose what?" I ask.

"Choose. Choose who dies."

I look down at the cup.

"You want me to force one of my brothers to drink this? To kill one of them?" I ask.

"YESSSSSSSSSSS."

My heart hurts from beating so hard inside my chest.

I pick up the cup, and I move toward the old man. I hear Mast yell 'no', and I feel the tip of the spear press even tighter into my skin. It hurts so much that I stumble, nearly spilling the poison. I know that if I pour out the poison, I will be killed.

I cannot kill my brothers. Flot is so innocent, and Jet is so brave. Is that what this trial is supposed to test, whether I believe decency or courage is more important? Or is this old man just sick in the head, and he's angry over losing the first trial? Is he just punishing me?

There must be a way out of this, but I cannot see it. I look around the room, but there are no weapons. Mast may be slow of foot, but he is quick of spear. If I try to fight, I will most likely die.

It is impossible to choose between them, to choose which brother I will murder with the poison. I look at Jet, and he is crying. I look at Flot and he is calm. He just nods to me, as if he is saying 'it's okay, I know I must die. Choose me and let Jet live.' I think Jet is crying, because he is thinking the same thing too. That I will murder Flot, and let Jet survive.

I shake my head in disgust at the decision I must make. That is when I realize it was never really a decision for me after all. If I do what I am about to do, they will have no choice but to let Flot and Jet live.

"I love you both," is all I say.

I drink the poison.

It burns going down my throat. I close my eyes, waiting for my death. Waiting for the pain to take over. I hear

Mast drop his spear and move to me.

"Sam!" he yells.

Helm also hurries to me. They lay me on my back, trying to make me as comfortable as possible as I slip away. The dim light of the room grows dimmer. I can feel pain now, shooting through my entire body, like I've been thrown into the Great Fire. I hear Helm shouting at me, but the more he yells, the further away he sounds.

I panic, trying to fight the poison. My arms and legs shake as Mast and Helm try to hold them down. I can feel my eyes go wide, my mind trying to capture the last moments of my life. The room goes dark, and I can't feel anything anymore. I can't move, or hear, or see. I'm alone, inside myself, and afraid. I don't want to die. Sky Gods, please help me, I don't want to die. Don't want to...

* * *

I scream, and it tears my throat apart.

I can breathe again, but my entire body aches. I can still feel the poison moving through me, only not as painful as it once was. It burns, but I am glad for the pain, because it means that I'm not dead. But how am I not dead?

Helm is close to me. I can feel his breath on my skin, and see the surprise in his face.

"Sam, can you hear us?" asks Mast. I turn to look at him.

"How long was I dead?" I ask.

"You're okay now. That's all that matters," says Helm.

I rest for a moment. My body eventually starts to feel normal again. I'm still sore from my body shaking, but the burning inside disappears. I move slowly, just to make sure that the poison is not still affecting me. I push off from the ground, stand up, and start to walk toward the old man. This time I will kill him, and Mast won't be able to stop me.

"Not poison," says the old man.

I stop.

"What?" I say.

"Never poison. You lead," says the old man, retreating

111

to the other room.

I don't know how to feel. I have passed the trials. But I have been tricked into thinking I was killing myself. I am glad to know that no matter what I chose, I never would have killed one of my brothers. But I would have had to live with the shame of picking one of them. Things never would have been right between us ever again.

I am glad I'm not a coward, that I was willing to sacrifice myself for them. I would do anything for them, and I have proven that to them now.

I untie Jet while Helm unties Flot. Jet seems relieved to still be alive. I put one arm around him as he gets up, and Flot comes over to us. We all hug each other.

After we have calmed down, I send Flot and Jet back to our room. I stay behind with Helm and Mast so that I can talk to them about what had happened.

"Who is the old man?" I ask. "And don't you dare leave anything out. I'm the Leader of the Hunt now, which means you both must do everything I say."

"We will tell you now. You have definitely earned that right," says Helm.

"I know I've earned the right, now TELL ME!"

"The old man is named Stern. He was the Leader of the Hunt before Hammer. He has seen more snows than anyone in the Crag," says Helm.

"Why is he like that? Why is his voice so strange, and why doesn't he talk right? Why is he so evil?" I ask.

"Stern was injured very badly by a wolf once. It bit deep into his neck, and made his voice sound wrong. We were surprised that he survived the attack at all, because there was a lot of blood, and his head was very warm for a long time. It made him... different. He has never been the same. Even now, it hurts his throat to talk, so he doesn't say much," says Helm.

"What do you mean by 'it made him different'?"

"He is not quite right anymore. He is quick to anger, and he does not like being around people. Stern is very much like an angry new one. He is still clever, and understands things, but his emotions aren't normal."

"Has he been the one giving you orders?" I ask.

"No. There are rules that are passed down from leader to leader. We have been doing what we were told to do if our leader ever died. We hoped it would never come to this, because Lagan was a good man. We both owed him our lives."

"He was a good man, and I wish he was here. I would rather he lead the hunt instead of me," I say.

"You will make a fine leader, Sam. Maybe even better than Lagan," says Helm.

I just shake my head at them. Why can't they understand that I don't want to do this? It doesn't matter if I'm good at it, or even the best at it. I don't want to lead. I don't want to make decisions that might cost people their lives. I don't want to control people as if they were animals. I don't want to seem special, or different, or better than anyone else. I just want to be left alone.

"I'm going back to my room," I say.

I think I hear them trying to talk to me as I leave, but I ignore them. I throw the wooden door back as hard as I can, and as it hits, it sends a loud echo down the tunnel. I hope it gets my point across.

I walk to the Great Fire first and pray. I say a prayer of thanks for protecting me, and Jet, and Flot. I pray that people realize I am not the Sky Child. I pray that people leave me alone. And I pray that someone does something about Chaff.

I know that the Sky Gods won't listen to my last prayer, because the Sky Gods do not honor prayers for someone to be harmed. I feel ashamed that I even thought to pray it, but Chaff is so evil that I could not help it.

I decide instead to ask the Sky Gods to end his evil in the way they see fit. Maybe they can work a miracle in his heart, and he will become a good person. Somehow, I doubt even the Sky Gods are that powerful.

I get up off the ground that I have been kneeling on and walk back to our room. Inside are Jet and Flot, waiting for me to come back.

"Are you okay, Sam?" asks Flot.

"How I am doesn't matter. How are both of you?" I ask.

"Surviving," says Jet.

"My wrists are sore, but I am okay," says Flot.

"I want both of you to know that I would never kill either of you, even if I was forced to. You are my brothers, and I would rather die than hurt you," I say.

"We know, Sam, and you proved that," says Flot.

"Did you know that the cup wasn't poison?" asks Jet.

"No, I thought for sure it was poison. That is why I wanted the old man to drink it. Because he seemed evil, like the trials were his idea, and that he wanted to kill me," I say.

"Who was he?" asks Jet.

"A Leader of the Hunt from many, many snows before. He is not right of mind. He does not matter, for he does not rule over any of us."

"So you are the Leader of the Hunt now?" asks Flot.

"Yes."

"Don't think that we will do what you say now, or that we will listen to you," says Jet.

"No more than you normally do," I say.

I nod goodbye then walk to the loud waters with a bar of soap in my hand. I wash away the day, cleaning the dirt and sweat out of my clothes. I clean myself, but it doesn't clean the feelings inside me. I am glad to be alive. I am glad that I survived the trials, but I never should have had to go through them.

I am so tired that when I return to our room, I spend most of the day resting. The only thing I want to do is sleep.

## 21

Eventually, I get hungry. Flot and Jet have already left the room for the feast. I stretch, and yawn, and force myself to get up. I am tired, but I know that food will help me wake up.

As soon as I reach the feast chamber, people begin to clap. It startles me. I look around, not knowing what is going on. Then I realize, everyone is clapping for me.

Stop clapping. I don't want this. Just leave me alone.

I do not speak those words, but I feel them just the same.

I manage a very weak smile, and the clapping eventually disappears. I get in line for food. It is a soup filled with many different vegetables. Tomatoes, and onions, and potatoes, and celery. I take my food to the head table and sit down.

Chaff looks very unhappy that I survived. At least something good came from the trials. I stole the evil grin from his face. Maybe being leader won't be so bad if I can do that every day.

I set my bowl and spoon down on the table, and just as I am about to sit down, Helm stops me.

"People of the Crag," he starts, and everyone quiets down immediately. "Sam is the new Leader of the Hunt, both chosen by Lagan before the attack, and proven on the fields of battle. Sam has survived the trials, and made a fool out of Mast in the process."

Mast looks unhappy to hear those words, but the people of the Crag laugh. Mast stands up.

"Without Sam, many of us would have died in a field, burned to the ground by a dragon. For that, I am glad that we have Sam as our leader. Many good hunts to you, Sam," says Mast.

The crowd claps again. This time I'm able to make a real smile, because I'm glad that I could help save people's lives. I am glad that many of us did return from facing the dragon. And I am glad that the Sky Gods protected us, and brought us home.

I'm also surprised that after what Mast put me through, and what I put him through, that he would say good words about me. Maybe he is not a bad person. Maybe he is just doing what he feels is necessary to keep the hunters and the Crag safe. Maybe Mast is a better person than I realize.

I am now very glad that I did not kill him during the trials. I am even more glad that he did not kill me.

I sit down and eat my soup. It tastes very, very good. I finish it quickly. I am so hungry that I lift my bowl to my mouth to get the last few drops from the bottom of it.

I stand up and walk over to Ebb. I see that she has also finished her soup.

"Ebb, will you protect me as I walk back to my room?" I ask.

"Is that a command?" she asks.

"No, just a question," I say.

"It would be my honor," says Ebb.

I put a hand out to help her up from her seat, even though I know that she needs no help. We leave the feast chamber together.

Once we are a few steps away from the sound of others, Ebb turns to me and hugs me. It is a strong, warm hug, unlike any I have felt before. It surprises me, and it takes me a moment to hug her back. We stand there, holding each other for a while. Eventually, slowly, we pull away.

"Sam, I'm so glad you survived," says Ebb.

"Me too, actually," I say.

"What were the trials? What did they make you do?" asks Ebb.

"The first one wasn't very bad. They put glowing sticks under many buckets. One of them was on fire. They moved the buckets around very quickly, and I lost track of which one was still on fire."

"How did you figure out which one it was?"

"I waited until I was sure none of them were on fire," I say.

"Wait, how did the fire go out?" asks Ebb.

"I believe that fire has a breath of its own. If you steal its breath, then it dies, just like a person," I say.

"That's clever."

My cheeks feel warm because I'm a little embarrassed. "The next trial, Mast tried to kill me. I was able to beat him, but I would not kill him."

"I would have loved to have seen that," says Ebb, smiling.

"The last trial, I had to choose who I would give poison to, Flot or Jet," I say.

The smile disappears.

"Who did you choose? Did one of them die? I didn't notice them at the feast! Sam, did you kill one of your brothers?" asks Ebb, panicking.

"No, I drank the poison."

"You... drank the poison? How are you still alive?"

"The poison was never real," I explain.

"Did you know that it wasn't real?"

"No. I was sure it was real."

Ebb looks very sad for a moment. I think she realizes now that I value Flot and Jet's lives above all else. But her look of sadness changes.

"Sam, I'm proud of you. Proud that you were willing to risk your life to save the people you love," says Ebb.

"I always will," I say, smiling at her.

She walks me back to my room then stands guard,

protecting us as we sleep.

22

The next morning, I wake up and see that both Flot and Jet are already awake. It looks like they have made eggs, and have left enough for me to eat.

"Thank you both for the breakfast," I say.

"It was Flot's idea, but he made me cook it," says Jet.

"Well, thank you both anyway. But thank you less, Flot, for not really helping," I say.

Flot laughs.

"So what are you going to train us on today?" asks Flot.

"What do you mean?" I say.

"Well, Lagan would train us on something every day, so that we would be better hunters," says Flot.

"Oh, right," I say.

My mind races. I realize that I am not prepared at all to be the Leader of the Hunt. There is a lot more to it than I had thought. I guess I was so busy trying to stay alive, that I forgot to look ahead to see what needed doing.

I think about it for a while. I start to wonder what type of leader I want to be. Lagan was all about keeping the peace, and keeping people happy, so that they wouldn't kill each other.

Lagan wouldn't teach the hunters more than a few basic things about weapons, and he didn't have much of a grasp of strategy. He let people do what they wanted, so that everyone was happy, and again, so that no one died.

I don't want to be that kind of leader. I want people to learn how to hunt better, how to think better, how to use their weapons better. I don't want the trainings to be a waste. But if I do this, I really will need protection. I'm going to change things, and some people won't like it.

It makes sense to be true to what I think a good leader is. People already want to kill me for slaying a dragon and being the 'Sky Child', so what difference does it make if I change how we hunt? The same people that want to kill me want to kill me more? Dead is dead, so I may as well use what life I have left for doing what I believe in.

"Okay Flot, ask me again what I'm going to teach the hunters," I say.

"What are you going to teach the hunters?" asks Flot.

"How to be hunters."

"But they already *are* hunters."

"No, not really. None of them are trying very hard, because they are all worried about being killed by each other. I have to change that," I say.

"How do you plan to do that?" asks Flot.

"I'm not sure. I guess we will both find out today during training," I say.

After putting on our armor, we go outside before anyone else arrives for the training. The sun isn't high enough in the sky for people to be out yet. It isn't raining, but I can't make out the sun, as its edges have been blurred by the clouds. I can still see the bright spot where it hangs, though.

I look down at my armor and realize that I still look like one of the other hunters. Hopefully Anchor, Jib and Stanchion can finish the new armor quickly.

I help Flot and Jet work on their sky spear throwing. With a few suggestions, both are throwing their spears far, and fairly straight. After tossing the spears for a while, I show them both how to use a sling.

Neither of them can make their rocks go where they want them to, but that is normal. It can take a while to get a feel for when to release it. I try to show them how to do it slowly, so they can see what it should look like when you do it right. I can tell that they are improving, but they still aren't throwing the rocks far enough.

As we sling rocks away from the Crag, some of the other hunters start appearing. It is good to see that people are still willing to come out for training after what happened a few days ago. I think a lot of them are coming just to see what things will be like without Lagan, and whether I will be worth following.

I can understand that. Lagan was nearly a gray one, and I am still young. I don't have the amount of experience that some of the other hunters have. Honestly, if I didn't have to be the Leader of the Hunt, I would think either Mast or Helm would make a better leader. Both are strong, brave, true-of-heart, and are good hunters. They won't need very much training.

Mast and Helm come to the front and stand by my side. Once everyone has arrived, I talk to the crowd.

"Hunters, as you know, Lagan had a way of doing things. That ends now, because under Lagan we were not getting any better at hunting. We can be better. Lagan held back his knowledge on purpose to keep the peace, so that jealousy wouldn't lead to murder among us. I am telling you now that a hunter's life will not be threatened because they are better at something than you."

The hunters look around at each other, not knowing yet how to react, or what this means.

"If you attack another hunter out of jealousy, you attack us all. If you try to put a hunter to death, we will stop you, and put you to death. You will not go free. You will not be left alone. If I must see to it myself, you will die by my hands. If you have a problem with this, come see me and my guards, for we will end your worries with the tips of our spears."

I hear whispers in the crowd. I see faces with many different reactions. Most of the hunters look relieved by my words. But I look for those faces that hold anger and rage in them, because those are the ones I will need to deal with.

I turn to Helm, and I can tell that he is surprised by my words. I even see a bit of a smile on his face. I whisper to him the people who I think may cause problems. A few of the names I do not know, but he helps me with those. I ask him and Mast to remember those people, so that we can protect ourselves from them.

"So, now that you have had a moment to think," I say, "are there any of you that would like to fight me and my guards right now? Would you like a spear in your heart? A stone in your head?"

I look across the crowd again. Most of the faces that I saw rage in have calmed down. Apparently, no one is dumb enough to try to fight us. That is a good place to start.

"Also know that these rules protect you from those that are not hunters. If you see another hunter being attacked, it is now your duty to protect them. If you are murdered, the hunters will do their best to find and put your killer to death. You should not live in fear anymore. None of us should."

Smiles appear on most hunter's faces.

"As you may already know, one of Lagan's protectors, Port, was killed in battle. I have already chosen someone to replace her. Ebb, please step forward."

I watch as Ebb makes her way from the back of the crowd to where we are standing. The hunters move to let her pass. She carries her helmet under one arm, and her spear in the other.

She smiles at me as she approaches, but I can tell that she is worried, because there is always the concern that one of the hunters might hurt her because of it. I hope that I'm not making a bad decision, and that my threat about what I will do to murderers will be believed.

Ebb takes her place next to Mast.

"Hunters, I have chosen Ebb because she has shown great bravery by protecting me. Ebb has already proven herself worthy of this honor, and I ask that you show your loyalty to her," I say.

I turn and face Ebb then place my right fist over my heart and slide it downward. I watch out of the corner of my eye as the other hunters do the same to Ebb. A few hesitate, but eventually join in with everyone else. Ebb returns the gesture.

"I would also like to thank Mast and Helm for protecting me as they had protected Lagan. I will keep them as protectors, for they have also shown loyalty and bravery."

This draws some cheers from the crowd, as Mast and Helm are both well liked and well known by the hunters.

"I will be changing more things, making more rules, but I believe you have seen enough change today. We will not be hunting tonight, as you all deserve to spend some time with your families. Go to them, enjoy the feast tonight, and pay honor to the Sky Gods as you see fit," I say.

The crowd seems happy that I have cancelled the hunt for the evening. I thought it would help the hunters deal with the loss of Lagan better, and it might give them time to let the new rules sink in. It could also give some of them a better chance to plan my murder, but I will be staying close to my protectors tonight.

"Mast, Helm and Ebb, would you mind staying behind a moment?" I ask.

Each of them waits with me as the rest of the hunters return to the Crag.

"That was rather brave of you to do, Sam, threatening the hunters like that. Or very stupid," says Helm.

"Maybe both," I say. "I suppose we will find out if it works. The hunters who would be angry by my changes already want to kill me, so I don't believe this does much. It may make them think that if they were to kill one of us, the rest of us would put them to death. I hope no one tests my new rules, because I don't want to take another person's life. That kind of justice is for the Sky Gods to worry about. But if it comes down to it, I will put a murderer in the ground to prevent more deaths," I say.

"Then it wasn't just a threat. Good. There are some that believe you aren't strong enough to lead, that you will say one thing, but when you are pushed you will do another," says Helm.

"I won't be that kind of leader, even if it puts me in the ground," I say. "We have more than that to worry about right now. Tonight, there is a good chance that someone will try to kill either me or Ebb. Helm and Mast, I think you are probably safer than us, since things haven't changed for you, and people still think of you as Lagan's protectors. I am sure many would like to see me dead so that one of you would lead instead."

"Then why do you trust us, even after I tried to kill you in the trials?" asks Mast.

"I trust you because you didn't kill me when you had other chances. I trust you because so far you have proven yourselves trustworthy. But more than that, you seem like good people when you aren't being hunters. You both have families and new ones. Your wives seem to care whether you live or die. I saw the happiness in their faces when we came back from facing the dragon. If you had died in battle, it would have hurt them. It is sad, but the same cannot be said for Cannon. I spoke with Cannon's wife, and she told me that he was a monster. There were no tears, just worry over how they would survive now that Cannon was dead," I say.

I can tell that both Mast and Helm are glad that I took notice of how they got along with their families. There are few things more important to people than their families, and it says much about people that do not treat their wives and husbands, sons and daughters well.

"So what is your plan then, Sam?" asks Mast.

"I think tonight will be just as dangerous as the last few nights were, maybe even more. At least for tonight, Ebb should stay with me and my brothers. There is more than enough room for her there. Mast and Helm, I ask for your help in protecting us. Will you take turns tonight, standing outside our door?" I ask.

"Of course," says Helm.

"Thank you. Ebb and I will also take turns protecting the room with you. That way we all can get some rest tonight, but we will still be well-guarded," I say. "Until then, Mast, can you watch over Ebb as she rests? She has not had much sleep. Helm, can you stay with me as my protector until this evening?"

Both Helm and Mast agree to their duties.

"Sam?" says Ebb.

"Yes?"

"Thank you for making me your protector. I will give my life for you, if need be," she says.

"And I will do my best to protect your life in return," I say.

Ebb turns and walks away with Mast.

## 23

"So what is your plan?" asks Helm.

"To make the hunters as good as they can be, and stay alive," I say.

"I was meaning, what is your plan right now?"

"Oh. Well, I haven't talked to Crook and Vault yet. Since they are also leaders, they may be willing to share some wisdom on how to lead. Maybe they have ideas on how to deal with Chaff," I say. "Who do you think we should visit first?"

"Probably Crook, since she is almost always outside, and it will be easier to talk to her in the daylight."

"Then let's talk to Crook."

It doesn't take us long to find her. I follow Helm to the door where the chickens are kept. He opens it up and looks inside, but then steps back, closing the door.

"Not there?" I ask.

"No. No one in there but the chickens," says Helm.

"Should we check the sheep?"

"I think she is probably tending to the goats. They take more work."

Helm and I walk side-by-side until we reach the goat pen. I open the door this time and look in. I can see Crook inside, fighting with a goat over someone's shirt. Helm and I go inside, shutting the door behind us.

"Crook?" I say.

Crook turns around and finally notices us. She is taller

than me, which fits her strong personality well. She has her long red hair tied back so that it doesn't get in the way of her work.

"Hello, Sam. It is good to finally talk to you. What brings you to the pens?" asks Crook.

"You do, actually. I was hoping to talk to you, maybe get some advice. Find out how to be a leader," I say.

"What is the advice you need?"

"I want to know how to handle Chaff. How to avoid him as much as possible."

"Well, the only advice I can give you is try to stay on his good side if you can. If he feels like he can't control you, he will bury you. There is no use in trying to avoid him, because then he will come to you, and he will be even more of a monster to you. Chaff is lazy and predictable, but also manipulative and dangerous," says Crook.

"How have you gotten along with him for so long?" I ask.

"I don't know that we get along, but I will say that I've had to bribe him to get what I need from him. He loves being bribed. It not only makes him feel powerful, but he feels like he's stolen something important from you. He always makes a big deal about whatever it is you've bribed him with. I always have extra of anything he could possibly want, so that it never actually effects me."

"That is smart."

"I always act upset, but that is all it is: an act. Chaff is a child. All he does is throw fits when he doesn't get what he wants. He makes ridiculous threats, steals things, hurts people. Even though he acts like a child, he is very, very smart. He knows how to see through people, how to manipulate them into doing what he wants. Honestly, it's better to just let Chaff have his way. It's not worth trying to fight him," says Crook.

"I don't know if it is within me to do that," I say. "I have always had to fight for what I have, whether it is food, or clothing, or a place to sleep. I do not have many things I could give him anyway. I'm not going to give him weapons or armor, and he already has plenty of food. I don't have any objects that he would want, and I have never had anything of value."

"Then you will have a hard time with Chaff. He might try to turn you into his slave, or have you deal with people he doesn't like," says Crook.

"What do you mean 'deal with'?" I ask.

"Threaten. Frighten. Beat up. Kill. Who knows?"

"I won't do any of those things for him," I say.

"Then I am sorry, Sam, but you probably won't last very long as a leader. I hope you're successful, but I have never seen Chaff lose," says Crook.

"There is a first time for everything," I say.

"Yes, and I hope you are that first time," says Crook. "My advice on how to be a leader is really simple: don't die. It's hard to lead when you are dead. Also, every new leader makes mistakes. Learn from them. Try not to change too much too quickly. People hate that," says Crook.

"It may be too late for that," I say.

"Why, what did you do?"

"I told the hunters that if any of them killed another hunter, the killer would be put to death. I also added a new protector who isn't very old."

"Well, at least you won't have to worry about Chaff anymore," says Crook

"Why, what do you mean?"

"You're a walking corpse. You'll be lucky to survive the night."

"That's why I'm posting guards in front of my room, just in case."

"You might live to see another sunrise then."

"I hope so," I say.

I reach out and shake Crook's hand. Her palms and fingers are like mine: callused and dry. She shakes back very firmly, more than I was expecting. Helm also shakes her hand, and then the pair of us leave.

As we walk back to the Crag, Helm talks to me.

"Crook's advice didn't sound very helpful," says Helm.

"No, not really. Or at least it wasn't anything we didn't already know. But that's okay, at least we know that Crook is smart and patient, and plans ahead so that she isn't harmed by Chaff. It's good to know your enemies, but it is just as good to know your friends."

"Crook is your friend?" asks Helm.

"She's not my enemy. That much I know," I say.

"So we are heading to Vault's room now?" asks Helm.

I look up into the sky. The clouds seem to be getting darker. The rains will be coming soon.

"Yes, Vault's room," I say, "and we should hurry."

## 24

Vault's room is very close to the mouth of the Crag. He chose it so that he could watch people come in and out, and protect the Crag from animals that may wander near. As we approach his room, I realize he isn't there. His glowing stick isn't burning, and even in the darkness I can tell no one is home.

"Let's check with one of his neighbors," says Helm.

Across the tunnel, I see a room with a glowing stick burning brightly. I come up to the opening of the room and look in. Inside is Lock, one of the other protectors of the Crag. She is laying on her bed mat, reading one of the few books we have in the Crag. I have never read that book, but I can tell by the cover it has something to do with a cat that wears a hat. Lock seems to be enjoying it, and I hear her laugh as she reads it.

"Lock?" I say.

She doesn't react to my voice.

"Lock?"

Helm and I stand there for a moment, trying to decide what to do. Lock's light brown hair flows down her shoulders and onto the ground. She looks to be younger than me, but older than Flot and Jet. Her face is thin but soft, and her skin looks very smooth. Eventually Lock notices us.

"Oh, I'm sorry, I didn't realize you were there. I was just finishing what I was reading. Sometimes I forget that there is a world outside of books," says Lock.

"It's okay, I enjoy reading too," I say.

"Wait, you are Sam, aren't you? You are the Sky Child!" says Lock.

"My name is Sam, but I'm not the Sky Child."

"That's not what I have heard. I've heard that you are here to save us! Can you... can you heal my mother?"

My heart starts to hurt. I am not the Sky Child. I can't heal anyone. I don't have any powers, because I'm not a god, and this poor girl thinks I can heal her sick mother. I would give anything to be able to help them.

"I don't think I will be able to do anything for your mother," I say honestly.

"Please, just try. It couldn't hurt, could it?" says Lock.

I look over at Helm. He looks at me like he doesn't know what to do.

"Okay, you can take me to your mother, but I can't promise that I can help her."

"Just being there will help. Thank you, Sky Child. Or I mean... Sam."

I cringe when I hear 'Sky Child'.

Lock leads us away from her room, down a small side-tunnel. The walls are very close together, causing us to walk down the tunnel sideways. There aren't many passages like this one in the Crag, and it reminds me of the tunnel I took to get to Anchor's room. Even though I live in a cave, small spaces still bother me. I start to panic and move down the tunnel faster, until I bump into Lock's back.

She stops and looks at me. I think she can see the worry on my face. Lock turns back around and continues down the tunnel, this time moving faster than before. Finally, we come out the other side. I put my hands on my knees and take many deep breaths. I try to think of the sky, and the grass, and the clover outside of the Crag. It seems to help, but it takes a while for me to calm down.

I look around and notice that we are in what looks like a room, but it isn't being used as one. It is empty, except for a piece of wood that stretches between a pair of rocks. It seems like it is meant as a place to sit. I can see another room connected to the one we are in, and I notice the familiar flicker of a glowing stick coming from inside.

Helm and I follow behind Lock, into the smaller room. Lock's mother rests under a blanket on her bed mat. Her head is held up by a stack of clothes.

"Mother? I'm here with the Sky Child," says Lock.

"Oh, Sam, you're here! Of course I know Sam."

I realize that Lock's mom is Harness, one of the women that took care of me when I was a new one. It is nice to know that she has a daughter, but I still feel a pain inside me from losing her as a mother. Her skin is very pale. Her hair is short, and white with age.

"Harness, I am sorry to hear that you are not well," I say.

"You know, Lock, Sam here was such an interesting child. Always getting into things, trying to figure things out. Very smart. I have known for a long time that Sam would be something special. Now look at you: a dragon slayer!" says Harness.

I force a smile, feeling even more uncomfortable. I look over at Lock and I don't see any jealousy in her eyes. Instead, I see the fear of losing her mother.

"Can you help her?" asks Lock.

"Harness, do you know what you are sick with?" I ask.

"Oh, it's alright, Sam. I'm sure you have more important things to do than worry about an old woman like me."

"You helped me so much growing up, and there is nowhere I would rather be right now," I say.

"Thank you, but I will manage. I always have."

"Harness, I don't even know if I could help, but I would at least like to pray to the Sky Gods for you. Will you at least let me do that?" I ask.

"Yes. That will be fine. You don't need to bother though," says Harness.

"It is no bother at all," I say.

"Well then, they say I have something wrong with my heart. It sometimes hurts in my chest and my arm, and I feel like I can't breathe. It only started a few days ago, when it was at its worst. Now it comes and goes. Some days are better than others."

"I am very sorry to hear that Harness. I will do my best, but I do not know if the Sky Gods will listen," I say.

"Your best is more than I could hope for," says Harness.

I kneel then place a hand over her heart, and raise my other hand to the sky. I pray silently to the Sky Gods, asking that they heal poor Harness. Lock needs her mother. After a moment, I lower my hand.

"It is done. I will also keep you in my prayers every time I visit the Great Fire," I say.

"Thank you, Sam."

"Thank the Sky Gods when you are healthy, for it is them you should thank," I say, smiling a sad, but real smile.

Harness reaches out and holds my hand for a moment. I just keep smiling, even though on the inside I am afraid for her. I squeeze her hand then turn away, leaving the room and making my way back down the narrow tunnel.

I move as quickly as I can, trying to get away from the sadness. Trying to run from my fear of losing Harness again. I have seen heart problems before in some of the gray ones, and it almost always kills them. I wish there was something more I could do for her.

I trip and fall, hurting my arm on the tunnel wall where my armor doesn't protect me. I get back up and move faster than I should, until I finally reach the end of the tunnel. As soon as I make it into the larger tunnel, I fall to the ground. I try to blame the tears in my eyes on my scratches, but inside I know better. I dry my eyes quickly as I hear Lock and Helm approach.

"Sam, are you alright?" asks Helm.

"Yes, I am fine. I tripped in the tunnel, but I am okay

now. I'm just resting a moment."

"Thank you, Sky Child, for visiting my mother," says Lock. "If there is any way I can ever repay you, please tell me."

"You don't owe me anything, Lock. But I would be grateful if you could tell us where to find Vault," I say.

"Oh, yes, I can do that. He is probably out visiting his wife. He does that every day, you know," says Lock.

"I did not. Do you know where she is then?" I ask.

"Yes, she's in the cemetery."

Suddenly, I find it hard to swallow.

"Thank you, Lock. I will keep praying to the Sky Gods for your mother," I say.

"Thank you!" says Lock.

As I stand up, she jumps and wraps her arms around me. I don't know what to do. I just stand there, trying not to pull away from her, because I know that would hurt Lock's feelings. After being very uncomfortable for a moment, I start to relax some and put my arms around her. She cries into my leather armor. I let her hold on until she is done crying away her fear.

"Take care," I say.

"You too, Sam," whispers Lock.

25

Helm and I follow the large, curved tunnel until we finally reach the mouth of the cave. The dark clouds have already passed, and only a few small drops fall from the sky. I follow Helm to the cemetery, because I do not go there often, and I cannot remember the way.

I see some wildflowers growing along the way, and I stop a moment to gather some. It is normal for us to bring flowers to the cemetery, and we place them on our loved one's graves. I have to run to catch up to Helm, because he didn't realize I had stopped.

The cemetery is kept far from the Crag, in a safe area away from dragons. Animals also stay away for some reason. The smell of death may keep them away. But trees grow there, beautiful trees that cast long shadows over the dead.

In the middle of the cemetery stands Vault, who is looking down at a grave that is covered in fresh flowers. Much nicer flowers than the ones I have brought. I start to wonder if bringing them was a good idea.

Helm stands outside of the cemetery, watching me as I walk up to Vault's side. Vault ignores me, until I place my flowers on his wife's grave. I can see tears in his eyes, but it is hard to tell if they are real tears, for he is completely soaked with rain. It feels strange to me that someone so tall, so strong and broad of shoulder would be crying. Vault looks like he was carved from a mountain. His light hair is cut short like mine, much like his beard. He turns to me and stares hard into my eyes.

"Thank you," he says.

I break away from his stare, down to the flowers. I just nod, because I do not know what to say. I look down at the piece of wood that marks her grave and the name that is carved into it: Flora.

We stand in silence for a moment, until Vault startles me when he finally speaks.

"Her parents hated me," says Vault. "Her whole family were harvesters, and they looked down on the protectors and hunters. They thought it was horrible that we sometimes kill, both for food and to protect the Crag from predators. I have never been ashamed of what I do. I believe it is noble to stand guard, to protect others. Protect people that may not be able to protect themselves."

"I agree," I say.

"Even though it was difficult for her, Flora still chose to join with me. She was so beautiful that she could have chosen anyone to be with. I still do not know why she picked me."

Vault looks up into the sky, as if searching for an answer.

"How did she die?" I ask.

"No one knows for sure. I worry that someone poisoned her with wolfsbane. There were many that were jealous of her, and hated her, even though she was sweet, and kind, and loving. Sometimes people die for no reason, but she was young and healthy. She had no wounds that I could see, and there was no blood on her body."

"I am very sorry that you lost her," I say.

We stand there for what seems like forever. I close my eyes and say a prayer to the Sky Gods, asking them to watch over his wife. I also pray again for Harness, so that she will be healed.

Eventually, Vault turns to me.

"Come. We will talk more," he says.

Vault and I leave the cemetery. Helm follows behind us, looking out for dangerous animals and people that might try to hear our words. We walk to a place halfway between the Crag and the cemetery, but away from the normal path.

I have never been there before. It is a beautiful field of wildflowers, about the size of the Crag. Across the field, I see an old tree. Its branches twist around its trunk, as if it was trying to scratch its own back. I also see some large rocks resting in the field. I wonder if the rocks know how lucky they are to live in such an amazing place.

"How did you find this field?" I ask.

"One day I came to visit Flora's grave, and a strong wind grabbed the flowers I had picked for her. I chased after them, and they led me here. When I looked into the rows of flowers, I could see Flora's name, written in reds and yellows and blues. So now when I visit Flora, I only bring her flowers from this field. And every time I am at her grave, and the wind howls, I hear her name."

"Is that story really true? Did you really see her name in the flowers, and hear her name in the wind?" I ask.

"No," he says, "but isn't it a lovely story?"

"Yes. It is a very lovely story, Vault."

"So what brings you to me, Sam?"

"I was hoping you might have some advice for me. On how to be a good leader," I say.

Vault closes his eyes and takes in a deep breath. I watch as his muscles relax, his body perfectly still. He seems to be at peace with the world around him, something I have never felt. I have always felt tense, worried, afraid that something bad was going to happen. It has kept me alive, but it has also made me miserable.

"Yes, Sam. I can tell you how to be a good leader."

Vault opens his eyes and turns to look at me.

"Be a good person, Sam. In the end, that's all that really matters. Not if you are powerful, or important, or the Sky Child. What matters is being good to the people around you. If you make all your decisions with other people in heart and in your mind, then you will truly accomplish something."

I am surprised by his words. It doesn't surprise me that Vault would say something so important and true, because Vault is a good man. What does surprise me, is that I had never thought like that before. I realize the truth in what he has says, and I feel ashamed. I have always considered myself a good person because I've never meant anyone harm, but it is something else, something more to live for other people.

"I understand. Thank you, Vault," I say.

"Thank me by listening to my advice. Be a good person, and the hunters will follow you into the mouth of a dragon."

"I will, Vault."

I turn to walk away.

"I am glad that you are the Sky Child," says Vault, which causes me to stop.

"Why?" I ask.

"Because you can be so much more than what you already are, and because I know you are willing to die trying to do what is right," says Vault.

"All I really want to do is survive," I say.

"It is easy to see yourself that way, but there is more to you than you know," says Vault.

"What if I don't want to be the Sky Child, or the Leader of the Hunt. What if I just want to be left alone?"

"We almost never get what we truly want, Sam. Life is about making the best out of what we have, not living in a dream all the time. Right now, you must be the Leader of the Hunt, but what you do with that opportunity is up to you."

I nod at Vault then turn and head toward the Crag.

26

Helm and I walk slowly back to the Crag. I spend the walk thinking about what Vault and Crook had said. It amazes me how both are wise, but in different ways. They both gave me good and important advice, and yet they each had something different to say.

When we get close to the Crag, Helm breaks the silence.

"Sam, I've been thinking. I would also like to offer you some advice on how to lead. Don't listen to what other people say. Do what you think is right. Follow your instincts. You are smart. You will be able to figure things out on your own. You don't need advice from anyone. What will make you a better leader is ignoring the way things were done in the past. Keep changing things. Make things better."

"I will try, Helm. I want us to be better, not just as hunters, but as people. And I can live with making mistakes, if they are my own mistakes. Thank you for the advice," I say.

"That wasn't advice. That was me telling you to ignore advice."

I laugh.

"I guess that is true. Well, thank you then for the not-advice."

"You are welcome, Sam."

We reach the mouth of the Crag, and Helm follows me to my room. He stands guard outside. Inside, Flot is working on his armor.

"Flot, where is Jet?" I ask.

"Oh, he's probably watching that girl he likes," says Flot.

"Till?"

"That's the one."

"Do you know when he will be back?" I ask.

"No, I have no idea," says Flot.

"You aren't very helpful," I say.

"Well, if you're going to be mean about it, I won't tell you that someone came by."

"Someone came by? Who was it?"

"Not telling."

"Really? Do you want me to tickle it out of you?" I ask.

"Haven't I seen too many snows for that?" asks Flot.

"Apparently not, because it still works."

"Do your worst!" says Flot, challenging me.

"Fine, I will!"

I slowly creep up to him. He drops his armor on the ground and curls up into a ball. I move slowly, because it is the waiting that makes it worse. Finally, I reach him, and I start to tickle his sides. He writhes around on the ground, trying to avoid my tickles. He laughs until his face turns red.

"STOP! Stop, I can't take any more. You win," says Flot, trying to catch his breath.

"So who came by?" I ask.

"It was Anchor. He says they need you to try on your new armor, so that they can make the final adjustments. He's waiting for you in his room."

"Thank you. Now was that so difficult?"

"Yes! It was!" says Flot.

"Well you deserved it," I say.

"Just go away," says Flot.

"Fine," I say, leaving the room.

Helm follows behind me.

"Where are we going?" asks Helm.

"Anchor's room," I say.

"Have they finished your armor then?"

"They need me to try it on to make sure it fits."

"I'm excited to see what it looks like," says Helm.

"So am I," I say.

It doesn't take us long to reach Charm's room, which is how I found Anchor's place before. Thankfully, from there, Helm knows which tunnel to take to reach Anchor's room.

We walk down the narrow tunnel, and I try to keep my eyes closed, feeling along the walls to know where I'm going. I open them sometimes just to make sure that I don't run into a curve in the wall, or scrape against a rock that is sticking out. It's not as narrow as the cave that leads to Harness' room, but it still bothers me. The feelings of panic seem to be worse now. I eventually make it out of the tunnel and into Anchor's room, but it takes me a moment to calm down.

"Sam, you made it! Great, I am very excited to have you try on your armor," says Anchor. "Also glad to see you, Helm."

"Hmph," is all Helm grunts.

"Right, anyway. Sam, have you ever met Jib and Stanchion before?" asks Anchor.

"No, I have not," I say, reaching my hand out toward Jib.

I notice her hair is the color of bread, and even though she has tied it back, the tight wavy curls stick out in all directions. She barely comes up to my shoulders, but is thick in the arms and legs. Jib shakes my hand.

Jib is very sturdy looking. She is not a gray one yet, but there are streaks of gray in her hair. She looks old for the number of snows she has probably lived through.

"And this is Stanchion," says Anchor.

Stanchion is not at all what I expected. He is very tall, and thin, and hasn't seen many more snows than me. His short black hair is smoothed back. His face is clean, which isn't normal, because most men in the Crag wear hair on their face. He smiles a very big smile. I suddenly feel very awkward around him.

"Sam," says Stanchion, reaching out his hand.

I shake it, but maybe a bit too roughly.

Stanchion's hands are strong, but they do not feel rough like mine. I can tell that he uses them a lot, but not for things that require pulling or lifting or throwing.

"It's an honor to meet you," I say.

"And what, it isn't an honor to meet me?" says Jib.

"Uh... "

She just laughs.

"Don't worry, Sam, I'm not offended. Most people react that way when they meet Stanchion. He is very famous for someone that tries to hide from everyone," says Jib.

Stanchion's cheeks turn red.

"I'm really not famous," says Stanchion.

"Of course you are, boy. People always talk about your creations, saying this and that. I'm kind of sick of it, really," says Jib.

"I will try to do worse then, so that you do not have to hear it as much," says Stanchion.

"No, don't do that. Your skills are too important to the Crag to have you hold them back. But you sweet thing, you probably would do that just to make me happy, wouldn't you?" says Jib.

"I do like to make people happy, when I can," says Stanchion, smiling at me.

I don't really know what to say. We are uncomfortably quiet for a moment. Finally, Anchor breaks the silence.

"So, Sam, are you ready to see your new armor?"

I nod.

Anchor walks over to what must be the armor, which is covered by a blanket. Jib and Stanchion each put a hand on my shoulders, waiting for my reaction. Anchor finally pulls away the blanket.

The armor looks better than I could have hoped for. It is a deep green color, very close to clover. In the middle of the chest is the symbol of the Crag. I can tell by looking at the symbol that it is Stanchion's work. It is made of metal, and it looks like a very pale gold color, almost white.

"It's incredible! I will wear it with pride, and with honor," I say. "Can I ask a question about it?"

"Of course," says Anchor.

"What kind of metal is on the symbol?" I ask.

"It is a blend of gold and silver. Do not worry if the symbol gets damaged, because I have much more of both. It is too bad that gold is so soft, and that silver tarnishes, because I have more than I will ever need of both. All I can make is beautiful things with them. Nothing useful," says Stanchion.

"Sam, you still need to try it on," says Anchor.

"Oh, right," I say.

I take my clothes off and they help me into the armor. It fits differently from my other armor. It is a bit heavier, and this one has long armored sleeves. My normal armor does not have sleeves, so that I can still use my sling.

"How will I use my sling if my arms are bound?" I ask.

"I've made a few changes to the armor," says Jib. "Your arms should be able to move as if you weren't wearing any armor."

I try it out for myself. I can move my arm in any direction: up, down, sideways, twisting. I cannot believe how well it works. I even spin my arm as if I had a sling in my hand, and I can do everything I normally would. I may have to practice to get used to it, since it does add weight to my arm. But once I get used to it, I shouldn't have any problems.

"I can feel that. It feels almost like the armor is a part of me," I say.

"There are a few other things we added," says Anchor. "There are sheaths on each side of you that we placed near your stomach. They are meant to hold these knives."

Anchor hands them to me. Both are very sharp, with edges on both sides of the blade. They have the Crag symbol on them as well, with dark green handles. The blades are colored with the gold and silver I have on my new armor. Their shine is so bright that they don't seem real. I carefully slide them into their sheaths.

"I made the knives so that you can protect yourself up close, but they can also be thrown if necessary. They are meant to protect you as much from wolves as from people. I heard that you'd been attacked, and I wanted you to be able to defend yourself from anyone, and anything," says Stanchion.

"I also made some changes to the armor to help protect against knives and spears," says Jib. "That is why the armor is a little heavier in the chest. There are thin pieces of metal between the layers of leather that should keep it from being damaged by most attacks. The only thing that might get through the armor is a big spear, and only the strongest person would be able to pierce it."

"I added pouches to the tops of your legs," says Anchor. "You can carry your sling and rocks in them. There is also a sheath on the back for holding a pair of sky spears."

Anchor picks a pair of sky spears up from the ground, moves to my back, and slides them into the sheaths. He must have made the holders fairly long, because I can feel as the tips of each spear hit the bottom of their sheaths.

"I owe you each a debt. If there is ever anything I can do for you, let me know," I say.

"You owe us nothing, Sam. Just be the leader you were meant to be," says Anchor.

I place my hand on my heart, and slide it down to each of them. Jib, Stanchion and Anchor each return the salute. I pick up my clothes then Helm and I head back down the tunnel we came from.

27

"I want to test out the armor," I say.

"I think that's a very good idea," says Helm.

"We will need to stop by my room first, so I can leave my clothes there."

"And maybe show it to Flot and Jet?" asks Helm, smiling.

"Yes, maybe for that reason too," I say.

When we arrive at the room, both Jet and Flot are there.

"Wow, you look really dangerous!" says Jet.

"I can't believe that's actually yours!" says Flot. "What is the symbol on it made from?"

"It's a mix of gold and silver. Stanchion says that if it gets damaged he has more."

"Wait, you met Stanchion?" asks Flot. "I didn't think he ever talked to anyone."

"What are those?" asks Jet, pointing to my knives.

I pull them out of their sheaths and show them to my brothers.

"I can't believe they made those for you. Now you're going to get a big head. I don't think there's enough room in here for your head as it is!" says Flot.

I punch Flot in the arm.

"Ow, okay, maybe I deserved that."

"Maybe?"

"Alright, I deserved that."

"And don't worry, I'm not going to treat either of you differently, now that you must obey my every command," I say.

"Yeah, because you don't boss us around all the time anyway," says Jet.

I raise my fist.

"Sorry," says Jet.

"So, when are you going to test it out?" asks Flot.

"Helm and I were just heading outside to see how it works," I say. "Did you want to come along?"

The twins look at each other then hurry to put on their own armor.

"Wait, why are you guys putting on your armor?" I ask.

"Just in case something goes wrong," says Flot.

"Yeah, with your aim, you might accidentally hit one of us with a rock," says Jet.

I give Jet a punch.

"Ungh," he says, rubbing his arm.

Helm helps Flot into his armor, while I help Jet get his straps tied. I place my sling in the pouch on my right leg, and fill the pouch on the left with stones. Jet and Flot both pick up their big spears and carry them out into the tunnel. Finally, we are ready to head outside. Flot and Jet run ahead, trying to be the first to make it to the mouth of the Crag.

We go walking, not too far from the caves, just to make sure we don't run into any animals. We also make sure we aren't close enough to hit anyone coming or going from the Crag.

The first thing I have them do is throw rocks at my chest with their hands. I put my helmet on backwards, so that even if they miss and hit my face, it will be protected. I can barely feel the rocks as they hit my armor and bounce off. It is much stronger than the old armor.

I also have them hit my chest with the dull end of their big spears. The armor does such a good job at protecting me that I can barely tell I was hit at all. I don't have them hit me with the pointed part of the spear, because I don't want to ruin the armor. I also don't want to get hurt. I'm sure I will find out soon enough if it's stronger than the old armor.

"Looks like it will protect you, but how well can you use your sling?" asks Helm.

I reach down and pull out my sling, and a very smooth stone. It should fly true.

"Okay, everyone, you want to be behind me and to my left," I say.

Once they are in place, I give the sling a try. It feels right. I launch a stone at a faraway rock, but one that I should be able to hit most of the time. The rock falls just a little short, but it was straight on. I try another stone, and the same thing happens.

"It feels good, but it does weigh my arm down a little. I will try aiming a bit higher and see if that helps."

I launch my next stone, aiming a bit higher than what I first tried. It works, and my stone hits the target exactly where it should.

"I will need to keep aiming high, until my mind and my body get used to where the rocks are actually going," I say.

"Still, not bad," says Flot.

"Try throwing one of the sky spears now," says Jet.

I pull one of the sky spears from my back. I grip it in the middle, start running, and throw it with all my strength. It goes very far, and sticks in a patch of grass.

"Not bad," says Helm.

I run and pick up the sky spear. After removing the dirt and grass from the tip, I slide it back into its sheath.

"Try the knives now," says Flot.

"Okay, but I need a target," I say.

"Oh, what if we got a pumpkin from the garden?" suggests Flot.

"I think Chaff would be unhappy with us, and I don't think the pumpkin plants have any large enough to use as a target," I say.

"Well, do you have any ideas?" asks Jet.

"What if we use a wolf skull," says Flot.

"That would probably work," I say. "But where would we get one without hunting down a wolf?"

"Easy! We just grab one from the boneyard," says Flot.

"Good idea," I say. "Here, take a sky spear with you and go grab a skull."

I pull one of the sky spears out of its sheath and hand it to him.

"Be careful. You don't know what kind of animals might be there," I say.

"I will," says Flot.

We watch as he heads toward the boneyard.

"You think he will be safe?" asks Helm.

"Yes. I also think it is good to give him a chance to face dangers alone. It teaches him how to be strong without help. It also gives him a sense of freedom. Flot is very good with a spear, and he's very smart, so I am sure he will be fine," I say.

While we wait, I have Jet and Helm hit me on the legs and arms with the dull ends of their big spears. They don't seem as heavy as the chest piece, and I want to make sure that they are just as strong. After a few hits, I decide that the armor is the same across my whole body.

I also practice with my sling more. After many tries, I'm able to hit where I'm aiming at, instead of having to aim high. It will still take me a while to hit the target every time, but for now I am doing well.

Flot comes back with a very white skull. It looks like the black birds had picked away the remaining meat, and the rains must have washed away the blood that had been coating it.

He takes the skull and places it in the grass, not too far away from me. Flot returns the sky spear, which I slide back into its sheath. He then stands over where Helm and Jet are. I pull out one knife and throw it at the wolf skull.

I miss, and not by a small amount. I throw the other knife, and it also misses my target completely.

"Finally! Something you are terrible at," says Flot.

"Did your arms break?" asks Jet.

I stare at them until their smiles disappear. I walk over to the skull, pick the knives off the ground, and go back to where I was standing. Instead of holding the knife by the handle, I hold it by the point of the blade.

I steady myself, line up my throw, take in a short breath and let go. This time the knife goes deep into the skull, making a disgusting crunching noise. I hurl the other knife. This one lands just below the first, splitting the skull clean in half.

"What, no words?" I ask.

Flot and Jet stare at me.

I walk back to the skull, pick the knives up then place them back in their sheaths.

"I think I'm finished for today," I say.

"Good, you were getting annoying," says Jet.

"Isn't Sam normally?" says Flot.

"I wonder how funny a pair of sore arms will be for both of you," I say.

Both Flot and Jet start running back to the Crag.

"Cowards!" I yell.

Helm laughs.

"It is amazing how well you take care of them," says Helm. "My parents did not care as much for me and my brothers."

"I am sorry to hear that," I say.

"Well, it made me strong, and independent. I never really had a father until Lagan. He would spend time training me when we weren't hunting. He was more than just a teacher, though."

"I understand how hard it was to lose him, Helm. I cared for Lagan, too. He is the reason why I became so good with my sling. Like you, he spent time with me, helping me get better. He was the closest thing I ever had to a real father. So now you are not just my protector. Helm, you are my brother."

I reach out my hand and place it on his shoulder. He places his other hand on my shoulder. We both do our best to fight back the tears, trying to stay strong, because that is what Lagan taught us to do. But it helps knowing that there is someone else feeling the same pain that I am.

"Okay, enough of this. We should head back," I say.

"Yes, we should," says Helm.

We walk back to the Crag. Helm and I both turn away from the other for a moment to wipe the tears from our eyes. Cannot allow anyone to see them.

"Helm, will you walk me to Ebb's room?" I ask. "I will have her watch over me for the rest of the evening."

"Whatever you want, Sam."

## 28

Once we reach the Crag, I follow closely behind Helm. He is not as careful about protecting me as Ebb is. I think because he is so strong, people stay away from him out of fear of what he might do to them. Instead of looking down side-tunnels he simply walks straight ahead, confident that he will handle whatever may come.

We arrive at Ebb's room. She is asleep. I peek inside without making any noise, but she suddenly wakes up. I watch as Ebb pulls a knife out from under her blanket and turns around to aim it at me.

"Ebb! It's just me!" I say.

Thankfully, Ebb stops her hand from throwing the knife. Although my armor would probably deflect a knife, I would rather not take the chance.

"Sam? You startled me!" says Ebb.

"I'm sorry, I didn't mean to."

"It's okay. I'm just glad I didn't stab you."

"Me too," I agree.

I turn to tell Helm that he can leave, but he has already disappeared.

"Do I need to get out of bed already?" asks Ebb.

"Yes, and I am sorry that you do. If I could, I would let you sleep longer. Unfortunately, the feast should nearly be ready now. I will need your protection."

"Alright. It should only take me a... "

Ebb finally looks at me, and notices my new armor.

"It's beautiful," she says, pointing at my chest.

"Thank you. Anchor, Jib and Stanchion made it for me," I say.

"I don't think I've seen anything so amazing before," says Ebb. "How do you throw rocks with your arms covered?"

"They designed it so that my arm can move freely," I say. "It took some getting used to, but I've fixed my aim with it."

"I very much like the symbol of the Crag they put on it. How did they make it that color?"

"Stanchion told me he mixed silver and gold. It's my favorite part of the armor," I say.

"I can see why," says Ebb. "And did they give you knives?"

Ebb points to the blades on my stomach.

"Yes, they made these as well," I say.

I pull one of the knives out and twist it around in my hand, so that the blade is aimed at me. I pass her the blade, which she grabs by the handle. She lays it out flat in her palm and moves it up and down, trying to feel how heavy it is.

"They are not very heavy, and they have good balance," says Ebb.

"I was able to split a wolf's skull at distance with one," I say.

"I don't doubt it. Make sure you take care of them, because they would be almost impossible to replace."

"I will," I say.

"Did you get to pick the color yourself?" asks Ebb.

I nod.

"I like it. Reminds me a little of clover."

"I wanted something that would look good, and help protect me. I figure I can lie down in the grass, or in the clover, and hide from a dragon. I think wolves will still smell me, though. It might help me hide from people too, if I am on the ground," I say.

"The good thing is, when you're standing up and

leading us, you will be easy to see with the sky to your back," says Ebb.

"I hope so. But I will use a strong voice to make sure I am heard."

"I bet you will also be hard to see in the dark tunnels. Except for the symbol. That will give you away."

"Probably. So, will you be ready to go to the feast soon?" I ask.

"I would like to wash first," says Ebb.

"That sounds like a good idea. Can we stop by my room so I can grab my soap?" I ask.

"Yes, of course, Sam. Just let me put on fresh clothes."

I decide to turn around, so that I can't watch Ebb put on her clothes. I don't know why I am shy around her now. Everyone changes their clothes in front of everyone else, and it has always been that way.

"Okay, I am ready," says Ebb.

She looks at me with a curious look on her face. I can tell she is wondering why I turned around. Her look of curiosity grows into a smile.

"Are you ready?" she asks.

"Why wouldn't I be?"

"I don't know, why wouldn't you be?"

"Right. So, let's go then," I say.

Ebb hurries to catch up to me, because I'm walking a little faster than I normally do. I'm not sure why I am, though. I also find it strange that I don't understand why I am acting this way. I normally know exactly why I'm thinking, or feeling, or doing something.

When we reach the room that I share with my brothers, neither of them are there.

"They must have already headed to the feast," I say.

I take off my armor and pick up a set of clean clothes, grab my soap, then follow Ebb to the loud waters.

It is busy when we arrive, because people are trying to get cleaned up before the feast. If we had come much earlier though, it would have been worse. Many others have already bathed and left for the feast.

I wash up. Every so often I look over at Ebb, but then quickly look away. I don't want her noticing me looking at her. One time, though, she sees me looking and smiles. I try even harder not to look at her now. Ebb goes back to her washing and so do I. Once I am ready, I look over and see that Ebb is already getting out of the water.

We both hurry to the Great Fire to dry off. It doesn't take very long to get dry, and the clothes we brought are already clean, which makes things easier.

I am still a little wet when I put my clothes on. Ebb notices that I have already dressed, and after ringing her hair out, she puts her clothes on too. I think she is still more wet than me, because her clothes cling to her, and mine do not.

We make our way to the feast chamber. Half the food is already gone, but what is left looks delicious. I don't know that anyone has come up with a name for them yet, but Cleave created a new food not long ago. She takes a few pieces of bread and puts meat between them. She's tried adding different vegetables to see what works best. It seems that the vegetables people like to use are lettuce, tomato and cucumber. I tried one with squash and broccoli once, and it wasn't very good.

I grab a pair of the bread and meat things and take them to the head table. Helm and Mast are already there, waiting for me. I try to ignore everything else and focus on my food.

They are the best meat and bread things cleave has ever made. This time she used leftover wolf meat that she'd cut into very thin slices. She also added onion, lettuce and a fried egg.

I bite into one of them, and I can feel the yellow egg center creeping into the bread. It makes the bread a little softer, and makes the food easier to swallow. The flavor is also amazing. The lettuce is crisp and the onion makes it spicy. I can taste the rosemary that Cleave added to the wolf meat. It is one of the best things I have ever eaten.

I finish the other one just as quickly as the first. I

finally decide to look over at Chaff, and this time he is looking straight at me. We lock eyes. He stares at me, and I stare right back. I wait to see if he will look away first. My eyes start to burn, but I will not give in. I eventually realize that we are both acting like new ones, and that I should be better than that. I break eye contact and shake my head in disappointment for playing his game.

I realize that while I was eating, both Helm and Mast had been talking with the other advisors. Mast finally turns to me.

"Sam, Chaff would like to meet with you privately tomorrow when the sun rises. He says that he has things he would like to discuss with you personally, and that advisors can stand guard outside the meeting, but are unnecessary for what he has to say."

I think about it for a moment. It seems like there is more good than bad in meeting him that way, because then I wouldn't have to deal with Sickle and Scythe. And even though Chaff may be dangerous, if we are alone together, I am not afraid of Chaff attacking me. He is so slow that I believe it would be very easy for me to kill him if it became necessary. He is dangerous only because he can control people, because he controls something that people need.

"Yes, I will meet with him. Tomorrow at sunrise," I say.

"I will let his advisors know," says Mast.

I am sure that Chaff just wants to meet with me to show me who is really in control of things. He will try and scare me into doing what he wants. But I can't be afraid anymore, not with so many people depending on me.

## 29

I wake up the next morning still tired. I went to sleep early so that I could be up for the sunrise. I get out of bed and put my clothes on as fast as I can. I have no idea if I've missed the sunrise, or if it's still dark out. When you sleep in a room that's far back in the Crag, you have a hard time seeing the sun.

I tell Ebb to go back to her room and get some sleep. I thank her for watching over us again. I head out toward the front of the cave, and see that the sun came up a while ago. Great, if Chaff didn't want to kill me before, he will definitely want to kill me now. I follow several twisting tunnels until I reach Chaff's room. Outside, both Mast and Helm are waiting for me.

"He's ready," says Helm. "If you need us, just yell."

"I'm pretty sure I can kill him if necessary. Let us hope it comes to that," I say, smiling.

Mast pulls the curtain to Chaff's room back and I walk inside.

The first thing I notice is that Chaff is sitting behind his table, and he looks angry. Not really a surprise. I also notice that he is busy sharpening one of the tools they use for the harvest. He runs a stone along the blade a few times then looks up at me.

"Sam, please sit," says Chaff.

I sit down on one of the rocks he uses as chairs. It seems strange that the words he says to me are polite, but I can tell from his voice that he has murder in his heart. Of course, to be the kind of leader that Chaff is, you must be able to say one thing and think, or feel, or do another.

"So, you think that you are the Sky Child?" says Chaff.

I am surprised by the question. I know the answer, but I didn't expect him to ask me about it.

"No. I'm not the Sky Child," I say.

"That is what people believe right now. That you have been brought here to save us."

"I really don't know why they would think that."

"Oh, come now. You saved the hunters, and you slayed a dragon with a stick. You also survived the trials. Who else but the Sky Child could do such things?"

"You and I both know I'm not the Sky Child. It's just a legend," I say.

"Yes, you and I both know, but unfortunately that doesn't matter. People in the Crag aren't like us. They are slow of mind, and believe anything they hear. There have been whispers of you being the Sky Child ever since you were found outside the Crag. Their belief that you are the Sky Child poses a problem. I know you are smart enough to understand that the people of the Crag will try to protect you from harm, which is why I think that you were so defiant last night. Why you decided to provoke me, instead of trying to form an alliance with me," says Chaff.

"I provoked you because I despise you. You and your sons. And I wanted you to know that you don't control me," I say.

"That is my worry, yes. So I needed to do something to make sure you understand who is really in control here. Who really runs The Crag. If you are unsure of who that is, let me explain it to you. I control the harvest. I control the food that comes in and out of the Crag, even the meat that you hunters bring back. Because anyone that defies me knows they will starve. You are young, and it wasn't that long ago that you were a new one, so I understand that you might still act like one. You tried to stand up to me the way a brat would stand up to their parents. Let me explain it to you plainly. I am your new father. You will do as I say, without question, from now on," says Chaff.

"Or else what?" I ask.

"Since you obviously won't listen, I think it will be easier for me to show you. I asked Sickle and Scythe to leave a gift in your room. When you get there, I think you will understand who really has control of the Crag."

I look at Chaff's eyes, and for the first time he seems happy. It makes my stomach sick. Something isn't right. I hadn't even realized that Sickle and Scythe weren't around. I need to get back to my room, now.

I run through the door to Chaff's room, nearly pulling down the curtain as I pass through. Helm and Mast realize something must be wrong if I am running through the tunnels, and follow behind me.

I can hear their footsteps as I take several turns, but I can tell they are having a hard time keeping up. The footsteps get quieter, until I almost can't hear them. As I run, I say a silent prayer to the Sky Gods that all is still well in my room.

I turn the corner to go into our room and see blood on the ground. Not the normal red of dried animal blood, but the dark, shining blood of a person. I look down at the body and start to cry. I scream for help as I slide my arms under Jet's lifeless body. I shake him and shake him, trying to get him to wake up. I put my ear over his heart, but I can't hear it beating. I panic, because I don't know what to do. I realize that it's too late. Jet is gone.

"No, no please. No. No. No, he can't, he can't, he can't..."

I lose myself to the sadness, and cry and scream and gasp for air. I grip Jet with all my strength as Helm and Mast appear. I see the horror in their faces as they realize what has happened, and what I am holding in my arms.

Mast and Helm pry me away from Jet's body while I kick and scream, then they drag me down the hall. Mast pins my arms to the ground, and Helm goes back into my room to get a bucket of water. He comes back and throws the water at me, washing some of Jet's blood away. It shocks me, and I stop trying to fight, but I can't stop crying. I don't think I will ever stop crying.

"Which one is it?" asks Helm.

"J-jet. It was Jet," I say.

"Where is Flot?"

"I... I don't know."

"I'm here," comes Flot's voice from down the hall.

It is hard to hear him. Helm walks off in the direction of Flot's voice. I hear a groaning noise. I twist my head to look down the tunnel, and watch as Helm returns with Flot in his arms.

Mast releases his grip on me and I stand up and run to Flot. He looks injured, but he is still alive. He has a cut lip, his neck is red, and he is holding his stomach.

"What happened young hunter?" asks Helm.

"It was Sickle and Scythe," says Flot with a rough voice, tears running down his cheeks. "They came looking for me. Jet was off getting water. They didn't say anything, they just smiled and stared at me. Then Sickle punched me in the mouth. I fell to the ground, and then they kicked my stomach as hard as they could. Scythe picked me up by my throat and pushed me against the wall. He held me there, and I couldn't breathe. That's when Jet came back. He was so angry at them, I thought he might kill one of them."

"What happened next?" asks Helm, setting Flot carefully on the ground.

"Jet jumped on Sickle and knocked him to the ground. He punched Sickle so hard that I think he broke his eye. Scythe got ahold of Jet though, and pulled him off of Sickle. He threw Jet to the ground then stomped on his head. He just kept kicking Jet, over and over. Sickle got up and started kicking Jet too. They kept kicking him until he stopped moving. Jet died trying to protect me."

I lean back against a wall and slide down it, covering my eyes. I cry harder than I have ever cried before. This is all my fault. If I hadn't tried to make Chaff angry, Jet would still be alive. Sickle and Scythe never would have come to hurt Flot. I should be the one that died, not Jet. Jet never did anything wrong. Jet was true of heart and strong and loyal, and he didn't deserve to die.

"Sam, Jet died because of me, because I'm not as strong, and I don't stand up for myself. It's all my fault," says Flot, as he starts to cry harder.

I move on my hands and knees to where Flot is on the ground, and I wrap my arms around him.

"No, Flot, it isn't your fault. You didn't do anything wrong, and neither did Jet. It was my fault that Sickle and Scythe came and attacked you. I am so, so sorry," I say.

But is it my fault? Chaff is truly evil, and would have sent Sickle and Scythe anyway. Chaff is the real cause of this, and he must be stopped. Tears turn to anger. I set Flot down on the cold stone floor.

"Mast, Helm, take Flot back to our room and put him in bed," I say.

I stand up, and start moving in the direction of Chaff's room, but a hand reaches out and grabs my arm. I pull away from it, but I can't free myself from the grip.

"Don't do this, Sam. I know you want to kill Chaff right now, but the Sky Child would never kill anyone unless they had to," says Mast.

I pull with all my strength and weight away from Mast's hand and break free, but I fall to the ground. I get back up, still filled with anger.

"I am not the Sky Child! The Sky Child isn't real, it's just some stupid legend, made up by people that aren't even alive anymore. Don't you think that if I was the Sky Child I would have seen this coming, and I would have stopped it? The Sky Child is supposed to bring hope and happiness to the people of the Crag. I have only brought death," I say.

"No, that was Chaff. He did this, not you. Jet's death isn't your fault," says Mast.

I stand there, staring at Mast. I am quiet for a moment.

160

"I'm going to kill Chaff for what he did," I say.

"If you do, you will doom the Crag. You won't just be killing Chaff, you will be killing all of us, because we need the harvest to survive. Otherwise, there just isn't enough food for everyone. Chaff knows that, which is why he is such a monster. He can get away with it, because he knows that he controls everything," says Mast.

"I have to end Chaff's evil."

"Then find another way."

I look at Mast for a moment longer then turn and head down one of the tunnels that lead outside.

30

I leave the cave and go to where we normally hunt. I know that no one will bother me, because the hunters will not leave the Crag without their leader. The other people in the Crag will not come out here either, because it's too dangerous. Most of them don't know how to protect themselves from wolves and other predators.

I keep walking, until I know I am so far away from the Crag that no one could possibly hear me. I lie down in a patch of clover and cry. I cry until I choke and feel like I can't breathe. Until my eyes hurt and my throat burns like fire.

No one can see me like this. That is why I left the Crag. They can't see me weak, or emotional. They can't see how much this hurts me. Especially Chaff. I will hide it, because I know he will think he can control me if I can't control myself. I must be strong, or at least seem strong, even when I am weak and dying inside. Chaff took away one of the only things that has ever really mattered to me.

Thank the Sky Gods that Flot still survived, and for him I need to be strong. He lost the only blood family he had, his brother, the person he cared about most. I cannot take that pain away from him, but I can be there for him. I will do what I can to help him.

Eventually, I stop crying. I just lay there, on my side, not caring about anything going on around me. Thinking about how stupid I am for not protecting Jet. For putting him in danger. For not keeping him safe.

I have failed. I forgot the most important rule of war. The lesson that I learned from jump stones: protect what is most important to you.

That thought hangs in my mind for a while, until I hear an animal growling. I slowly roll over onto my other side and see a wolf that has snuck up on me. My heart hurts from the pounding in my chest and my mouth goes dry. I get onto my hands and knees, and I grab a loose rock off the ground.

The wolf growls louder, acting like he wants to attack me. I stare him in the eyes and show him my teeth. I grip the rock, ready to protect myself if I must. He sniffs the air, and then his growling stops. The wolf stares back at me, back at my eyes, and tries to decide whether I am worth it. He cocks his head, holds his stare for a moment, and then walks away.

I have never seen a wolf act like that. They have always attacked us in the past. Something happened. Something was different. I wonder if maybe it was me. Maybe I am different now, since I have lost someone as important to me as Jet. Maybe the wolf could smell my anger and hatred. Maybe it could tell that I would fight it, and kill it, because I was desperate for revenge. Maybe. I will never know, because I cannot ask the wolf. But if the wolf could speak, he would likely be too proud to tell me.

My thoughts drift to Chaff. There must be some way that I can get revenge for what he and his sons did to Jet. I can't kill him. As much as I might feel like I want to kill him, I don't really want to kill him, because I don't want to murder anyone. I don't want to be like the jealous ones that kill simply because someone has more than them.

I could take something from him. There are only a few things that matter to Chaff. His sons, and the harvest. I can't take away his sons, because that would mean killing one of them. Would that make us even? Yes. But I don't want to take a life, even if that life is evil.

The only thing I can take away from him is the harvest. But how can I do that, when he is the only one who knows its secrets? I realize that he must have learned somehow, or figured out on his own how to grow vegetables and grains. So, I think about how he might have learned to grow things. Maybe he got it from the Book of Knowledge.

I hope that the Book of Knowledge somehow explains how to grow things. I wipe my eyes with my shirt and run back to the Crag as fast as I can. I try to stay quiet, even as I hurry through the tunnels, and I try to make sure that I am not being followed.

I reach the reading room, and I am very lucky that no one is there reading. I carefully pick up the Book of Knowledge, because it is old and worn, and looks like it could fall apart very easily.

I look up the word vegetable. It takes me a while to find, because I am still not very good at the order of the alphabet. I can read well enough, but for some reason, I have never tried remembering what order that letters go in.

The book tells me that a vegetable is 'a part of a plant that is used for food'. It takes me a while to find the word 'plant'. It reads 'to put a seed or flower in the ground to grow'.

I smile, because now I understand that you put something into the ground to make it grow. But I am not sure what a seed is. I flip through more pages, searching for the one that would have the word 'seed' on it. Someone has torn out that page.

Either Chaff has kept the page for himself, or he has destroyed it. Either way, I will need to find out what he knows. I can't torture it out of him, no matter how much I might want to. Even if I did, there is no guarantee that I'd get the answers I was looking for. So I will need to be clever to find out what I must know.

I close the Book of Knowledge and set it back down on its stand. I will need to search Chaff's room to see if he keeps the missing page there. Once I have the information, I may finally be able to rid the Crag of the evil monster that took Jet from us. And it will hopefully also rid us of his evil sons, forever.

## 31

I head back to the room to check on Flot. Mast is standing outside, protecting it.

"You didn't do anything stupid, did you?" asks Mast.

"No, I did something very smart," I say.

Mast looks me in the eyes and can tell that I didn't kill Chaff. Killing someone changes your eyes. It takes the shine away from them, because part of you disappears forever. Even the evil ones seem to be different after killing someone, like they aren't alive anymore. It makes me feel sad for the ones that have only killed for good reasons, like to protect someone, because they still deserve to be whole.

"Sam, I have taken Jet's body to Pyre so that he can prepare it to be buried tomorrow," says Mast.

"Thank you," I say, as I fight back the tears.

I walk into our room. Helm is there, watching over Flot. Flot is asleep, but seems to be doing okay. His skin is a normal color, and he seems to be breathing better.

"How is he?" I whisper.

"He will survive this," says Helm. "But what he saw will live inside him. He may not be the same Flot you remember, and he may want his own revenge against Sickle and Scythe."

I hadn't thought about that. How Flot might have murder inside of him, or even think of killing someone. I doubt he would ever do it, because he is good, and good people do not murder. At least that is what the Sky Gods tell us.

Flot is so soft-hearted, I can't imagine him doing it. But he may think that his soft heart is why Jet died. That he doesn't stand up for himself enough. Maybe more than just revenge, he wants to prove that he is not a victim.

Flot will need to be watched and protected from himself. But he can't know that he is being watched, because he is smart, and will only find a way around our attempts to stop him. For that reason, we will need to stop him while he is trying to carry out his plan. The possibility of Flot trying to kill Sickle and Scythe means that I will need to work fast to carry out my own plan. I'll have to start tonight.

I let Helm and Mast get some rest. I thank them for everything they've done today, and send them back to their rooms. I also ask them to tell the other hunters that there will be no hunt today. That they should say that Jet is dead, but that they can't tell anyone he was murdered, who killed him or why.

Jet had friends in the Crag, and people that liked him, and those same people may try to deal with Chaff, Sickle and Scythe on their own. I can't allow that, because for this to work, and for the Crag to survive, I must make good on my plan.

I lie down next to Flot. For a while I just lay there, staring up at the rough ceiling of our room. Sometimes I cry for a while, but I make sure that I don't make any noise when I do. I hold his hand, not because I think it will help him, but because I think it will help me. It lets me know that he is still alive. That he is okay. That I haven't lost him too.

I hear footsteps near our room. They stop just outside. "Sam?"

It is Ebb.

I stand up and leave the room, so that we won't wake up Flot with our talking.

"Sam, is it true? Did they kill Jet?"

I reach out and wrap my arms around her. I use her

balance to help keep me upright. My tears pour into her shoulder. I can feel her hand on the back of my head, stroking my hair. It only makes me cry harder.

"I am so, so sorry," says Ebb.

She holds me. I can tell she doesn't know what to do. How to help. But she is doing what I need: she is there for me.

Eventually, I calm down enough to talk.

"I am sorry you have to see me like this," I say.

"There is no reason to be sorry, Sam. Your tears show how much you cared for him. There is no shame in that."

I wipe the tears from my eyes.

"Thank you," I say. "Oh, Ebb, you must be tired! I forgot you haven't slept much."

"I am fine. This is more important than sleep."

"I think I will be okay now. Please, get some rest," I say.

She looks into my eyes.

"Don't you think someone should stand guard?" asks Ebb.

"No, it's alright. Chaff would not be dumb enough to attack us now. If anything happened to Flot, or to me, he would be a dead man, regardless of the harvest. There are enough people in the Crag that would kill Chaff for either murdering Flot, or the Sky Child, that he wouldn't dare take the chance. He has sent his message, and I am sure he feels like he got his point across."

"Are you sure you don't want me to stay?" asks Ebb.

"I do want you to stay, but I want you to rest. We will be fine. I promise," I say.

She gives me one last hug then leaves.

I go back inside our room and lie down. I find myself sleeping, even though it's in the middle of the day. My body is so tired from crying so much. I am fortunate that it helps my plan to get some sleep, because I do not expect to sleep tonight. I will only be able to carry out my plan once everyone else is asleep.

Eventually, I wake up to hear people going down the

tunnels for the dinner feast. I look over and see that Flot is still asleep. Instead of walking to the feast chamber like everyone else, I head to the cooking room, where many people are busy making food. I grab a large bowl from a stack and fill it with whatever stew that Cleave has been making. I notice that Cleave isn't there. I ask one of the other cooks about it.

"Corriander, where is Cleave?"

"She went to pray at the Great Fire for a moment, but she said she would be right back. She said she felt bad that you lost your brother. I am also sorry for that."

A tear flows down my cheek, but I quickly wipe it away.

"Thank you. I will go find her then," I say.

I take the bowl of food back to the room, but leave it there to cool. I am worried about Cleave, so I decide to visit the Great Fire. When I get there, though, she is not there. To be able to go from the cooking room to the Great Fire, you have to pass by our room. Cleave hasn't yet. I am worried about her, so I decide to head toward the mouth of the Crag.

As I arrive, I see Cleave coming back inside with something in her hand. She sees me, and quickly puts it in her pocket.

"Cleave, there you are. Are you okay?" I ask.

"Oh, Sam, I'm okay. I am so sorry about your brother. He was such a good boy. I liked him very much. He would bring me wild herbs that he found while he was out hunting."

I didn't know that he did that. I try to fight back the tears when I realize that there were some things I will never get to learn about Jet.

"Cleave, I am sorry, but I have to ask: what is it that you put in your pocket?"

Worry is on her face.

"It is just some herbs I picked," says Cleave.

"Can I see?" I ask.

Cleave hesitates, but pulls out the stems and roots that she is hiding from me. I recognize them immediately.

"Wolfsbane," I say.

Cleave's face twists with anger and sadness.

"Cleave, it's okay. I know that you want to poison Chaff, and I won't tell anyone about this. But I have a plan that will deal with Chaff and his sons forever. The Crag will still have food. Can you let me do that?"

She thinks for a moment then nods in agreement.

"Okay. Then take the wolfsbane back outside, and leave it far enough away from the Crag that no one will know it was picked," I say.

Cleave nods her head in understanding. She reaches out and hugs me briefly then goes back outside.

I return to our room and find that the food is still warm. I wake Flot up so that he can eat. It takes him a moment to realize where he is and why he is in our room. Fresh tears roll down his cheeks. I hug him and let him cry. I cry too. Eventually, I pull away.

"I brought you some stew," I say.

"I'm not hungry," says Flot.

"You need to eat, even if it feels like you don't," I say.

Flot is so tired that he doesn't argue with me. I watch as he forces himself to spoon some food into his mouth. He chews very slowly on it then swallows. I can tell that his throat still hurts, because as he swallows, his eyes close and his brow wrinkles in pain. I make sure that he takes a few more bites. After that, he starts eating more normally, but it is still difficult for him.

"Flot, I need to ask you something," I say.

He looks at me, searching my eyes for what it could be.

"Are you planning to hurt Sickle or Scythe?" I ask.

His eyes water. I can see in his eyes the shame that he feels. He feels bad that he wants to kill them, and he doesn't want me to know that he has those feelings.

"It's okay," I say. "I feel the same feelings that you do. We lost Jet, and it's because of them. They can never fix that. They can never make it right. They can never apologize enough for it, even if they feel sorry for killing him. Jet is gone,

169

and it's because of them. But I have to ask you not to hurt them."

Flot quickly looks away from me.

"Flot, there is a reason why you can't kill them. I need you to be patient. I have found a way to get rid of Chaff and his sons forever. But I need you to wait. I need you to hold back, just for a little while. If my plan doesn't work, then I will help you with yours. But I need you to wait so that I can see if it will work. Can you do that for me?"

Flot slowly turns back to me.

"I can do that. I can wait. But you will help me if your plan fails?" he asks.

"Yes, I will help you," I say.

I don't know if I mean it or not. I would like to think that if my plan failed, that I would take matters into my own hands and deal with Chaff myself. But if my plan fails, then all hope is lost.

## 32

Once Flot finishes eating, I return to the cooking room and fill the bowl with my own dinner. I take it back to our room and eat while Flot tries to fall asleep. As I finish my meal, I can hear him quietly snoring.

Now I wait. I need to make sure that everyone has left the feast, and that they are all asleep, before I carry out my plan. I cannot be seen, not by anyone if this is going to work. I wait until I stop hearing noises, and then longer after that.

While I wait, I think about all the horrible things that have happened recently. I spend part of the time crying, the other part trying not to cry. Finally, after what feels like forever, I am sure that everyone is asleep.

I walk down less used side-tunnels, and hide in the shadows as much as I can. Some of the protectors of the Crag walk the tunnels during the night, making sure that animals haven't come into the cave, looking for food. I didn't really pay attention to them much before, but now I must avoid them. It would be very difficult to explain why I was up when everyone else is asleep.

It is not their job to protect people from each other, but if one of them sees me, it might get back to Chaff that I was wandering the halls at night. That would make him suspicious, and it could ruin my plan.

As I move along a well-lit tunnel, I hear very faint footsteps coming near me. I notice light moving around a corner. It is probably one of the Crag protectors.

I turn and move as fast as I can, away from the protector and down a side-tunnel. I see a large rock toward the end of the tunnel that points at the ceiling like a spear. I panic, because as I go past the rock, I realize that I am at a dead end.

I lie down on the floor, on my side, trying to make myself as small as possible. That way, when the protector comes by, he won't see me around the rock. I stop moving, and I pray to the Sky Gods that I'm not found.

The footsteps grow nearer and then stop. I watch as light dances around the rock, throwing its shadow against the cave walls behind me. I never see any part of my own shadow on the wall, which makes me think that the protector can't see me. I'm relieved when I finally hear the footsteps of the protector disappear.

I look around the rock slowly, just to make sure that I wasn't wrong. Thankfully, I am alone. I move back down the tunnel and turn toward Chaff's room, leaving the dead end behind me.

As I walk, I do my best to walk quietly. Some tunnels can make sounds louder, or travel a long distance. Because of that, I must be careful not to make much noise.

I stay in the shadows, jumping across light only when I must. I pass by several rooms that still have glowing sticks burning in them. I do my best to stay hidden as I look into them, making sure that I am not being watched. As I come up to the room nearest Chaff's, I hear someone moving inside.

I look down on the ground in front of the room, and watch the shadow of the room's owner move back and forth in front of the light. I try to figure out what they are doing from the shadow, but the movements are so quick that it is hard to tell. That is when the shadow suddenly gets much larger.

I jump away from the shadow and push myself against the wall near the opening of the room. Several bumps in the wall crash against my back, knocking my breath out of me. I start to panic, because I can't breathe right. But I know that if I make a sound it will mean the end of my plan. If the shadow that I am hiding from is a killer, it could also mean the end of me.

I wait. I slowly draw a breath, using all my strength to stay quiet. It causes my body to shake, but I make no noise. Finally, the shadow goes back into their room and puts out their glowing stick.

There is very little light for me to see by, so I have to use my feet to feel for my next step. I see Chaff's room ahead, but not much light comes out of it. At least I can see where I am heading. I realize now that there was one part of my plan that I hadn't yet figured out: how do I search Chaff's room if Chaff is in it?

If he puts out his glowing stick, I won't be able to see well enough to search his room. If I look into his room and his glowing stick is still lit, and he sees me, then I am dead. But I would rather he catch me than need to protect myself, killing him and dooming the Crag.

As I get closer to Chaff's room, I hear loud snoring. The Sky Gods have smiled on me. I move around the corner, pull back the curtain, and look into his room. He is asleep, flat on his stomach. Next to him is a pitcher that is nearly empty. I can smell the beer inside it from many steps away. I am very lucky, because I know that people who drink too much beer sleep very deeply. I should be able to look through his room without waking him.

I step inside, and the first thing I notice is the smell. It smells like rotten food. As I move closer to Chaff, I realize that it's him that smells, and not something in the room. I try hard not to throw up, but I start gagging from the odor. I have to pinch my nose and breathe through my mouth just to get air inside me.

I look around Chaff's room. It is the largest in the Crag by far. I see the table I sat at, with the big rocks that look like chairs. Further into the room is a space where Chaff hangs his clothes. He also has a set of shelves, with many odd things on it that I have never seen before. Some of them are made from metal, while others look like they are made from something shiny and brightly colored that I haven't seen before.

I pick up one of the shiny objects, and I'm able to bend it in my hand. It seems strong, almost like metal, but it's lightweight. I wonder what this strange thing is. It looks like a handle, with some sort of flat spoon at the end, but it wouldn't work at all as a spoon because it has slots in it.

I resist the urge to take it with me, and instead I keep looking. I try to look for an object that could hold things. There are only a few objects that look like they might.

The first object I try seems like it's made of the same stuff that some of our bowls are made from. It's shiny, and has an odd blue creature on it with a pair of large white eyes. The creature looks like it is holding a light brown circle of food up to its mouth. The food has dark brown spots on it. I have absolutely no idea what it is. I pick the creature's head up from the top and look inside, but I find nothing.

I hear a loud noise and jump, but I realize it's just a change in Chaff's snoring. It startles me so badly that it takes me a moment to catch my breath.

The next thing I look at is a box made of metal. It has a red handle that is made from the same stuff that the flat spoon thing was made from. On the outside of the box is an image of a man standing next to what looks like some large evil creature with a long, sideways red eye.

I open the box and inside is a smaller, round container. I shake it, and there doesn't seem to be anything inside. I can't easily remove the top of this container, so I twist it, trying to force it off. As I twist, it loosens. I keep twisting, and it finally comes apart. Inside, just like the metal box, it is empty.

The last box I check is just that: a box. It is brown and made of wood, and has many small shapes on it. I try to find a lid, but it doesn't seem to have one. I shake it, but it does not open. I twist it, but still, nothing happens. Just as I am about to give up, my thumb moves a piece of wood on one of the sides.

I try pulling on the piece, but it won't move. It only

slides back and forth. I leave it pulled out, and check the box for other pieces to move. After playing with the box for a while, I find another piece that slides. I pull it all the way out too. The next piece I find is by the first piece that moved. Even with many pieces pulled out, I can't get it to open.

I start to get frustrated and accidentally drop the box. I can feel my heart pounding in my chest as I turn my head to see if Chaff is awake. Thankfully, he is still asleep on his mat.

I pick up the box, and the entire side of the box with the first moving piece slides down. I can see that the top of the box could pull out, if the side that slid down could move down even further. I try moving more of the side, but only the pair of pieces can move.

It takes me a while to realize that maybe the pieces shouldn't be pulled out all the way. That maybe they only need to be pulled out some. I start moving the pieces in and out, until finally the side moves down and I can slide off the top. I look inside, but there is nothing.

I get angry that I wasted so much time trying to open the box. I put the box back together the way I found it and set it down on the shelf. It only takes me a few more moments to realize that the paper isn't hidden on the shelves.

I look around the room, trying to find some other place where he might be hiding such important information. That's when I look down at Chaff, sleeping on his bed mat. What better place to hide something important than underneath you?

It makes sense. Someone would have to be a fool to try to move a sleeping person, especially one that might wake up and kill you for it. Also, with Chaff's large size, it would take many people working together to move him.

I decide to leave because I have nowhere else I can look. I am now certain that the paper is hidden underneath him. I very carefully make my way past Chaff, pinching my nose and holding my breath as I go by. I still cannot believe how bad he smells.

Once I leave his room, I move as quickly as I can until

I am sure I can breathe the air again. I cough, realize my mistake, and cover my mouth with my hands. I can hear a protector coming down the tunnel that I'm in. Thankfully, it is long and curved, but I won't be able to escape with the protector walking so quickly.

I come to a room that has its glowing stick still burning. I look inside, and a pair of girls are asleep. They both look like they have seen the same amount of snows as me. I slip inside, and lay on the stone floor next to them, pretending to be asleep. The footsteps of the Crag protector stop right in front of the girls' room.

I keep my eyes closed and my mouth open a little to breathe. Sometimes I look at Jet and Flot when they are asleep, and that is how they look. Or at least how Jet used to look when he slept. The feeling of loss from Jet's death overwhelms me. I can feel a tear running down my cheek. I hope that the protector doesn't see it.

I can hear him breathing now, staring at each of the us. It sounds like he is making a noise with his mouth, like he is licking his lips. I am disgusted by the sound, but I don't really know why.

Eventually, the protector leaves the room. I look over and see the girls, and they are still asleep. Rolling over onto my stomach, I push myself up and off the ground. I decide to follow the protector, but I keep him far ahead of me, and take my steps at the same time he does so that he cannot hear me.

It helps that the big tunnels in the Crag almost form a circle, with both ends meeting at the mouth. Sometimes the protector goes down a side-tunnel, so I have to stop and wait for him. But then he comes back into the main tunnels, and I can follow him again. It seems to take forever. I have a hard time holding in my yawns as I get more and more tired.

Finally, I reach our room. Flot, thankfully, is still asleep, although I can tell he is having a rough time of it because of his injuries. I can only imagine how bad his nightmares must be after losing Jet. I wish there was a way I could make him feel better, if only a little.

I take off my clothes, throw them in a pile on the ground and slip under my blanket. Even though I am tired, I have a hard time falling asleep. I can't help but feel that I have failed Jet; that it's all my fault he's dead. I know it was Chaff and his evil sons that killed him, but it was my stubbornness that pushed them to it.

I also lose sleep trying to figure out how I am going to get the paper I need, if it even still exists. I worry that once he had the knowledge, Chaff destroyed the missing page. I know if I wanted to keep a secret, that I would do everything I could to destroy any proof of it.

At the same time, Chaff may want to make sure that at least one of his sons runs things after his death, and you never know when you might meet your end. You can be sure that Sickle and Scythe would turn Chaff's room upside down looking for the secret of the harvest. They would probably find the information if it was hidden under Chaff's bed mat.

I am also sure that neither Sickle nor Scythe know how to grow things. If they did, they would have killed Chaff long ago. I hold onto that thought as I finally force myself to rest.

## 33

It is late when I finally wake up. I know what's coming, and I don't want to face it. Because I know that when we bury Jet, it will mean that it's real, and he won't be coming back. I won't ever be able to talk to him again. I won't be able to wrestle with him, or teach him how to hunt, or be there to celebrate with him when he joins with someone.

In my pain, I had forgotten about Till, the girl that Jet had liked. If she liked him back, she's having a hard time dealing with his death, too.

I check on Flot, and he's still sleeping. Thankfully, he seems to be breathing okay, and his snoring isn't as loud as it was last night. I get up out of bed and make my way to Helm's room. I see him moving around inside, so I go in.

"Helm?" I say.

"Yes, Sam. What is it?" asks Helm.

"Can you please watch over Flot this morning? I have someone I need to talk to, and I want to make sure that Flot has help if he needs it. I also want to know that he is protected, so that no one else tries to harm him."

"I will do that," says Helm.

"Thank you."

As I turn, Helm stops me.

"You aren't going to talk to Chaff, are you?" asks Helm.

"No. I'm going to try to avoid him and his sons for

now."

"That seems very wise. Remember that it isn't just you and Flot that you're responsible for now, it is also the hunters, and in some ways the entire Crag."

"I know," I say. "It's strange; I had told Lagan that I didn't want to lead. I have never wanted to lead, or be responsible for other people."

"He told me. Probably part of the reason he thought you would be good at it. That, and ever since you arrived, he believed that you were the Sky Child," says Helm.

"I wish I was the Sky Child. Maybe I could have saved Jet."

My eyes feel heavy, and I feel weak and tired. I leave Helm's room and make my way to the room that Till's family lives in.

It takes me a while to get there, because it's across the other side of the Crag, on the side that Chaff and Sickle and Scythe live on. Thankfully, Till's room is down a different set of tunnels, so I don't pass near Chaff's room.

Once I reach her room, I see fresh flowers sitting in front of the door. This is how we mark the loss of someone special. I need to pick some flowers too, but in my pain and anger I had forgotten. It seems like such an empty thing now, because flowers will never bring Jet back.

I look inside and see Till talking to her mother, Leaf. Leaf notices my arrival, and understands immediately why I am there.

"Till, are you up for seeing Sam right now?" asks Leaf. Till nods her head slowly.

"Okay. I will let the pair of you talk. Till, if you need me, I will be outside our room," says Leaf, kissing her daughter on the forehead.

"Thank you," says Till.

As Leaf leaves the room, I try to give her a smile. She puts her hand on my shoulder, letting me know that she cares, and that she is sad for what I have lost. I nod, then step inside.

"Hello, Till. I'm sorry that we haven't met before," I

say.

"Is Jet really dead?" asks Till.

The question takes me by surprise, not because of what she is asking, but because of the urgency of the question.

"Yes, Till, I'm sorry. Jet died yesterday," I say.

Till cries, and I sit next to her, putting an arm around her.

"I didn't know whether to believe it or not," says Till. "I overheard Sickle and Scythe talking about it in the tunnels nearby. I wasn't sure if it was true, because they are always lying. But I put out flowers just in case."

"That was very sweet of you. How well did you know Jet?" I ask.

"Not very. The first time I had even said more than a pair of words to him was a few nights ago, at the feast. He came up to me and started talking to me."

"What did he say?"

"Well, he was trying to act very brave, but I could tell that he was nervous. He had a hard time getting the words out at first. He said some very sweet things about me. It made me blush. No boy has said those kinds of things to me before."

I smile at her. I'm proud of Jet for working up the courage to talk to her. Talking to someone you like is always difficult, but when you've only seen as many snows as they have, it is much harder.

I realize that as she's telling me this, tears are coming down my face too.

"I hope it is okay that I ask, but what did you say to him?"

"I told him that I thought he was cute, and nice, and that maybe he could come out to the gardens with me some day. Maybe we could talk there, and get to know each other," says Till.

"That sounds nice," I say, swallowing hard.

"He also said that he thought he'd enjoy working in the harvest. That he was good at hunting, but he didn't enjoy it very much. He only did it because he wanted you to be proud of him."

Those words cut me deeper than any spear could.

"I had no idea that Jet didn't want to hunt, and I don't think I ever pushed him into it," I say, tears pouring from my eyes even harder.

"No, I don't think it was like that. It was just that he was so proud of you, and he wanted to be like you. He even told me so," says Till.

Whatever control I had over myself fails me. I cover my face with my hands and let the tears come. I can't believe that I'm letting Till see me like this, but I feel like I can trust her. She won't tell anyone how badly Jet's death is affecting me. She has lost him too, even if she barely knew him. Jet was like that, someone that people never forgot.

It is Till's turn to put her arm around me. I can feel her head against mine as she cries out her pain. We sit there together for a while until we both calm down. I give Till a final hug then make my way out of her room. Before I get to the tunnels, she speaks.

"Sam?"

"Yes, Till?"

"Thank you for coming and talking to me. It was very nice to meet you," says Till.

"And you," I say, doing my best to give her a smile.

As I leave her room, I see Leaf still waiting in the tunnels for us to finish.

"Thank you, Sam, for talking with her. It was better to hear about losing Jet from you. It will help her to know that someone cared about her feelings, and that she isn't the only one missing Jet," says Leaf.

"I understand why Jet liked her," I say.

Leaf smiles, and I give her a tear-filled smile back.

I head down a tunnel, and turn into a dark corner so that I can dry my eyes without anyone seeing.

## 34

I'm feeling a little better, now that I've talked to someone else who cared about Jet. I think it helped me to talk to Till as much as it helped her, and I will make a point of talking to her from now on. Leaf, too. They both seem like very good people, which there aren't a lot of in the Crag.

I walk down the long, shadow-filled tunnels, until I finally get back to our room. Flot is out of bed, unclothed, and he is trying to scrub the red floor of our room. Trying to get the blood out. Jet's blood. I rush to his side.

"Flot, no, please, you don't have to do this. You shouldn't have to do this," I say.

"Sam, it's okay. It's just blood, like any other day," he says.

"Okay, Flot, okay. I will help you clean then," I say.

I take off my clothes and put them on my bed, so that I don't stain them any worse than they already are. I grab a brush and start cleaning the dried blood off the stone floor. It is hard work, but together, Flot and I get the blood up. We do such a good job that the stone is no longer red; it's a dark gray now.

We both take our soap bars and clothes to the loud waters and wash away the dirt and blood that clings to us. It's the first time I see all of Flot's wounds. I see the deep bruises on his stomach where Sickle and Scythe kicked him, and the redness around his neck. I can feel the anger inside me building, but I need to hold it in, for Flot's sake. I must stay in control. I have to be like the Sky Child.

Only, I don't want to be the Sky Child. I don't want to lead. I don't want people to know who I am. I just want to live in peace, and I want Jet back. It makes me sad to realize that Vault was right. People almost never get what they truly want, and it seems like that is especially true for me.

I'm feeling sorry for myself. I need to think of something else, do something else to keep my mind and my heart from giving up. There is nothing I can do to bring Jet back, but I can make sure that his life wasn't meaningless.

I will do what needs to be done, to honor him and his memory. Because Jet wouldn't want me to give up. He would want me and Flot to be happy again someday. He would want us to miss him, of course, because we loved him and he loved us. But he wouldn't want us to give up on life because we were hurting so much.

Once I finish cleaning myself, I start to wash both of my shirts and pants. I want to make sure I have clean clothes for when we bury Jet. It takes a while, but eventually my clothes look better than I can remember.

This time I wait for Flot to finish, but I don't have to wait long. I don't want him alone and outside of our room right now. Not after what happened. I'm still worried, even after our talk, that he might try to find and attack Sickle and Scythe on his own. If they come by to harass him, he might lose control, maybe even kill one or both of them. I can see them saying things about Jet, and Flot trying to hurt them for it.

I don't think Sickle and Scythe will try to kill Flot though, because once I have lost both of my brothers, there is nothing else that they can take from me. There is no way to control me. Chaff knows this, and he knows that a person with nothing to lose is a person that can't be reasoned with. That they can and will do anything, even kill. I am sure that Chaff has told his sons to stay away from Flot because of it, but I'm not willing to take that chance.

After wringing out our clothes, we walk back to our room. I hang up one set of clothes for each of us, and we carry our other sets to the Great Fire. When we get there, I notice that Gravel is watching over the fire, not Moss. I was hoping Moss would be watching it, because he is nice. I don't like Gravel as much, because he almost never smiles, and he ignores people when they try to talk to him.

Flot and I hang our clothes up on the tree limbs that have been stretched between holes in the cave walls. Flot and I also spend a few minutes drying ourselves off with the heat of the Great Fire. When I'm close to finally being dry, Flot asks me something.

"Sam, why did the Sky Gods let Jet die?"

My mind thinks hard on that question.

"Even though we pray to the Sky Gods for help with things like hunting, and the harvest, and with healing, they allow us to still be people. They do not control us. They let us make our own mistakes, and our own decisions. Unfortunately, sometimes people make bad decisions, like what Sickle and Scythe did. Jet's death isn't the fault of the Sky Gods. It isn't your fault, and it isn't my fault. It's the fault of the people that killed him, and the person that told them to attack you in the first place. They are the ones that have made decisions so bad, that they will soon lose everything," I say.

"I hope so," says Flot.

"Me too."

"Do you think that Jet is with the Sky Gods right now?" asks Flot.

"I am sure of it. He was a good person. He didn't listen very well, but his heart was always true. Jet always wanted to help, always wanted to do the right thing, and wanted to make people happier. But we still need to bury him, so that he will be at peace with the Sky Gods. Otherwise, he will toss and turn forever while he sleeps," I say.

"Do you think Sickle and Scythe will be with the Sky Gods when they die?"

"Only if they try very, very hard to become good

184

people, and deep in their heart want to be good people. But right now, I don't think that they will," I say.

"That's good. I don't want them to be anywhere near Jet when they die."

"I don't either."

"Is it okay that I hate them?"

"Yes, Flot, you can hate them, but you can't let that hatred control you. It is always okay to have feelings and emotions, but sometimes it is very wrong to act on them. Sometimes it is even wrong to share those feelings with other people. You will find out on your own what is fine to share with others, and what is not," I say.

"So I shouldn't go tell Sickle and Scythe how much I hate them and want them to die?" asks Flot.

"I think that would be a bad idea right now. You can feel that way, but do not act on it."

"Are we going to see Jet before he is buried?" asks Flot.

"We can. Was that something you wanted to do?" I ask.

Flot thinks about it for a moment.

"I think we should see him. That way we can talk to him without anyone being there. When we bury him, other people will come."

"Okay, Flot. We can do that. Do you want to see him right now?"

Flot nods his head 'yes'.

"Then we will go visit Jet," I say.

Flot and I hold our clothes over the fire, doing our best to make them dry faster. Eventually, they are dry enough to wear. We put our clothes on then travel the crooked tunnels to Pyre's room.

When we get close to the entrance of Pyre's room, I tell Flot to stay there. He asks me why, but I explain that there may be things he doesn't want to see. Thankfully, he understands. I speak into Pyre's room before I go in, just so that he can cover whatever needs covering.

"Pyre? It's Sam. May Flot and I come in to visit Jet?"

"Yes, of course, but please give me a moment."

I hear Pyre moving around his room.

"Okay, you may come in now," says Pyre.

"Thank you," I say.

I turn to where Flot is standing, and put my arm around him to guide him inside. I keep him in front of me, so that I can hold him back if necessary, and to hug him from behind if he needs that.

On Pyre's table is Jet. He doesn't look like himself, not the way I remember him. He is very pale, and his lips aren't the right color. They are a blue color. Pyre has covered most of his body with a blanket. Flot moves forward and reaches under the blanket to hold Jet's hand. Fresh tears roll down my cheeks. Flot turns to me.

"This isn't him," says Flot.

"What do you mean?" I ask, confused.

"This isn't Jet. It's just his body. He is with the Sky Gods now. So I don't have to remember him this way, because it isn't really him."

"Okay, that isn't really Jet," I say, doing my best to smile through the tears.

"We can go," says Flot.

I turn to Pyre, who is standing there, watching us.

"Thank you, Pyre," I say.

"Of course," replies Pyre.

"When will we be burying him?" I ask.

"When the sun is at its highest in the sky. Not long."

We leave, and make our way back to our room.

35

Flot and I prepare for Jet to be buried. I look at my clean clothes, but wearing them doesn't seem right. I decide to put on my suit of armor, because I want to honor Jet for being a hunter, even if it wasn't what he wanted to do with his life. I hope it will also show the other hunters that I'm strong, and that I will still fight for them, and treat them well. That I will honor them if they die.

Flot notices me putting on my armor, and decides to put his on as well. It is not normal for people to wear their armor when someone is buried, but I am not worried about what people might say or think.

I help Flot with his armor, tying the pieces together the best that I can. In return, he helps me tie the last few straps on my new armor.

"Thank you, Flot."

Flot hugs me. I hug him back.

"The others are probably starting to gather outside. We should go," I say.

"Okay."

It seems like the walk to the mouth of the cave is the longest walk I have ever taken. I don't want to go outside, because once we do this, Jet will really be gone. We will never see him again. But I know that we must do this, and that I need be here for Flot.

When we reach the entrance to the Crag, everyone is

there. I see the other hunters, and every one of them is dressed in their armor. My knees weaken, and I swallow hard, because no one has ever had this many people turn out for their burial before. Normally, a hand's worth of people will bury a person. It says so much about the kind of person that Jet was, that everyone would come. I'm also struck by the fact that the hunters are all wearing their armor. I could never thank them enough for that.

I look around, searching for Sickle, Scythe and Chaff. They did not come to the burial, which was wise of them. I wouldn't doubt that there are many people who are wanting to kill them for what they've done. It also makes me wonder if some of the people have shown up just to see a fight. To see what I might do to the people that killed Jet. I realize that Chaff and his sons aren't the only evil people in the Crag, and that a fight would be their only reason for coming.

I ignore those thoughts though, push them out of my mind, and hope that everyone is there because of Jet. Because Jet was good, and decent, and respected by people. I do believe that about most of the people that have showed up. Many people in the Crag are good, but those that are evil are truly evil.

I look for Pyre and see him outside, standing in the sun. It is warm and beautiful, and the blue sky seems endless. The world seems so filled with life. Inside my heart though, I am filled with pain and sadness, and my thoughts are of death and loss.

Next to Pyre are his assistants, Tomb and Eulogy. Tomb is big like Helm and Mast, and Eulogy is beautiful in a different sort of way. She has hair as black as night, and pale skin like the moon. Eulogy is a quiet person, and only leaves the Crag when a burial happens.

In front of them is Jet, wrapped in a blanket. He rests on a stretcher made of straps and tree limbs. Pyre has used the colors from plants to make Jet look more like he used to. His skin seems pink and alive. Pyre notices me and Flot. He then asks Tomb and Eulogy to pick up Jet's body and follow him.

The entire Crag follows behind, as we go away from the Crag to our cemetery.

A place for Jet has already been dug out of the ground. Tomb and Eulogy carry Jet over to the hole and set him down next to it. They lift him up by the blanket he's been wrapped in and carefully lay him inside. The crowd moves around the grave, circling it. Flot and I make our way to the front, as Pyre also comes to the front of the crowd. He speaks to the people of the Crag.

"Jet was a hunter, and a brother. He has died too young, having only seen a few snows past being a new one. We are less as people, because he is no longer a part of our lives. We are sad because we miss him, but he is somewhere better. He is with the Sky Gods now, resting, and we put him to ground and cover him in a blanket of grass and clover so that he will rest peacefully."

Pyre nods to Eulogy and Tomb. They start covering up Jet with dirt, then handfuls of grass and clover. Helm speaks.

"Hunters, salute."

I look around the crowd as the hunters place their fists over their heart then slide them downward. I have been trying very hard not to cry, but tears stream down my face. Flot and I both do the same, placing our fists on our hearts and moving them downward. Flot turns around and wraps his arms around me. I watch as they place the last handfuls of grass and clover on top of the grave.

The crowd slowly makes their way back to the Crag. Till and her mother Leaf both stay behind to talk to us.

"Flot, I am sorry about Jet," says Till.

"I am sorry too," says Leaf.

"Thank you. Life won't be the same now. He was more than my brother, he was my best friend too. I almost never went anywhere without him. I feel like I've been cut in the middle, like a part of me is gone forever," says Flot.

"I feel a part of my heart missing," says Till. "It's like I can't feel the part of my heart that is filled with love and happiness, like someone took it away from me."

"Someday it will heal, Till. Someday you will find someone to put in your heart again," says Flot. "You may not feel about them the same way you felt about Jet, but you will love them in a different way. I know Jet would have wanted you to be happy again. He would want all of us to be happy again. We need to try to be happy, for him, so that he can rest with the Sky Gods. Otherwise, he will spend all of his days up there worrying for us."

"I will try," says Till.

To my surprise, Till moves in close to Flot and kisses him on the cheek. It looks like Flot is just as surprised. It is very sweet of her to do, letting Flot know that she appreciates his kindness. I hope that Flot never loses that: his good heart.

Till takes her mother's hand and they walk back to the Crag. Flot and I stay for a while. We eventually walk over to the stone that marks Jet's grave. Eulogy has stained a large rock to look like Jet's face, so that we will know him when we come visit him. It looks like him, very much. Once our eyes are dry, we walk back to the Crag.

# 36

On our way back, I see that Ebb is waiting for us. She comes up to Flot and gives him a hug.

"I'm so sorry, Flot. I very much liked Jet," says Ebb. She turns to me.

"If there is anything I can do, anything at all, I will do it."

I was about to give her a simple 'thank you', but I consider her words.

"There might be," I say. "Flot, can you catch up with Till and Leaf, and make sure that they reach the Crag safely?"

He nods to me that he can. I wait until Flot is far enough away that he can't hear us talking.

"Ebb, I have a plan. You are the only person I trust right now. Flot may be too filled with anger and sadness to make good decisions. I trust Mast and Helm, but I don't know that they would be able to help."

"I am willing to do whatever I can," says Ebb.

"I need a distraction. I need Chaff to leave his room when there is no one else around. There is something inside that I need."

"What is it you need?"

"I am trying to learn how to grow vegetables, so that Chaff won't be in control anymore."

I can tell by the look on her face that she is both surprised, and excited.

"And you think the secret of the harvest is in his room?" asks Ebb.

"I do. I snuck in while he was asleep from beer, and I searched everywhere I could think to search, except for one place. The only place I couldn't look while he was asleep."

"Where?"

"Underneath him. I think he keeps a page he'd stolen from the Book of Knowledge under his sleeping mat."

"That's clever," says Ebb.

"Chaff is smart, but hopefully not smart enough. If he sees through our trick, we may not get another chance. He has kept his secret this long, and it is difficult to keep secrets in the Crag," I say.

"So, what is your plan? How can I help distract him?"

I think for a moment.

"Do you think you could lure him out with beer?" I ask.

"I don't know. He has as much beer as he could ever drink," says Ebb.

"Can you think of another way?"

Ebb is silent for a moment.

"What if I made him think that I want to join with him?" says Ebb.

"No."

"Sam, I won't actually join with him, if that is what you're worried about. I could make it seem like I'd had too much beer to drink. He will follow me."

"How do you know?" I ask.

She just smiles at me.

"I don't like it," I say.

"Sam, please let me do this. There is no way I'll let him hurt me, or even touch me. And you know that I can defend myself. I will lure him outside, in the dark. Then I'll come back to the Crag."

"But what happens if he tries something later? Asks you about it the next day?"

"I'll just tell him I was so full of drink that I don't

remember any of it."

It makes sense, and I can't see any other way.

"I don't want you to risk your life," I say.

"It is my life to risk. I will do this for Jet, and for Flot... and for you. I will also do this for the Crag. If we succeed, we will be rid of Chaff forever."

"I just realized something. Maybe *you* are the Sky Child," I say.

"Maybe I am," says Ebb. "When do you want to try?"

"Tonight. The sooner we do this, the better chance we have."

"Then I will rest during the day, so that I will be ready for tonight. We can meet after everyone is asleep, just outside the mouth of the cave."

"Thank you, Ebb."

We make our way back to the Crag.

37

When I get back to the room, Flot is waiting for me.

"I think I'll spend some time with Till and Leaf. They wanted to teach me about the harvest," says Flot. "Till could use someone to talk to, and I could too."

"Okay, Flot. Whatever you need. Just be careful," I say.

"I will. And I'll make sure to stay away from Sickle and Scythe. Leaf and Till said they will meet me near the Great Fire to talk. I don't think Sickle and Scythe go there much."

"No, they don't. I have never seen them there, other than to dry themselves. I don't think that they believe in the Sky Gods much," I say.

Flot leaves our room.

I try to get some rest during the day. I'm able to sleep some, but not much. Helm stops by to check on me. I get up and go to the entrance of our room to greet him.

"How are you feeling?" asks Helm.

"Sad and tired," I say.

"I am as well, Sam. Are you planning to lead the hunt today? We are running low on meat, because we haven't hunted in many days now."

"I don't think I can," I say. "Helm, will you and Mast lead the hunt today? I know that the hunters trust you, and will listen to what you tell them."

"I will do that for you. Are you sure that you don't

want to go? It might help," says Helm.

"I am sure. And Helm, thank you."

"You are welcome, Sam."

Helm leaves.

I'm finally able to get some sleep. When I wake up, I can hear people coming back to their rooms from the feast. It's okay that I missed it, because I'm not very hungry. I start to put on my clothes as Flot appears. He's carrying a bowl of food.

"You need to eat," says Flot.

"I'm okay," I say.

"If I were the one that slept all day, you would make sure that I ate something."

It's true.

"Then I will try to eat some," I say.

Flot hands me the bowl. It isn't very warm, but it doesn't bother me. I barely notice. I scoop some of the soup into my mouth. The soup has fresh meat in it. Deer meat. Helm and Mast must have had a good hunt without me. It is good to know that I can rely on them if I ever need to again.

"How are Till and Leaf?" I ask.

"Till seems better. I think I cheered her up. Probably because I remind her of Jet," says Flot.

"I hope she knows that you are very different people," I say.

"I think she does."

"Is Leaf okay?"

"She seems sad, but I think she's mostly worried about Till," says Flot.

"A mother always worries about her children," I say.

Flot just nods at me. He looks so tired. His eyes are dark and sore from crying. It isn't normal to see someone so young look so empty of life. I hope that soon he will be full again.

"I'm going to try to sleep now," says Flot.

"Okay."

I pretend to rest. I wait until I don't hear any footsteps

outside of our room, and then I wait some more. Once I am sure that everyone is asleep, I sneak out of our room.

I follow the tunnels to the mouth of the Crag, making sure no one sees me walking around. Outside, I can barely make out Ebb, who is waiting for me. She's wearing her normal clothes, and she's carrying a large cup that is half filled with beer.

"Are you sure you're okay with this? Because we could always think of something else," I say.

"Sam, you know that this is the only way. I will be fine. You worry too much," says Ebb.

"Worrying has kept me alive. So far."

"And your..." she trails off.

"My... what?" I ask.

She won't answer me. But I think I know what she was going to say: my brothers. Only that isn't true anymore. I know she didn't mean anything by it, but it still cuts me inside. I should have thought about them more. I should have had someone protecting them.

I need to stop hating myself for what happened. I didn't kill Jet. It's not my fault. It's not my fault. I keep thinking that, over and over again: it's not my fault. Maybe someday, if I think it enough times, I might even believe it.

"I'm sorry," says Ebb.

"Are you ready?" I ask, ignoring her apology.

Ebb stares at me for a moment.

"Yes," she says.

"When you're done, meet me back at my room."

She nods.

We walk down the twisting tunnels until we reach Chaff's room. His glowing stick is still on fire, and we can hear him snoring. I find a dark shadow and hide.

I watch as Ebb takes a drink of the beer. She walks into Chaff's room, pretending to stumble. She spills some of the beer on her shirt, and onto Chaff's face.

Chaff is startled awake. He looks up at Ebb, who is bent over, looking into his face.

"Oh, I am so sorry! I thought this was my room!" says Ebb, loudly.

Chaff rolls over and sits upright. Ebb slowly moves back. I can see in the light that her shirt is now clinging to her body.

"It's okay, beautiful," says Chaff, an evil smile on his face.

"I think I've had moo touch beer. I mean too much beer!" says Ebb.

She takes another drink.

"Hey, you're cute," says Ebb.

Chaff's evil smile gets even wider.

I watch as Ebb slowly walks backward, keeping her eyes staring right into Chaff's. Chaff stands up and follows her down the tunnel.

I look around to make sure that no one sees me, and then go inside. I head straight for the sleeping mat and lift it up. It's there. Oh, thank the Sky Gods, it's there!

I pick up the missing page, and I try to find the meaning of 'seed'. It takes me a moment, but I find it:

**Seed** – a flowering plant's means of reproducing; develops into another plant of the same type.

So, vegetables must have seeds that make them grow. And it sounds like they are part of the plant. I wonder what they look like.

I think about keeping the page, but I realize that all I need is the information. I don't need the actual paper. I put it back exactly how I found it then move Chaff's sleeping mat back into place. I leave Chaff's room excited, because there is now reason to be hopeful.

I make my way back to our room. Flot seems to be sleeping, but I think he's having nightmares. He moves in his sleep, making noises, saying words that don't make any sense.

I stand near the entrance of our room, waiting for Ebb to appear. She finally does, and her shirt is still soaked.

"Are you okay?" I ask.

"Yes. It worked very well," says Ebb.

"I'm glad that you're back safe," I say.

"Me too. Did you get the page?" asks Ebb.

"I read it, but I left it there."

"Why'd you do that?"

"So that Chaff wouldn't know someone had been there. I need to use what I've learned to show people I can grow food. They might not believe me otherwise. I don't know how long it will take to grow it, so Chaff can't know that he's been tricked yet," I say.

"He seemed so full of drink, I doubt he will even remember me," says Ebb.

"That would be even better, but I think it would be hard to forget you."

"That's sweet," says Ebb.

I smile a nervous smile.

"Will you watch over us tonight?" I ask.

"There's no place I would rather be," says Ebb.

I take off my clothes and slide into bed.

# 38

The next morning, I realize I should take the hunters out on a hunt. What good is a leader if they are never there to lead? I would have done it yesterday, if...

I let Ebb go back to her room to get some sleep. She looks tired, and I share that feeling, too.

I collect some eggs from the chickens, but I grab too many. When I finally realize it, I freeze. It takes all my strength to fight back the tears. I decide to set a few back down on the ground.

When I return from cooking the eggs, Flot is already awake. He's set out cups for each of us and filled them with water. He looks up at me and realizes he's made the same mistake that I did.

"It's okay, Flot. There are things that will change. But we will deal with them, together," I say.

"Can... can I keep pouring him a cup? At least for a while?" asks Flot.

"Sure. You can do that, if it helps."

"Nothing really helps."

"I know."

We eat our breakfast in silence. Every few bites I have to wipe the wetness from my eyes.

When we've finished eating, I finally speak to Flot.

"I was going to take the hunters out today. Would you like to join us?" I ask.

It takes Flot a moment to think.

"Yes. I think it might help to do something normal," says Flot.

"Okay. I will also put them through training."

"I will be there for that too, then."

"If you need anything..."

"I won't. I will be okay," says Flot.

I pick up the pan that I cooked the eggs in, and walk to the loud waters to clean it off. When I get there, I see Sickle, but not Scythe or Chaff. His head is wrapped in a piece of fabric, with a patch over his eye. I am glad that Jet stood his ground, and fought to protect his brother. That eye patch will stand as a reminder of Jet's strength and bravery.

Sickle notices me staring at him. He has a blank look on his face; no expression. He just stares back with his one good eye. I look away. I don't want to start something with him. Not now. And I must remember that it's his father who I really need to stop. Do you blame the knife, or the person holding it?

I rinse the eggs out of the pan then take it back to the Great Fire. I use the bottom of my shirt to dry it out. Once I'm sure that it won't rust, I place it in the stack of pans next to the fire.

I turn and stare into the flames. They pull me in closer. I find myself on my knees, praying. I pray for protection for Ebb and Flot. I pray for courage to do what is right, and the strength to keep going. And I pray that no matter what happens, the people of the Crag will be okay.

I get up off my knees and walk to Helm's room. When I get there, I see flowers outside the entrance.

"Helm?" I say.

"Sam, come in," says Helm. "Did you need us to lead the hunt again?"

"No, I will lead them today. I'm also planning on having a training. Can you and Mast let everyone else know?" I ask.

"We can. Are you sure you're ready after what

happened?"

"What happened cannot be changed. We can only change today. I won't let what they did to Jet be an excuse to hide. I will make myself ready. The hunt is too important. The hunters need someone to lead them if they are ever going to improve."

"I think they are ready to listen now."

"Good. You haven't heard of any attacks on the hunters, have you?" I ask.

"No, not since your new rules. Everybody seems to be getting along. At least for now," says Helm.

"Pray then that this peace holds. Because if it breaks now, things may be worse than before. It would be like loosing a wolf from a pen. They will be wild, and dangerous, and won't stop until they taste blood."

"Do you need someone to guard you now?" asks Helm.

"No. I don't think Chaff is going to send anyone after me, and my new armor should protect me against another attack. I am as safe as I can be."

"Then be smart."

"I will."

I leave Helm's place and head back to our room. Flot isn't there, but I see that he must be wearing his armor, because it's also gone. I put on my new armor. It's easier to put on than my old armor, because they made the straps that hold it together work much better. They are easier to reach, and easier to tie.

I wonder just how much work they put into making this armor. There are many things that are different than the old armor, things that are much, much better.

I head out to the mouth of the Crag. No one has come outside yet. I practice with one of the sky spears, trying to throw it as true as I can. I can tell I'm improving, but I am still better with my sling.

I ready the sky spear for my next throw, when I stop and look down at it. I realize what made it better than the old spear. Lagan had taken what we already had and made it smaller. I wonder if it would be more useful if I could make it even smaller.

I think about what a smaller spear would look like. It could be as long as my elbow to the tips of my fingers, and maybe as thick around as my smallest fingers. I could make one from a small branch, with a sharp point at the end. It would be easier to find small branches than large branches, so I could make many of them. And they wouldn't weigh much, so a hunter could carry many of them.

I walk toward the cemetery, because I know I will be able to find good branches there. When I get there, I collect many small branches that have fallen from the trees. I take one of my knives and make a sharp point at the end of a stick, just like the sky spears. I also take the knife and try to scrape the bark off the branch to make it as straight as possible. I hold the new short spear in the middle, take a running start and throw it.

It doesn't seem to go as far as the sky spears do. It also doesn't fly true. When the short spear starts losing speed, it just falls out of the sky. I watch as the tip hits the ground, but it doesn't stick into the ground like the sky spears. It makes me question whether the short spear will work at all.

I also think about my sling. I use small rocks that feel as heavy as a short spear. When I throw a small rock at someone with only my hand, it just bounces off them. They may say it hurts, but it won't kill anyone no matter how hard I throw it. I use the sling to make the rock go faster. Maybe I can make something like the sling to launch the short spears with.

I take my sling out and hold it how I normally would. Then I put the dull end of the short spear against the pocket of my sling, making sure that the sling stays tight against the spear. I reach back and try to throw the short spear. It gets tangled in the sling and goes nowhere.

I decide to give up for now. Maybe I can talk to Anchor, Jib and Stanchion, and see if they have any ideas for making my short spear work. I have a feeling that with their help, we could make an even better weapon than the sky spear.

Taking the new short spear with me, I head back to the mouth of the Crag. When I get there, no one is waiting yet. I decide that instead of waiting, I will go see what Anchor is doing.

I stop at the opening of the tunnel that leads to Anchor's room. Just thinking about the narrow hallway makes me start to panic. I close my eyes and feel my way down the tunnel. It helps again to think of blue skies and green clover. I just need to focus on those until I come out the other side. It takes a while, but I finally reach the opening to Anchor's room.

"Sam, I was just about to leave for training. Were you coming here to tell me, because Helm had already mentioned it," says Anchor.

"I am actually here for another reason. I've created this," I say, handing him my short spear.

Anchor moves it around in his hands, feeling the weight of it.

"So, you did this?" asks Anchor.

"Yes," I say.

"Interesting," says Anchor. "You could carry many of these with you, unlike the sky spears which you can only carry a pair of. Did you test it?"

"It doesn't work well when you throw it by hand."

"Did you try anything else?"

"I tried using my sling by placing the dull end of the short spear in the pocket then throwing the spear with all of my strength," I say.

"And how did that work?"

"Worse, so I thought I would come to you and see if you had any ideas."

Anchor looks more closely at the short spear then finally sets it down.

"I will show this to Jib and Stanchion, and see if they have any ideas."

I turn and head back through the narrow tunnel,

keeping my eyes closed, and hoping I come out the other side unharmed.

# 39

I come out of the tunnel from Anchor's room okay. It still takes me a moment to relax myself, until my fear of small spaces is no longer bothering me. I make my way back to the mouth of the Crag. Most of the hunters have finally appeared.

I look around and I see Jet.

Wait, no, it's Flot. I feel my hands turning into fists. I am sure that if I ordered the hunters to raid Chaff's room and bring him to me, they would. But if I did that, I would be no better than Chaff.

What would the hunters think? They would think that murder was okay. That the rules I made no longer meant anything. Things would get worse, and I would never be able to fix them.

I do my best to calm my anger. I open my hands so that they are no longer fists. After a handful of deep breaths, I am in control of myself again.

I look out into the crowd, searching, and I find Ebb. I wave her to come to me. Mast and Helm arrive at the same moment, and they take their places at my sides.

"Yes, Sam?" says Ebb.

"As my protector, you should be up here, with us," I say.

"Oh. Okay," says Ebb.

I finally turn and talk to the crowd.

"We are going to try something new today. I want

everyone who uses a big spear to stand over here," I say, pointing to my left. "Everyone who uses a sling stand here," I say, pointing straight ahead. "And everyone that uses a sky spear, stand here," I say, pointing to my right.

The large crowd splits. I can clearly see now how many of each I have. It seems that there are about as many that throw sky spears as there are that use slings. There are as many that use big spears as the other pair of groups combined.

"I am going to make you into smaller hunting groups. There will be a hunter with a sling, a hunter with a sky spear, and a pair of hunters that carry a big spear. If I put you with a person in your group that you cannot get along with, you must learn to get along with them. These people in your group are now your new family. You will hunt alongside them. They will protect you, and you will protect them, and not just in the killing fields, but in the Crag too," I say.

I listen for any comments, any arguments, but none come. My guess is that they are waiting to see what the groups are like before they argue.

I move into the crowd and start with the hunters that carry big spears. I try to pair people up so that there is one younger and one older hunter. I also try and put family together, because they are already connected outside of the hunt. I do my best to make the pairs fair, so that no one ends up with someone that I can tell they hate. I look around, and no one seems angry by the choices I've made.

"Now, does anyone have a problem with how I've selected these pairs?" I ask.

No one speaks up.

I turn to the hunters that use slings. I do my best to do the same things I did before. Families together, no enemies, and someone that would fit in with the pair I had already put together. This is a bit more difficult, but I make it work. I look around. This time, there are a few people that look surprised, but none that look angry. A few people even look happy and relieved.

It takes me the longest to work in the hunters that use

sky spears. After moving a few hunters around, I have the groups mostly set. I realize that I'm missing a few hunters to throw sky spears. We are almost a handful short. It takes me a moment to come up with a way to fix it.

"Is there a pair of big spear hunters, with a sling hunter, that would like to learn the sky spear? Realize that you will no longer be part of the group you are with now," I say.

I wait, listening to the crowd, and eventually a group raises their hand. It is the group that Flot is part of. They were one of the last groups I had put together, because they were people that did not have other family in the group of hunters. Although they were not enemies, they also were not friends.

"Come then. For those of you that carry more than one sky spear, share one with these new throwers," I say.

We are short a sky spear, so I give one of the hunters, Plank, a sky spear from my back.

"Practice well with it," I tell her. "Your new family's lives depend on your ability to use it."

She nods.

I do my best to place the new sky spear hunters in groups. Once I'm finished, I look around to make sure that again no one is angry. Every face seems to be okay with the groups I have made.

"Does anyone have a problem with their group?" I ask.

No one says a thing.

"Good. Get to know your new family. Know their names. Know what they love and hate. Soon you will learn how well they hunt. How they move and see and hear. The way they think. The way they live. I am going to say these words clearly so that everyone understands: if anyone tries to hurt someone in your new family, it is your duty to protect them. No hunter dies at the hands of another person. No hunter kills unless they are protecting themselves. Anyone that is found going against these rules will be killed," I say.

Still no comments from the crowd.

"Each new family will have a letter that I give you. It is

your duty to remember your letter. If you have a hard time remembering, scratch the letter into your armor. From now on, I may call on your group's letter. When I do, I will give you a command. I expect you to follow my commands immediately. If you have a hard time hearing my commands, the other members of your family will repeat my command for you. Does everyone understand this?" I ask.

Silence.

I walk through the crowd, assigning letters to the different families. I have a hard time remembering the order of letters, and I get stuck after the letter 'F'. Thankfully, Ebb whispers to me that the next letter is 'G'. From there I'm able to remember the rest of the letters. Eventually though, I run out. It takes me a moment to come up with an answer.

"The families that already have a letter will also have a color. Your color will be green. So the family that I said was family 'A' is now family 'Green A'. The families that do not have letters yet will use the color black," I say.

I walk over to the next family that needs a letter, and point at them.

"This family is now 'Black A'. The next is 'Black B'. Does everyone understand?"

Silence.

I continue giving families names, until I finish at 'Black O'. I go back to the front of the crowd.

"I want you to stay together as a family, but spread out from the others. Show them what you are capable of. Big spears, show them how well you can attack and protect with your spear. Slings, show them how far you can make rocks fly. Sky spears, show them how deadly your throw is. Take turns, watch each other, and give advice. The only way we get better is to practice and to learn from our mistakes. Mistakes make us smarter, failure makes us stronger," I say.

I turn to Helm, Mast and Ebb.

"Helm and Mast, do you want to keep using big spears?" I ask.

"I prefer it," says Mast.

"I want to try a sling," says Helm, surprising me.

"Ebb, which weapon do you want?" I ask.

"I normally use a sling now, but I would rather go back to using a big spear," she says.

"Ebb, hand Helm your sling. Helm, give her your spear. I will use the sky spear then. Ebb, can you show Helm how to use it?" I ask.

"I will do my best," says Ebb.

"I'm going to walk around and see if I can't help people that are having a hard time with the changes. Some people are using sky spears for the first time, and it isn't obvious how you should hold and throw them," I say.

I spend time talking to each group, getting to know them, trying to learn their names. I am surprised by how many names I had already known. I make suggestions where I can and try to be positive. I want to help these people, not make them angry. It is easy to become frustrated and discouraged when trying something new, so I do what I can to make it easier for them.

I take the people that have never used a sky spear before away from their groups. We walk far away from the other hunters, just in case something goes wrong. I show them the way that I hold the spear, and how I throw it. It takes a while, but I make sure that each of them know how to hold the sky spears, and that they each have at least one good throw. Then I send them back to their groups.

I watch a while longer then spend time with my own group. Ebb is already very good with a big spear. Mast is the best I have ever seen with one. Helm though is having a hard time learning the sling, even with Ebb's help. It takes me watching a few throws to figure out where he is going wrong.

"Helm, you want to release it earlier. Spin it around a few times and when you release it, watch how the rock flies. Keep changing when you release it, until you know when you need to let go. It just takes practice, but you will get it," I say.

I watch as Helm tries a few more times. He does much better, and after a hand's worth of tries it seems like he has got it.

I take the sky spear from my back and throw it a few times. I feel comfortable with it now, and I hit what I aim at almost every time. I also practice with my knives. I like throwing them, because they feel dangerous in my hands. Like I could take down a wolf with them.

"Okay everyone, we are done for now," I say to the crowd.

Some people stay behind to keep practicing, while everyone else goes back inside the Crag. I notice that Flot is among those that stay, and he continues practicing with the sky spear.

Out of the corner of my eye I see Plank running at me, as fast as she can, holding a sky spear. I put my hand on one of my knives, ready to pull it out of its sheath if necessary. Mast sees her and readies his spear. At the last moment, she holds the spear out sideways and slows down. Mast relaxes his grip on his spear, and I pull my hand away from my knives.

"Sam, thank you for lending me this," says Plank, handing me back my sky spear.

"You're welcome. Next time though, do not run at me with a weapon in your hand," I say.

Plank's eyes get big.

"Oh, I am sorry! I did not mean to worry you. I just wasn't thinking," says Plank.

"It's okay. Things are tense now, and we all have to be more careful," I say.

She nods but still seems worried. Maybe the worrying will keep her safer. I can only hope.

I put the sky spear in the sheath on my back and walk to my room.

## 40

"S̲am, wait," says Ebb.

She catches up with me right as I reach the mouth of the Crag.

"Everything alright?" I ask.

"I just wanted to thank you for letting me use a big spear again. I've been bored with my sling for a while. I like dealing with things up close," says Ebb.

"I've noticed," I say.

"So why did you break everyone into groups like that?" asks Ebb.

"It is a waste having all of the hunters attack at once. This way, if there are only a few animals to kill, we will not lose as many good throwing rocks, or break as many spears. It should also keep the skins we collect from being damaged," I explain.

"That makes sense," says Ebb.

"It will also make them easier to give commands to if we fight another dragon," I say.

"Do you really think we will see one again? What if you killed the only dragon left in the world?"

"Then I did it a favor. I cannot imagine what it would be like to be the last of my kind. It would be very lonely," I say.

"That is very sad. I don't think I could be alone like that either," says Ebb. "So, when do we start growing food?"

"Sorry Ebb, but I have to do this alone. It will be

easier for me to sneak around by myself than it would be if you came with me," I say.

"But wouldn't things go faster if I help?"

"Some, but it will still take many sunrises for the vegetables to grow. What I need is someone to protect Flot. I am not as worried about killers coming after him. I'm afraid he might still try and get revenge on Sickle and Scythe."

"I will protect him then," says Ebb.

I can tell Ebb is sad that I said 'no', but I really do need someone to watch over Flot, and I trust her. I also trust her not to tell anyone that I'm leaving the Crag late at night. If Helm or Mast guarded our room, they would at least ask me where I was going, and the fewer people who know what I'm doing the better.

"We should get some rest before the hunt. You haven't had much sleep, and I need to get some sleep now so that I can stay awake tonight. If you want, you could rest... in our room," I say.

Ebb looks at me in an odd way. Her moon eyes are almost closed, and she only has a smile on half of her mouth.

"Yes. I'm okay with that," says Ebb.

As we reach the room, I realize that Ebb won't have her own mat to sleep on. Jet's is still there, where it has always been. I wonder if I should offer it to her. Then I realize that it might hurt Flot to have someone else resting on it, so I decide it would be better to share my mat with her. It should be large enough for both of us, but just barely.

"Where should I sleep?" asks Ebb.

"Well, I don't think it would be a good idea to have you sleep on Jet's mat," I start to say.

I can tell that hearing his name has made her sad again, and honestly, my heart breaks every time I say his name out loud. It takes me a moment to collect myself and try to smile through the pain.

"I think Flot would kill me if we used his. But I could share mine," I say.

"That would be fine."

My face feels very warm.

I work on taking off my armor. Ebb helps undo some of the straps. Once I am out of my armor, I help her out of hers. Mine is now easier to remove, thanks to the changes that Anchor, Jib and Stanchion made.

We lie down on the mat together, and I pull my blanket over both of us. We both lie on our backs, next to each other. I close my eyes and try to fall asleep, but I can't. Ebb though falls asleep quickly. I can hear her breathing change, and it sounds almost like when Flot and... when Flot falls asleep. Her breathing is quieter, and a little faster than Flot's. I can tell that she's dreaming now.

Ebb rolls onto her side and puts her head on my shoulder. I stay flat on my back, and I don't know what to do. I place my arm on her side and rest it there. It is more comfortable than I thought it would be. For as strong as Ebb is, she feels very light resting on me. I finally relax then fall asleep.

It feels like we are asleep for only a short while. I hear Flot's voice, as if he was far away. It takes me a moment to fight off the effects of sleeping in the middle of the day. Flot has come back from training finally.

"Sam. Come on, wake up Sam," says Flot.

"Go away, I'm sleeping," I say.

"You have to get up, because you have to lead us now," says Flot.

"What are you talking about? You just got back from practicing."

"No, I came back here too. I took off my armor, rested for a while, then put my armor back on."

I start to worry. I carefully shake Ebb. She seems startled by it, but she eventually wakes up.

"Are we supposed to hunt now?" asks Ebb.

"That's what Flot is saying."

I pull the blanket off us and start putting on my armor. Ebb stretches then stands up and starts putting her armor on too. Flot helps both of us get our straps tied.

I look over at Ebb, and her golden hair is a mess. Before she fell asleep, she had taken out the thin strip of leather she uses to keep her hair pulled back. I kind of like her hair messy, but she finds the piece of leather and ties it back again.

I pick up my sky spears and place them in the sheaths on my back then do the same with my knives in the front. I am ready now. Flot helps Ebb with the last strap of her armor. As soon as she is done, we hurry down the tunnels to the mouth of the Crag.

Everyone is waiting. I feel bad, because it is obvious that I should have been outside long ago. Flot must have been worried when we didn't show up and came back to wake us.

There is still enough sunlight to hunt, but we should have left sooner. We will need to find deer quickly. Thankfully, the weather is warm and the sky mostly blue. We should be able to see animals from a very long distance.

"Thank you, hunters, for your patience," I say. "We will leave now."

I walk to the front of the hunters, and Mast and Helm both walk at my side. Ebb finds her way to me, and walks just in front. She carries her spear straight out, ready to protect me from wolves.

I make sure that we walk to one of the better places for hunting. It is near a stream that the animals drink from.

Sometimes when we hunt near water, it turns red from the blood of our kills. I am hoping that on this hunt we will be more careful with our kills, so that we do not cover the green grass and clover in red. It is a beautiful place, and seeing death there seems wrong. To me though, hunting has always felt wrong.

As we near the stream, we see many deer drinking from it. The sky gods are smiling on us. I don't know if I remember seeing so many deer in one place before. I have the hunters stop. I try to speak loudly enough so they can hear me, but not so loudly that we scare away the deer.

"All families, I want you to spread out by the letters I

have given you. Green A should be on the left, Green B should be just to the right of them, and so on. Black O should be the family that is furthest on the right."

I watch as everyone finds their place. I bring Mast, Helm and Ebb with me to the middle of the group, so that I can see everything that is going on.

"The deer are lined up, just as we are. I want everyone to focus on a deer that you see. If you are on the left, find a deer on the left. If you are on the right, find a deer on the right. If you are in the middle, and you haven't figured out you should pick a deer in the middle, you should go home," I say.

There is some laughter at my joke. Thankfully, no one seems angry by my words.

"Those who have slings, move in front of your family. When I say 'now', I want you to fire your rocks."

I watch the deer, and I wait for them to be spread out along the stream. Finally, the moment comes.

"Now!"

I watch as many rocks fly through the air. Some of the rocks find their targets. Deers fall to the ground. Those that aren't hit by rocks scatter, running away from the rest of the herd.

"We are going to try something new. I want all sky spear throwers to come together in front of our line, in the middle. Move!" I say.

The sky spear throwers each leave their groups and head toward the center.

"Big spears of families Green A through Green F, and Black A through Black F, I want you to surround and protect those that throw sky spears."

Hunters break away from their groups and position themselves around the sky spear throwers.

"This new group, which I will call Group Red, I want you to move forward until you are close enough to hit the deer, then stop. Throw your sky spears then come back and reform into your normal families. Go!"

The hunters follow my commands, but the timing isn't

very good yet. They aren't moving at the same time. Some of the sky spear throwers throw their spears too soon, missing the deer, and they end up retreating back to the big group early. But I want them to practice coming back to the big group, because once a sky spear thrower has used their spear, they are defenseless.

Once the last of Group Red has returned, I yell out a new order.

"To understand what comes next, I need a person from each group to see this," I say. "Sling throwers, circle around me."

I wait until they have gathered near the patch of wet dirt I'm standing on. I take one of my sky spears and draw small circles. Then I draw a line to show them where the stream is.

"I want families Green A through Green O to go toward the stream, but I want you to move away from the rest of the group, to your left, and come back to the kill place as you come near, like this," I say.

I take the tip of the sky spear, and draw a rounded line from their group to the stream.

"Do you understand?" I ask.

Finally, someone speaks up and asks a question.

"Why do you want us to do that?" asks a man named Row.

"That's a very smart question. If you have ever been attacked by a pack of wolves, you know that they come at you from many sides. It makes your target panic, the way that we panic, because we feel surrounded, even though there are more of us than there are of them. It also makes the attacking group spread out, so it's harder to hit more than one at a time."

"Oh, okay," says Row.

"Now I want Black A through Black O to come in from the right, curving from the right in the same way," I say, drawing another rounded line to the stream.

"What about the rest of us?" asks a woman named Bell.

"Another good question. Families Green P through Green Z should walk straight up the middle. That way we are coming at the deer from every direction we can."

Most of the hunters nod their heads in understanding.

"Go back to your groups, tell them what we are doing, and when I signal, I want you to do what I have just told you," I say.

The sling hunters go back to their families and explain what my plan is. I can hear some talking, but it is mostly just questions to understand what we are doing. Once I am sure that everyone understands, I yell.

"Now!"

This time the hunters do a better job of following orders. They aren't perfect yet, but they are getting better. I have Ebb, Mast and Helm follow me behind the middle group, so that if I need to give orders, I can still be heard by both the left and right groups.

Once we reach the stream, the big spear hunters put the few deer that are injured but not dead out of their pain. Everyone pulls out their kill bags and collects their meat. There is enough to fill almost everyone's bag. We have had a good hunt.

"Everyone, you have done well today. Back to the Crag!" I yell.

I hear the hunters cheer. Mast comes up to me and hits me with his hand across my back.

"Not bad, Sam," he says. "Not bad at all."

My excitement fades when I realize that I am wishing Jet could be here to see it.

## 41

I let everyone get ahead of me. Ebb tries to stay behind. I think she can tell that I'm sad, but I just need to be alone for a while.

"Are you sure I shouldn't stay with you?" asks Ebb.

"I just want to walk alone, but thank you. I will see you at the feast."

"Okay. I will see you then."

I watch as she walks off, and I make sure she catches up to the rest of the hunters.

I stand there, surrounded by green in every direction. My eyes close, almost as if I am not the one closing them. I can feel the wind on my lips, but it is not enough, so I take off my helmet. The breeze cools the sweat on my forehead. My body relaxes, and I start to feel at peace with myself.

I think of Jet and remember. I think back to when their parents died, and I took them in. How they were so small they could barely feed themselves when they were given food. I had to tear their bread into pieces so that they wouldn't choke on it. How Jet would wiggle out of my arms when I tried to get him to do something he didn't want to. He was always a fighter, even at the end.

It is hard to have Jet gone when I still see him in Flot's face. His eyes and nose and mouth. The same hair. Flot is a reminder of how badly I failed Jet. It isn't Flot's fault; I know that. And I hope I'm not treating him differently because of it.

Because if I do, then I have failed them both.

I eventually decide that standing out in the field and being alone isn't going to help. Not really. I need to feel like I can change things. I can't change what has already happened, but maybe I can change what will happen from now on. I hope the rest of my plan works, because it is all I have now.

That's not true. I still have Flot. I have my friend, Ebb. I have other friends now too. Lock and Harness; Anchor, Jib and Stanchion; Cleave, Charm and Moss. Even Mast and Helm are my friends now. It is nice to finally have friends. To have people that care. Charm, I guess, has always cared. But it didn't always feel that way. It felt like she had given up on me.

I carry my helmet back to the Crag. I didn't fill my kill bag with deer meat, because if there isn't enough meat for everyone to carry some, the Leader of the Hunt will not fill their bag. I'm saved from having to skin my kill. It is a good thing, because I do not want to look at blood right now.

The reason why the Leader of the Hunt is the last to carry meat, is to keep the hunters from killing more animals than they need to. It is a kind of reward for the leader, so that they don't have to deal with the chore of cleaning their kill. When I finally make it back, I find Flot working on the deer meat.

I watch, just outside our room, trying not to let him know I am there. He works quickly, and his motions are violent. I can tell that he is angry. It seems like every cut, every pull, is something he wants to do to Sickle and Scythe. Tear them apart, chop them into pieces then throw them into a basket.

I don't blame him. I am angry too. I watch as he takes his frustrations out on the dead deer. At least the deer is out of its misery. We are not. But I will try to help him deal with his sadness, so that he doesn't do to his heart what he has done to the deer.

"Flot, are you okay?" I ask, still standing outside our room.

He doesn't answer me.

"Flot?"

"I heard you. No, I'm not okay."

"I can see that. That must have been one really mean deer to treat it like that. Did it step on your foot or something?" I ask.

As much as Flot doesn't want to let it out, a quick sharp laugh comes from his mouth. But he finds his anger again and doesn't let go.

"Flot, what do you need?" I ask.

"I need Jet back!" he yells.

I just stand there. There's nothing I can say or do. So I just stand there and nod, letting him know I understand that he needs some space right now.

"Okay. I will leave you alone. But you can always talk to me," I say.

He puts the knife down and turns toward me. His eyes look tired, like he hasn't slept in days. We just stare at each other. Eventually, I nod my head again and leave.

I decide to go see Anchor. I close my eyes as I take the narrow tunnel that leads to his room. About halfway there, I open them. I get very dizzy, and close my eyes again. I fall down on my knees, but my armor protects me from the hard stone ground. It is all I can do not to panic.

I get back up and blindly make my way into Anchor's room. When I open my eyes, I see that he is talking with Jib and Stanchion.

"Ah, Sam, we think that we have an idea for your new short spear problem," says Anchor.

"Do you know what a bow is?" asks Stanchion.

"You mean the things you can tie straps into?" I ask.

"No, not quite. A bow has few parts: a piece that bends, and a piece of thread. I've put one together to show you how it works."

Stanchion picks up a stick with a thread tied to both ends of it. He holds the middle of the stick then pulls back the string. When he can't pull it back any further, and the stick is curved instead of straight, he lets it go. The string is no longer stretched, but nothing seems to happen.

"Um, that's great Stanchion," I say, confused. "But how is that supposed to help?"

"When I let go of the string, it moved very fast, kind of like your sling. If you can take your short spear, or what you might call an 'arrow', and fling it with the bow, you might be able to make it work."

"Wait, an arrow? What is that?" I ask.

"Well, I spend a lot of time reading the Book of Knowledge. I remembered reading a long time ago about the word arrow. So I went back and looked up arrow, because that is what your new short spear sounded like. It mentioned the word bow, so I looked that up too. That's how I created this," says Stanchion.

I look at the bow, and then the arrow. Something about the arrow seems strange.

"Why are there feathers on the arrow?" I ask.

"Oh, that was something the Book of Knowledge mentioned. I think they help the arrows fly better. Makes sense, because feathers make birds fly better too," says Stanchion.

"Have you tried it out yet? Does it work?" I ask.

"We've tried it, but we have a problem," says Anchor. "We can't get the arrow to work with the string. It just slips off it."

I stare at the bow, and at my arrow, trying to think of a way to make it better.

"Did you try tying something to the string that would hold the arrow?" I ask.

"Yes, and it does sort of work, but probably not well enough to be useful. The arrow goes flying wherever it wants to, instead of where you aim it," says Anchor.

I think for another moment.

"It may be a dumb question, but did you try putting the holder on the arrow instead?" I ask.

All of them have a strange look on their face.

"What, was my question really that dumb?" I ask.

"No, Sam, we just hadn't thought of that yet. And it seems pretty obvious, now that you say it," says Jib.

"Well, you are all very smart. Maybe you were thinking about it too hard," I say.

"You are probably right, Sam," says Stanchion. "So how do we put the holder on the arrow then?"

"I don't know. Can I look at the holder?" I ask.

Stanchion puts another bow on the table, and this one has a small piece of wood tied to the middle of the string. It looks like he carved out a hole in the middle of it for the arrow to go into. It's attached to the string with knots. I can't see how the extra piece could be attached to the arrow to make it work.

"Maybe we are thinking too hard about this," I say. "Can anyone think of something easy we can do to either the string or arrow to make it work?"

It takes a moment for someone to finally come up with an idea. Jib starts laughing at herself.

"I've figured it out," says Jib, shaking her head.

"Okay, so what is it?" I ask.

"Cut a slit in the back of the arrow," she says.

I take out one of my knives and pick up the arrow. It takes me a moment to carefully cut a slit into the back of the arrow. After putting my knife back, I pick up the bow without the holder. I put the string in the arrow's slit and pull the string back.

It is difficult to get the arrow to stay in place. I rest the end where the top of my hand meets the bow, but it still doesn't want to stay put. After a moment of struggling, I twist it, so that my hand and the bow make a shape like the letter 'v'. I point the arrow away from everyone, down the narrow tunnel leading out, and let it go.

The arrow goes much faster than I would have thought. We can hear what sounds like the arrow crashing against the stone wall just outside of the tunnel.

"I shouldn't have done that! I hope I didn't hurt anybody," I say.

"I am sure it's okay, Sam," says Anchor.

"Can you check?" I ask.

"Sure," says Anchor.

I watch as he disappears down the tunnel. I can hear his footsteps get quieter in the distance. Eventually, he comes back into his room. The arrow is broken, but it is still in one piece. It has a very bad bend near the tip.

"Well, I would say that worked pretty well," says Jib.

"Better than expected," says Stanchion. "We need to make more arrows. Sam, can you give us a while to make more arrows for you?"

"I can wait for them. I should be getting ready for the feast," I say.

"Us too," says Anchor.

With that, I head out of Anchor's room, eyes closed, feeling my way down the tunnel.

42

I head to our room. Flot isn't there, but I didn't expect him to be. I take off my armor, grab a clean set of clothes and a bar of soap. I walk to the loud waters. I don't see anyone I know there, but that is normal.

I wash away the sweat that I worked up during the hunt. I rub the soap into my hair and my face then down my body, cleaning my legs, arms, and everything else. Then I lie down in the water, flat on my back.

I keep my eyes closed, and feel the water across my skin, much like I did when I felt the breeze near the killing fields. It makes me wonder if things wouldn't be better for the Crag if I just stayed here, underwater, forever.

I know it wouldn't, because even if Chaff died, his sons would just take over. Things would probably be even worse than when Chaff was alive. That, and I don't want to die.

I sit up, take a deep breath and go back underwater. I scrub what little soap still clings to my skin until I feel normal again. Once I'm sure that I am rinsed I stand up, collect my things, and head to the Great Fire.

I try to dry myself as quickly as I can. I wipe myself dry with my shirt then ring the water out of it. It is easier for me to hang my shirt over the fire to dry than my skin. Normally I don't like my clothes smelling like smoke, but it doesn't matter to me much right now. Finally, my body is dry, and eventually so is my shirt. I put on my clothes and make my way to the feast.

I stand in line for food, and I check to make sure both Ebb and Flot have made it to dinner safely. I see Ebb first, picking at her deer and some bread that is made from corn. It is one of my favorites, and normally it would make me happy, but nothing is normal right now.

I realize that this will be the first time since Jet died that Chaff will see me. I have seen him asleep, full of drink, and trying to have his way with Ebb. It makes my stomach sick just thinking about it. I hope he doesn't try to talk to me.

After I get my food, I walk over to the head table and sit down between Mast and Helm. I look up at Chaff. I am surprised, because he doesn't seem happy like I thought he would be. I would have thought he'd want to gloat about Jet's death, and how he got the better of me. But instead, he looks uncomfortable.

I look down at my food and eat. It tastes okay, but I don't enjoy it. Food doesn't have much flavor to me right now. I have another memory in my mind of Chaff following Ebb, and I gag on my bread a little. It takes everything to fight it, to make myself swallow the food, because I need it.

My eyes move upward, and I see Chaff whispering to Scythe. Scythe then turns to Mast and whispers to him. Mast turns to me, and before he even has the chance to say a word, I look up at Chaff, and speak.

"I understand."

My voice sounds dead and without emotion. Cold, and tired, and weak. Chaff stares at me for a moment then goes back to eating. He doesn't look at me the rest of the meal.

Mast whispers to me.

"How did you know what he was going to ask?"

"Because all Chaff cares about is control. He wonders if he finally went too far. He is smart enough to know that he can only push people so far before they kill. Chaff does not know me well enough to know if I will kill him, no matter how bad that would be for the Crag, or for Flot. So he is trying to find out if I will be weak now and accept his control."

"And have you?" asks Mast.

"I have made him think that. That is all that really matters," I say.

"You're not planning to kill him?" asks Mast.

"No. I won't kill him," I say.

Mast's shoulders relax.

"I am sorry, Sam, but if you tried, I would have to stop you. Even if it meant..."

"I know. You don't have to tell me. If that is the way I die, then I will be glad it is at your hands, and not his."

"I don't want to kill you, Sam. I don't know if I could live with myself after that. I would do it to protect the Crag, but it would destroy me. Do not try to kill him, not just for your sake, but for mine."

Mast's words surprise me. There have been times where Mast seems to like me, but this is the closest to real emotions I have seen him show.

I finish my meal. I can taste what I'm eating now, instead of just forcing myself to chew my food. The bread made from corn is good, and the deer meat is better.

"I am done, and I'm going to bed now," I say.

"Do you need someone to watch over you and Flot tonight?" asks Mast.

"Ebb is going to," I say.

"It seems like the pair of you have grown together," says Mast.

"She is a good friend."

I take my bowl to the stack of dirty bowls and add it to the pile. I walk over to Ebb and place a hand on her shoulder.

"Are you ready?" I ask.

"Yes," says Ebb.

Ebb stands up and follows me out of the feast chamber.

"So, you are going to start tonight then?" asks Ebb,

once we're alone.

"Yes."

"What are you planning to do?"

"I guess the first thing I need is seeds," I say.

"What are seeds?"

"They're what make plants grow."

"How will you get them? I would think that Chaff has to hide them somewhere," says Ebb.

"I am sure he does, but I don't know where. I haven't tried following him, because it would be obvious if I did. He would only go there in the day, and I couldn't follow him out in the open. He might also know if I took some. I'm hoping that I can steal some vegetables from the kitchen and use those. I don't think Cleave keeps track of things like that."

"I hope she doesn't. If you get caught stealing food, they will kill you," says Ebb.

"Only if someone were to tell the protectors. I don't think the cooks would," I say.

"Still, you don't know if they would."

"Cleave wouldn't."

"No, Cleave wouldn't. The others... it's hard to say."

"I also can't ask Cleave to gather the seeds for me. I don't want her to know what I'm up to, and I don't want to put her in danger," I say.

"I hadn't even thought of asking her, but I agree. Better not to tell anyone else what you're planning," says Ebb.

"You know, Cleave wants Chaff gone just as much as I do. She was going to poison his food with wolfsbane."

"Really? I like Cleave even more now."

"Me too. But I stopped her. I told her that I had a plan that would get rid of Chaff, and we would still have food to eat."

"Then you already told her most of the plan," says Ebb.

"I had to. It was the only way I could keep her from poisoning Chaff. If I hadn't told her, I think she would have tried killing him again. She loved Jet," I say.

227

"I didn't know that she really knew him."

"Most people loved Jet. He was very honest and brave. There isn't enough of either in the Crag, and I think people liked him for it."

We reach our room.

"Ebb, can you wait until you think that everyone else in the Crag is asleep, then let me know?" I ask.

"I can do that."

I go inside the room, take off my clothes and rest. Eventually, I hear Flot come in and do the same. I can tell he's still having nightmares. He moves around a lot in his sleep, and his face almost always looks worried. I wish I could save him from his dreams, but I need him to sleep if I'm ever going to try my plan.

Ebb comes into the room and puts her hand on my chest to wake me. I was only half-asleep, but it startles me just the same. I look up into her eyes and she smiles, then nods, telling me I need to go now.

I get out of bed, and as quietly as possible I put on my clothes. I look over at my suit of armor and notice my knives. Should I take them? Then I ask myself, what would I do with them? I don't have an easy way to carry them in my clothes. If one of them dropped, it would make so much noise that I would definitely be caught.

I also wonder what would I use it for. I'm not going to kill one of the protectors if I am found, so I decide to leave them there. I take my glowing stick though, even though it's not burning, so that I can see outside of the Crag.

I am finally ready. I look back at Flot to make sure he's still asleep, and it seems like his nightmares have passed. He is quietly snoring, and for the first time in a long while he looks how young he is. With everything that has gone on lately, he acts like someone who has seen many more snows than he really has.

I walk out of the room, give Ebb a sad smile, and then make my way down the twisting tunnels of the Crag. I make sure only to take a few steps at a time then listen for the protectors. It takes a while, but I can't risk making any mistakes.

I sneak into the cooking room. There are many baskets of vegetables sitting out, waiting to be made into dinner. I had thought I would pick some, but I have no idea how closely Chaff watches his gardens and fields. I take a few tomatoes, some cabbage, and some peppers.

I use the light from glowing sticks inside people's rooms to see my way around the dark tunnels. I do not chance lighting my own glowing stick yet. I make it to the room closest to the mouth of the cave and peek inside. I see Shackle, one of the protectors of the Crag. He sleeps on the ground, wrapped up in animal furs.

He is a large man, and his body is in the way of his glowing stick. It is burning dimly on the wall. I put a foot over Shackle, and against the wall that his glowing stick is attached to. It keeps me from falling over. I stretch as far as I can, and I'm just barely able to get my own glowing stick to light. I carefully push against the wall with my foot, pulling it back down to the ground. I then turn and leave his room.

A flicker of light and dark move in front of me, and I think that someone is there. It takes me a moment to realize it is just a shadow cast from my glowing stick. I make my way outside the cave, with the peppers and tomatoes in my pockets, and the cabbage in my hand.

Off in the distance I can hear a wolf howling. It sounds far enough away that it shouldn't bother me. I also don't plan to travel very far for what I'm about to do. I need to find a place where others will follow, because they believe it is safe, but people won't go to on their own.

I decide it should be somewhere in the killing fields. Only hunters travel there, and now that I am the Leader of the Hunt, they travel only where I tell them to. I will find a spot away from the cave, and I will make sure that I know where it is so I can avoid it when we hunt.

After walking to a place that I think will work well, I put the glowing stick in the dirt, standing up. I then carefully pull the tomatoes and peppers from my pockets. I only cook eggs sometimes for Flot and... Jet... so I don't really know much about vegetables.

I hold up one of the tomatoes, and I remember that I'm supposed to look for something called seeds. I look all over the tomato, but the only thing I see are leaves, and the round outside of the tomato.

I decide to tear open the tomato. I split the skin open, and inside is a slimy mess. I scoop out some of the goo and hold it close to my glowing stick. I see these little round things, like tiny stones inside. My guess is that these are the things that Chaff has told us were pieces of poison. The things he collects in baskets and gets rid of to keep us safe. Maybe he doesn't get rid of them at all. Maybe those are seeds. I do my best to pull a few out of the goo.

The other thing I remember from the Book of Knowledge is that I need to put the seeds in the ground. I have seen the fields before things grow in them, and I know that the dirt has been broken up where the plants eventually grow.

I hold the seeds in one hand, and dig with the other. I pull up grass, trying to make a large square to put the seeds in. I realize that with the cabbage and peppers, I will want to dig first before I try planting them, so that I can use both hands.

Once I have enough dirt turned over, and grass removed, I place the seeds in the dirt. I try to spread them out, because I remember that the plants in the harvest gardens are spread out, and I don't know how big they will get.

I pick up the cabbage and hold it up to my glowing stick. I don't see any seeds on the outside either. I tear into it, but the more I tear, the more it just falls apart. I am unable to find any seeds inside of the cabbage.

It bothers me, because I can't understand how it grows. Then I realize that maybe the seeds come from somewhere else on the plant, because the head isn't the only part of a cabbage plant. So I won't be able to plant any cabbage without stealing some from the gardens. I'm not going to risk Chaff figuring out my plan, so I give up on the cabbage.

I move on to the peppers. I had grabbed one red and one orange pepper. They are both the size of my fist. Some peppers are very hot, but these are not that hot. I do not see any seeds on their outsides, so I tear into the red one. Inside there are seeds. I'm excited to see so many, and I'm happy that they aren't covered in goo. I pull out all the seeds that I can, and plant them as quickly as possible. I do the same with the orange peppers.

After I am sure that I've finished, I bury the remaining pieces of cabbage, peppers and tomatoes away from my makeshift garden. I don't want animals to come near what I'm growing, because a deer could just as easily ruin my plans as Chaff.

That makes me realize I will need to build a small wall to protect the garden from animals. I can start working on that tomorrow night, because I know it will be a while before the vegetables start growing. I do my best to wipe the dirt off my hands, grab my glowing stick then walk back toward the Crag.

When I get to the mouth of the Crag, I put my glowing stick out in the wet clover. I look around and make sure that no one happens to be passing by right then. I don't see anyone, so I sneak back inside.

I stick to the shadows as much as possible to avoid being seen. I go past Shackle's room and see that he is still asleep, snoring like a new one. A very, very loud new one.

I keep walking further down the tunnel, passing rooms, avoiding the light of people's glowing sticks. It takes me a while, but I eventually reach our room. Ebb looks at me as if she had a question to ask. I smile and nod my head, letting her know that everything went well. Her body relaxes and she smiles.

Flot is still asleep, which is good. I put my glowing stick back in its place on the wall. I lie down under my fur blanket and pull it over my face. It takes a while to fall asleep, because I keep seeing Jet's lifeless body when I close my eyes.

## 43

For many sunsets, each day is like the next. I spend time with Ebb, train, hunt, and wait for my vegetables to grow. Ebb and I are growing closer. When we aren't training, or hunting, or sleeping, we talk. We play jump stones, or read to each other. Sometimes we go for walks outside of the Cave, just to get away from the darkness of the Crag. Spending time with Ebb is what keeps me going through the long wait of growing vegetables.

When the sun sets, and after everyone is asleep, I sneak out and work on my wall. I build it to protect the one thing that could save the Crag. I build it out of sticks and branches, because they are easy to carry. On dry days, I also bring water for the plants, because I have seen the harvesters do the same.

One night, when I visit the garden, I see that both the tomato plants and peppers are finally starting to grow. I remember seeing in the harvest gardens that they use sticks to help the tomatoes grow off the ground. I take a few twigs from the cemetery and place them standing up next to the tomato plants, hoping I don't damage them.

I visit the cemetery every day as the sun is setting. I talk to Jet, even though I know he can't talk to me. It helps visiting him, because then it feels like he's still here. There are times where I forget that he's gone. I will turn and look at Flot, and think that he's Jet. Just for a moment. That's when the pain is sharpest, when I see Jet in his brother. Flot is trying so hard now to be like Jet; brave, and strong, and fearless. I just wish that Flot would be himself.

I hope that things will change when my plants grow, when I have tomatoes and peppers. I hope that Flot will go back to being himself again, and not feel like he needs to fight so hard. That he doesn't have to keep his heart hidden from everyone.

As the tomatoes and peppers eventually start to grow, I notice something else growing. Flot and Till have formed a friendship. It seems that Till is able to learn more about what Jet was like from Flot, and Flot can talk about Jet with someone that also cared about him, even if her moment with Jet was brief. Young love can be like that: short and intense. I am glad that Jet found someone he liked, and who liked him back, before he died. I am happy to see that Flot is finally starting to open his heart some.

There are times when I see Till look at Flot, and I think that there might be more than just feelings of friendship there. I don't know that Flot sees it, but I can tell that he definitely likes Till.

It may be difficult for Flot to admit his feelings for her, even though he's trying to be so brave and strong now. It is one thing to be strong, and be good at the hunt, but when it comes to liking someone, fear is always a part of it. You have to win against fear just to talk to the other person and get to know them.

I check on the plants one night and find something that makes my stomach sick. One of the walls has been damaged, and the vegetables have been eaten. Even worse, I find the body of a dead deer in the garden. It looks like it's been chewed up and torn apart by wolves. The plants are trampled and ruined. I drop to my knees, cover my face and cry. I don't even try to hold the tears back. All of the waiting, all of the struggling, all of the pretending to be under Chaff's control. All of it wasted.

I grab a handful of wet dirt from the garden, look up

into the sky and throw the dirt at the Sky Gods.

"Why? Why would you do this to us? You take away Jet, then you take away the garden! What have I ever done to you?"

I wait, but no answers come.

I scream, letting out all the pain and anger inside. I throw more dirt at the Sky Gods.

"Why?" I yell.

I yell until my throat hurts and I can yell no more. I wipe away my tears then walk back to the Crag.

44

$W$hen I get back to our room, Ebb is standing guard. She sees the defeat on my face. I can't even look her in the eye. I start to go inside, but she grabs my arm and pulls. We sneak out into the night, into the moonlit world, and away from where anyone can hear us.

"The garden's destroyed. Animals got to it," I say.

Ebb swallows back her tears.

"I'm done."

"You can't be," says Ebb. "You can't give up! You were so close to making it work!"

"The Sky Gods hate me. If I try again, they will just tear down my garden."

"What happened wasn't the Sky Gods. They want to see you do good things, Sam."

"What have the Sky Gods ever done for me?" I ask.

"They gave you life, and brothers to love, and friends. And they gave you me," says Ebb.

I still can't look her in the eyes.

"Sam, you're stronger than this! You can rebuild the garden!"

"No. Better to just let things be like they've always been."

"Do you think that's what Jet would want?"

I look at Ebb finally, and she can see the anger in my eyes. Anger at her for using the memory of Jet against me. Her face twists in anger to match mine.

"Don't you EVER look at me like that again, Sam! I never thought you could be like this; feeling sorry for yourself. You're better than this! You're making my heart sick. You need to start over. That's what living is about. It's about doing what needs to be done, even when things are hard."

She shoves me backward. I just look at her, staring.

Ebb shakes her head in disgust then turns and walks back to the Crag.

She wasn't wrong; I shouldn't give up. It just feels like everything is working against me, no matter what I do.

When I finally reach our room, Ebb has gone back to standing guard. She won't look at me, so I walk right up to her, stand in front of her, stare her in the eyes, and make sure she can see my face.

"I'm going to rebuild the garden," I say.

She smiles.

* * *

The next night, I head for what's left of my garden. When I get there, it looks exactly like it did the night before. I search through the what is left of the plants, but there aren't enough seeds to start again. It takes me a few nights before I'm able to sneak back into the kitchen and gather more seeds.

I start another garden near the old one, but this time I build a wall of stone. The stones are heavy, and every night I am sore. My back hurts, my arms hurt and my legs hurt. As I put one of the last stones in place, I smash my fingers underneath it. They bleed for a day, but I use pieces of an old towel to keep the blood from pouring out. I wait a handful of days before I'm able to lift rocks again.

After many nights, I check on the plants and there are peppers, and even more tomatoes. It is finally time to rid the Crag of the monster that is Chaff.

45

I wake up and have no idea if the sun is out yet. I put on clean clothes then walk to the mouth of the Crag. The sun is high and the sky is beautiful, and I can only see as many clouds as there are fingers on my hand. Flot was not in our room when I left, but I could tell that he had breakfast already. My guess is that he's spending time with Till.

I walk to Helm's room and find him repairing his armor. It was damaged a few days ago, when a wolf surprised us as we hunted deer. Thankfully, the armor protected Helm's leg enough to keep him from being seriously hurt. The wolf's teeth made it through the leather though, and his leg bled some. I watch for a moment as Helm ties straps to the new piece so it can wrap around his leg and stay on tight. I finally interrupt.

"Helm?"

"Oh, it's you, Sam. You surprised me. Why are you here?" asks Helm.

"I have need of you. Can you and Mast have the hunters put their armor on, and have them bring their weapons to the mouth of the Crag? Before they do that, ask them to go around telling everyone they know to meet at the mouth of the Crag as soon as possible. It doesn't matter if they are hunters, or protectors, or harvesters, or keepers. Everyone needs to be there," I say.

"Why, what is going on?" asks Helm.

"I will tell everyone when I am sure that the entire Crag is there. But it is very important that everyone is there, even Chaff, Sickle and Scythe. Especially them. Can you do that?"

"Yes, I can do that, Sam," says Helm.

I make my way to Leaf and Till's room. They are both there, as is Flot, just like I'd guessed. Leaf is sharpening one of the tools that is used for the harvest, while Till and Flot play jump stones.

"Sam, why are you here?" asks Flot.

"It's ready," I say.

"What do you mean 'it's ready'? Wait, do you mean your plan?"

"Yes."

"Um, what do I need to do?" asks Flot.

"Put your armor on, grab your sky spear, then meet everyone outside the mouth of the Crag. Leaf, Till, it would be an honor if you would also come outside as soon as you possibly can. I promise, you won't want to miss what happens," I say.

"Oh, yes, we will come watch, whatever it is," says Leaf.

"I will see you soon then," I say.

I walk to the mouth of the cave. A few handfuls of people have already arrived, and the hunters are wearing their armor. I have decided not to, because I want to share this with everyone. I don't want it to be about the hunters, because it's more than that.

I want them to see that I'm just a person, and that I don't feel like I'm better than them. But I ask the hunters to bring their armor and weapons so that we can keep the peace if there are any problems.

I wait. It takes a while for everyone to come, because people have jobs that they do. Jobs that take time, and hard work. Sometimes it's not possible to stop what you're doing just to hear someone talk. Eventually I see Chaff, Sickle and Scythe come out of the cave. They all look angry that they were called away from whatever evil they were committing, or planning to commit. Once I am sure that everyone is there, I speak.

"People of the Crag, I have something important to show you. Unfortunately, I cannot easily explain what I need to show you. I ask that you follow me, so that you can see it with your own eyes. It won't take long, I promise."

I walk toward my garden and the entire Crag follows. It is odd to think that not long ago, people barely knew me. I miss being unknown. Hidden away in my room, except to hunt.

We finally reach the garden. Everyone moves around it so they can get a better view. I can see shocked looks on people's faces. The faces that look the most shocked are Chaff's, Sickle's and Scythe's.

"Thief! Sam has stolen some of the plants from the harvest!" yells Chaff.

"No, I did not," I say. "I grew them myself."

From the crowd, I hear gasps of surprise and whispers of happiness.

"That is impossible. Only I know how to make plants grow," says Chaff, looking worried.

"That was true until you took Jet away from us, Chaff. I went to the Book of Knowledge, and with some reading, I learned that plants have things called seeds. I tried to look up the word seed, but you had torn that page from the book and hid it under your sleeping mat. I snuck into your room and read it. I found out that seeds are what grow new plants. Sometimes they grow inside the plant, sometimes outside," I say.

"No, that's not true. You don't know what you're talking about!" yells Chaff.

"I do know what I'm talking about. I took tomatoes and peppers from the kitchen, and I took the seeds out then planted the seeds. They have grown into the plants that you see now," I say.

"Sam can grow food!" yells Mast.

"No, it's a lie!" says Chaff.

"I can prove it!" I say. "I will cut open a pepper and show you the seeds. I will show every person in the Crag how to grow things, so that no one will ever be able to control the Crag's food again!"

"Show us!" yells someone in the crowd.

I go over to one of the pepper plants and pull off a pepper. I then tear into it, and show people in my hand the small seeds that will grow many more pepper plants.

"No, those are poison, everyone knows that! You don't know what you're doing!" says Chaff.

Chaff comes after me. Thankfully, he is very slow moving. He is also unarmed. A pair of hunters grab him by the arms and hold him back.

"Everyone, Chaff's hold on our food supply is no more. You do not have to live in fear of him and his sons ever again. We should decide Chaff's fate together. I suggest that we banish them from the Crag forever," I say.

"Why don't we just kill them!" says one of the more vicious hunters.

"We should let nature take care of them, because they won't last a day outside of the Crag," I explain.

"Let us raise our hands to the Sky Gods if we agree that Chaff, Sickle and Scythe should be banished," says Mast.

Hands move slowly upward, into the air. I look, and everyone has raised their hands. Everyone except for Sickle, Scythe and Chaff.

"Chaff, Sickle and Scythe, I will save you the embarrassment of raising your hands to the Sky Gods in a sad attempt to spare your own lives. It appears then, Chaff, that you are banished from the Crag. You deserve a fate far worse than what is in store for you," I say.

For the first time that I can remember, Chaff looks defeated. His sons just look idiotic and confused, as if they don't understand that they will never be allowed to set foot in the Crag again.

"Now leave, and know that if you try to come back,

the people of the Crag will put you to death," I say.

Chaff nods his head in understanding. He thinks for a long moment, then turns and starts walking in the direction of the killing fields. Sickle and Scythe reluctantly follow him.

"Wait," I say.

Chaff turns to look at me.

"Here," I say, throwing him one of the tomatoes I had grown.

Chaff looks at it for a moment then crushes it in his hand out of anger. We all watch as they slowly make their way over the hillside, until they finally disappear from our eyes.

As soon as they are gone, I look around. Nearly everyone drops to their knees and raises their hands to the sky. I even see Ebb on the ground, looking up at me. I hear the crowd start to mumble 'Sky Child.' My stomach turns.

"People of the Crag, I am not the Sky Child! It's just a story made up by gray ones from long ago," I say.

"But you have fulfilled the prophecy, Sam! You have brought food and peace to the Crag," says Helm, loudly enough for everyone to hear.

"Stop! Everyone, please, stand up! Do not worship me! I am like you, and I do not wish to be anything more than one of you," I say.

"You will always be one of us, Sky Child. Thank you for delivering us from evil!"

The crowd starts chanting my name, over and over.

"I am not the Sky Child!" I yell as loud and as angry as I can.

That's when I walk away from them.

## 46

Flot follows behind me. I hear the chanting slow and eventually stop. I run as fast as I can to the Crag. To my room. Even though the sun is still in the sky, I lie down on my bed and cover myself with my blanket. Flot eventually comes into the room, completely out of breath.

"Why did you run off like that?" asks Flot.

"Because I'm not the Sky Child," I say.

"But, what if you are?"

"I'm not."

"Sam, who knows? Helm was right, you did fulfill the prophecy. You *have* saved us all."

"I didn't mean to. I didn't want to. I just wanted revenge on Chaff. I wanted him dead," I say.

"But you didn't kill him. You're better than he is."

"No, I am not. Without the Crag, Chaff and Sickle and Scythe will surely die."

"You don't know that, and you've at least given them a chance to live. A chance to prove that they can take care of themselves. That they aren't completely useless. You gave them more of a chance than I would have given them. I would have thrown rocks at them and stuck them with spears."

"No, you wouldn't, Flot, because your heart is better than that," I say.

"You don't know that either. You don't know how much hate I have in my heart for them," says Flot.

"I do know, because I feel it too. But if all you cared about was killing them, there would be no room left in your heart for Till," I say.

"What do you mean?" asks Flot.

I wait a moment before I speak again.

"Just think about what I have said. It is up to you to decide for yourself what you feel. But know that your heart is capable of amazing things, even when it is hurting the most. You think you didn't kill Sickle and Scythe because I asked you to wait. If you truly had murder in your heart, there was nothing I could say or do that would have stopped you. You would have done it, and the Crag would have fallen. But you chose the right way, Flot. You. Inside your heart."

Flot doesn't say a word.

"I'm tired. I just want to be left alone," I say, covering my face with my blanket.

Eventually, I hear Flot walk out of the room. I fall asleep for a while. The many nights of staying up late, sneaking in and out of the Crag, have caught up with me. When I finally do wake up, I hear people passing by our room. It must be time for the feast. I force myself to get out of bed, because my stomach is killing me.

Instead of going to the feast, I go to the kitchen. Cleave is there.

"I was wondering when you would show up. People don't know what to make of you. Everyone believes that you're the Sky Child. Before, people had wondered. But now..."

"What do you think?" I ask.

"I think you're still the same old Sam you've always been. Maybe a little angrier with people, but still the same Sam."

"Thank you, Cleave."

"Don't thank me. It should be me thanking you. I don't know what I was thinking when I picked those wolfsbane stems," says Cleave.

"I do. You just cared about Jet. He would have appreciated you trying to kill Chaff."

Cleave laughs, but part of her laughter is mixed with sadness. I can tell that she feels bad for what she almost did.

Cleave hands me a plate of food.

"Oh, is this new? What is it called?" I ask.

"It's called Steak Chaff," says Cleave.

"Wait, why?"

"It's cooked in a tomato sauce. And I added some beer to make it bitter."

It takes me a while to stop laughing.

"Thank you. I needed that," I say.

"Glad I could help. Do you know when you might be hunting again?" asks Cleave.

"Soon, Cleave. But I want to give things time to go back to normal," I say.

"They will. You have already done everything in the prophecy, so people will slowly start to forget, or not care anymore. That is the great thing about people: memories fade over time. That is why we can forgive."

"Some things still can't be forgiven."

"No, no they can't," says Cleave.

I turn and take my plate back to our room.

## 47

Ebb shows up at our room and waits as I finish my meal.

"So, I guess I'm not the Sky Child," says Ebb.

"I don't know, you still could be. If it weren't for you, I might be dead. You also helped me get the information I needed to get rid of Chaff forever. Beat some sense into me. How about we say we are both the Sky Child?"

"I guess that would be okay," says Ebb. "What will you do now that everyone thinks of you as a sky god?"

"Well, I think the harvesters will probably need some help figuring out how to make things grow. We still need to find out where Chaff kept his seeds. Once those are taken care of, I guess I will keep hunting," I say.

"So you aren't going to lead the Crag?"

"No, the Crag doesn't need another Chaff."

"You aren't Chaff," says Ebb.

"Maybe not, but I don't like the idea of one person being more powerful than everyone else."

"That is because you are a good person, Sam."

"I don't know that I am, Ebb. I still feel like I've killed Chaff and his sons. Maybe I didn't use a knife, or a spear, or a sling to do it, but I sent them off to their death. Maybe that makes me a murderer and a coward, because I didn't even bother to kill them myself, with my own hands," I say.

"You know that what you did was best for everyone in the Crag," says Ebb. "No one sees you as a killer but yourself."

"In the end, whose opinion matters most?" I ask.

"The people that love you."

"If only that were true. Thank you for trying to make me feel better, but I don't think I will ever forgive myself for this."

"Then learn to deal with the guilt. Flot still needs you," says Ebb.

"No, he doesn't. He is ready. Flot is stronger now, and he has Till," I say.

"The hunters need you."

"No, they don't. Mast and Helm can lead them. I will lead the hunters, but they would survive without me."

We sit in silence for a while.

"I..." Ebb starts to say.

"You what?" I ask.

Ebb stares at me for a moment, like she has something to say, but can't say it. The look on her face changes though. I can tell she has given up on whatever it was she wanted to say to me.

"I guess I don't need to protect you anymore," says Ebb.

I hadn't even thought about that.

"I guess you don't," I say.

Ebb turns to leave.

"Wait, Ebb," I say.

"Yes?" she says, still turned away from me.

"Thank you for being there for me. For being the one person I could trust. I... have a hard time with trust. I just want you to know I really couldn't have done any of it without you."

"Is that all?" she asks.

"I don't understand what you mean."

"Is that all you had to say?"

I think for a moment. Was there anything I forgot to say? I can't think of anything. Was there something she wanted me to say?

"That is all I can think of."

"Then I will see you tomorrow at training," she says,

and walks off.

I feel like I said something, or didn't say something, and it bothered Ebb. My mind goes back over what we'd just talked about, and I can't understand what I said wrong. Sometimes I have a hard time understanding people, and I think that maybe I hurt her somehow. I just wish that she would talk to me, and tell me what is bothering her.

I try my best not to worry about it as I take off my clothes and lie down. I pull the blanket up to my face and roll onto my side. It doesn't take me very long to fall asleep, because the food has made me tired. I start to dream, and finally my dreams aren't of Jet dying.

## 48

Even though I'm awake, it takes me a while to force myself out of bed. Flot has already left our room. I put on my armor and stretch my neck, because it's stiff from sleeping so long. The cracking sound comes, and I feel much better.

I put my knives in their sheaths. I no longer carry sky spears. Anchor made me a holder for my arrows, which I strap on my back. The other hunters that used sky spears have switched to using a bow and arrows. Now that I am used to how it works, and Stanchion and Jib have improved it, it is more accurate than the sky spears. I can even hit birds now, although there isn't a lot of meat on a bird.

After I pick up my bow, I make my way to the mouth of the Crag. A few people have already started gathering, waiting for training. When I make it outside, and people see me, they cheer. I shake my head back and forth, and put up a hand, which tells them to stop. The cheering dies down. We wait together, until all the hunters have arrived.

It surprises me that Flot is almost the last to arrive. It makes me sad when Ebb is the last to arrive. She does not look happy, and the closer she gets to me as she walks to the front, the unhappier she seems to be. Unfortunately, I cannot worry about that now, because people are counting on me to lead.

Part of me wants to give up. To let someone else lead. To let someone else hunt. But I don't know what I would do with my life if I wasn't hunting. Maybe, like Jet, I would be happier with the harvest. Bringing things to life, instead of killing them. No more blood on my hands. My floor would finally be gray again.

I think these thoughts, but I know that the Crag needs me and my skills at the hunt. People rely on me for food, and now they also rely on me for safety. The rules that protect the lives of the hunters are my rules. People listen to me because they believe I'm the Sky Child.

Everyone believes it now, except for me. If I leave, there is no way of knowing if the hunters will go back to their murdering ways. Only a few of the hunters would kill a person, but it is a big enough problem that I am not willing to take the chance.

For now, I will continue doing what I have always done: survive. It is not what I want to be doing, but I see no other way. Maybe, eventually, all the hunters will become good people. People I can trust not to kill. But for right now, I don't trust them. They are dangerous.

The training goes well. I spend most of my time calling out different group names, and having them attack imaginary animals, so that the hunters get used to working as families. I also have everyone practice with their weapons. I am not the best with a bow, a girl a few snows younger than me is. Her name is Riley. She almost never misses, just like me with my sling.

I am better now with the bow and arrow, but it doesn't feel like a part of me yet. Maybe with experience I will improve. But now I am just okay with it. I also realize that some of the bows are better than others. I don't think Anchor, Jib and Stanchion have figured out the best way to make them yet. Since my bow is one of the oldest, it doesn't seem to shoot as far as the newer ones.

Once training is over, I watch as Ebb quickly leaves to avoid me. Flot cuts through the crowd and walks up to me.

"Sam, is everything okay with Ebb?"

"It doesn't seem like it, but I am not sure why. I don't think I did anything wrong," I say.

"Well, you are kind of dumb. Maybe you just aren't smart enough to realize what you did wrong," says Flot.

I resist the urge to hit Flot. He hits back harder now than he used to.

"Yeah, well you aren't the brightest either, Flot. You still haven't realized you're in love with Till."

"Yes I have," says Flot.

"Finally!" I say.

"Yeah, well, what about you and Ebb?" asks Flot.

"What do you mean? She's just my friend."

"Yeah, you are dumb."

Now I really want to hit Flot.

"Anyway, I'm heading in," says Flot.

He turns and walks away. Now I'm standing outside the Crag, all by myself. It still feels that way sometimes, like I'm all alone. Even when I had both Jet and Flot in my life, it always felt like something was missing. I have heard people say that when you join with someone, it feels like you are one person. I don't know if I will every truly feel whole.

I go back to the Crag and take off my armor, and then decide to wash off in the loud waters. I stare at the Great Fire as I dry off. After a while, it feels like the Great Fire is looking back at me. Gravel is there, and his stare also makes me feel uncomfortable. I look him in the eyes, and eventually he looks back down at the fire.

There is nothing for me to do but wait. Flot doesn't want to talk to me, and neither does Ebb. Most everyone else wants to ask me about what it's like to be the Sky Child, something I definitely don't want to talk about now.

I go back to our room and rest. I lie down on my mat, but I can't sleep. I look up at the ceiling and wonder what it would be like to live outside of the Crag. It doesn't seem like there is much keeping me here in the Crag anymore, now that Flot is strong, and trying so hard to become a man.

But where would I go? I don't even know if there is anyone else out there. People in another cave, like us, or in homes like before the End War. There must be someone out there, someone else. I guess it doesn't really matter, because if I left the Crag, I don't know how I would find them.

When I am sure that I finally need to leave for the hunt, I put on my armor. I don't hurry to put it on, because I want to be the last person that shows up for the hunt. Once I am finally ready, I find that I got my wish. I am the last to arrive.

I look over at Flot and smile at him. He returns the smile, but it seems like his heart isn't in it. When I look at Ebb, I can tell that she's still upset with me, but has calmed down some. Hopefully, that means she has started forgiving me for whatever it is I have done. I just want things to be like they were. I miss having her as a friend.

Instead of giving commands, I start walking toward a place I know where the hunting is good. I can tell that the hunters don't know what to make of things right now, but they decide to follow me anyway. I just keep walking, and they keep following, until we reach the place where I know we will fill our kill bags. Only there are no animals there.

In the distance, I hear a sound. My mind flashes back to Lagan's death. All I can think to myself is 'please, not this, not now.' It is the sound of a dragon. It is strange, because we are in a place I know to be safe from dragons, otherwise I wouldn't have brought us here.

I realize that I have made a mistake. I look down at the bow I carry. An arrow will never take down a dragon. It was a miracle that I took one down with a sky spear. I must have found a weak spot on the one that I killed. I think the size of the spear I used may have helped take down the dragon. But even if I hit the same place again with an arrow, I do not think it will be big enough to kill it.

I look over at the other hunters. Everyone that was using a sky spear now carries a bow. We have nothing that we can use to protect ourselves. We are doomed, and it is my fault. I hadn't even thought about needing to protect the hunters from another dragon. Part of me hoped that the one I killed was the last of its kind. I was wrong.

"Everyone, stay in your families, but hide! Try to find a large rock to hide behind, or a tree. Spread out as far as you can, so that the dragon cannot hurt all of us with one breath. And remember, aim for the back of the dragon as it passes over us. That is where it is weakest," I yell.

The hunters do a very good job of staying together in their groups, and the groups spread out far enough that it will take the dragon quite a while to kill us all. But that is what the dragon will eventually do. It will kill every single one of us unless I come up with a plan.

I turn to look at Ebb. She stayed with me, and so have Mast and Helm. We are hiding behind a small rock. There is not enough protection for us if the dragon comes straight at us. I have an idea, and I hope that the other hunters can distract the dragon long enough that I can make it work.

"Ebb, Mast, use these," I say, handing each of them a knife. "I need you to turn your big spears into sky spears."

I can only watch as they both start to scrape the bark from the spears. They work as fast as they can. I just hope that it's fast enough. I yell to the rest of the hunters.

"If any of you carries a knife, use it to turn a big spear into a sky spear. If you finish, go on to the next big spear. Do not stop making sky spears. We need them if we are going to survive the dragon."

The dragon is still far off, but I can hear its roar very clearly now. I can just make out its pair of evil glowing eyes in the distance, searching for us. It knows we are here. How, I do not know. But it doesn't seem like it has seen us yet.

I watch Ebb scraping as fast as she can. She now has a sharp tip at the end, but there is still too much bark on the spear. It will make it too heavy to throw well.

She looks up at me, looks toward the dragon, and starts scraping even faster. I worry that she will slip with the knife and cut herself, but she is doing a very good job. I just hope she can finish before the dragon reaches us.

It grows closer. I can now see the shiny, hardened scales of its skin. Its wings look different than the other dragon's, as does its color. This dragon is black like a moonless night, but the dragon I killed was red like the color of blood. Maybe there are many kinds of dragons.

There is something else that is different about this dragon. It's not moving as fast toward us as the other one. It also isn't breathing fire. The other times I have seen a dragon, they already would have been breathing fire at us. That's when the dragon does the strangest thing: it lands. It is far enough away from us that we cannot hit it with our arrows or stones.

"Hold," I yell, telling the hunters not to attack. "But stand ready!"

Even stranger than it landing in the middle of the field is that the dragon's mouth opens, and a person walks out.

## 49

The dragon's eyes make it hard to see the person. They are a shadow, surrounded by bright light. The shadow walks towards us, very slowly. Then the mouth of the dragon closes.

I look over at Ebb and Mast, and point at the knives. They hand both back to me, and I quickly slide them into their sheaths. I also take my bow, and put it over my shoulder so that my hands are still free, but the bow will stay with me if I need it.

"What do we do?" yells one of the hunters.

"Hold until I tell you otherwise. If this person hurts me in any way, you may attack. Do what you can to save yourselves. Just make sure that it doesn't follow you back to the Crag," I say. "I am going to try to talk to them."

"You are what?" asks Ebb, already knowing the answer.

"I'm going out there. I need to see who they are and how they survived being inside a dragon. If they can control dragons, then maybe we can learn from them. I also don't think this person is dangerous. If they were, they wouldn't be walking into a place where we can easily attack them, while they are unarmed. I don't see them carrying any weapons."

"You don't know that it's safe," says Ebb. "They might have a hidden weapon."

"I'm not going to send someone else in my place. This is my risk to take, my decision," I say.

I walk away from the rock I was hiding behind and put my hands up in the air. I am hoping that the stranger understands that I am not a threat, because I am not holding any weapons. I walk slowly toward them, as they continue walking slowly toward us.

It takes a while to get close enough to see them clearly. It looks like a man, but it is hard to tell through the helmet he is wearing. His armor does not look that different from ours, except it seems harder and stronger.

Finally, he is close enough that I can see his face. He stops, and I can tell that he is just as worried about me as I am of him. Carefully, he raises his arms and takes off his helmet.

His skin is light like mine. He looks like he could be someone from the Crag. Brown hair and blue eyes. Young. I doubt he has seen a handful of snows more than me. I slowly take off my helmet so that he can better see my face. I do my best to smile, hoping he understands that I will not attack him.

He does not smile back. Instead, he speaks.

"Are you Sam?" asks the stranger.

My stomach suddenly feels strange, like someone poured boiling soup into it. How can he possibly know my name, and how does he know how to speak like we do? It takes me a moment to calm down to where I can speak again.

"Yes. I am Sam," I say, wondering if I should have told him.

"Hello, Sam. I'm Carter."

I stare at him, not knowing what to say next.

"Hello," I say stupidly.

He finally tries to smile, but I can tell it isn't easy for him. He's looked at my knives many times now. I think he is worried that if he says the wrong thing, I will use them on him.

"I don't want to hurt you," says Carter.

"I don't want to hurt you either," I say.

"That's good. Sam, I've come to ask for your help."

"My help? You can control a dragon, and you need my help? How do you even know who I am?"

"It may be difficult to understand, but we've been

watching you for a while now, ever since you brought down what you call a 'dragon'," says Carter.

"How could you be watching me? I would have seen you."

"We have ways of seeing and hearing farther than your eyes and ears will let you."

My thoughts argue with each other, and aren't making any sense. It takes me a moment to fight through the noise in my head, to try to understand and believe what he's saying.

"What kind of help do you need?" I ask.

"We are at war, and we are searching for someone to lead us. We believe that person is you, Sam."

"And you want me to come with you? Inside your dragon?" I ask.

"Yes."

"Won't the dragon swallow me? Won't I die?"

"No, it's a very special dragon," says Carter.

"What about the hunters? They need me. And my brother needs me."

"There are millions of people that need you too, Sam. You don't know this, but your people are not the only people in the world. And if we fail, if we don't win this war, your people will die too. The people we're fighting control the dragons that killed your people."

I feel my body become stiff. It takes me a moment to realize I'm holding my breath. Could he really be telling the truth?

"Please, come with me," says Carter.

I think about his words carefully.

"What are millions?" I ask.

Carter looks surprised, but his face relaxes and I can tell that he's figured something out.

"You know all the people that live with you in the cave?" asks Carter.

"Yes."

"Now imagine that each one of the people in the cave had their own cave, filled with that many people."

I close my eyes and try to imagine it, but it's difficult.

"I think I can see it," I say.

"That's about a million people. And there are many, many millions of people out there. Good people. And they need your help," says Carter.

I turn around and look at my own people. The people I tried so hard to hide from before seem like the only thing important to me now. They are all my brothers and sisters. They are my family. How can I leave them?

I look at Flot and I am sure that he doesn't need me anymore. He is strong now. I can tell that he would fight this stranger, and this dragon, to save me. I look at Mast and Helm. They look as surprised and confused as I feel. I look at Ebb, my one true friend. The only person I trusted with my secrets.

I turn back to Carter.

"How can I trust you?" I ask.

I can see in Carter's eyes that he's thinking. He reaches behind him, to his lower back. Fear rushes through me. I spread my legs and bend my knees, and get low to the ground. I pull out one of my knives, ready to attack if I need to.

"Whoa!" says Carter. "Sorry, I'll move more slowly. I'm getting something from my back. It's a weapon, but I want you to have it. That way you know I'm not armed. That I won't hurt you."

I watch Carter slowly pull something metal and shiny from behind his back. He carefully places it on the ground, and takes a few steps back from it.

"I'll stand here. You can pick it up, but be careful; it's very dangerous," says Carter.

"Before I pick it up, tell me how it works," I say.

"Do you see the longest part of the gun?"

"Gun?"

"That's what that is. It's called a gun."

"What does it do?" I ask.

"You know the bow and arrows you use?"

"Yes."

"Well, imagine a very small arrow, about the size of

the tip of your finger. A gun fires small arrows, called bullets, very fast. So fast that your eyes can't even see them moving," says Carter.

"I can make rocks fly that fast with my sling," I say.

"Bullets move even faster than that."

"I don't believe you," I say.

"Well, I'll let you try it for yourself. Do you see the long part of the gun I was talking about? It has a hole at the end. That's where the bullets come out."

I look down at the gun, and I have to move a little to see what he's talking about.

"That long part is called the barrel. When the bullets come out, whatever you aim it at will get hit, so make sure not to point that at yourself when you pick it up," says Carter.

"What makes it fire the bullets?" I ask.

"There's a small, curved piece of metal called a trigger. Do you see it?"

"I think so. I think I see where your hand is supposed to go then."

"That's good. That's called the grip. When you pull the trigger toward the grip, and you pull it hard enough, a bullet will come out. Why don't you go ahead and pick it up now," says Carter.

"Why are you trusting me with your gun?" I ask.

"So that you know you can trust me."

"Is this the only weapon you brought?"

"Yes."

"You aren't very smart," I say.

"Not the first time I've heard that," says Carter.

I pick up the gun and make sure to point the gun's hole away from myself. I aim it away from where the hunters are, and away from Carter and the dragon. I point the gun at a rock that is many steps away, and I pull the trigger back like Carter told me to. Nothing happens.

"It didn't work," I say.

"Oh, that's because the safety is on. Do you see the metal piece just above your thumb, that looks like it might turn?"

"Yes."

"Take the tip of it and push down. It should show you a red dot. That means it's ready to fire," says Carter.

I twist the gun in my hand, so that I can see the metal piece he is talking about. Using my thumb, I slide it down, and I can see the red dot. Turning the gun so that the barrel is now pointing at the rock again, I carefully pull the trigger. The gun makes a sound like sky fire, and it moves back at me so hard that I almost drop the gun on the ground. I do see the rock I'd been aiming at, and a big chunk is missing from it.

"So now that you know you can kill me with the gun, and I gave it to you willingly, do you trust me?" asks Carter.

I look him in the eyes. I raise the gun up toward him then pull the trigger.

## 50

Carter grabs his shoulder then falls to the ground. I can see blood coming out of his armor where I shot him. I look up and I see the dragon. It starts to move upward, as if it's going to attack us.

I watch as Carter turns toward the dragon, and with his good arm waves it away. The dragon stops for a moment, waiting, then rests back on the ground.

"Why did you shoot me?" asks Carter, his teeth held tight together from the pain.

"If you gave me a weapon that couldn't actually hurt you, then you really wouldn't have given me control. You wouldn't have shown that you trusted me at all. I had to see how important I am to you. To see if I can trust you. That you really don't mean us any harm," I say.

"Yeah, well, I wish you could have done it without shooting me. I don't feel so good."

"I'm sorry I hurt you Carter, but I had to know that I could trust you with the lives of my people. It was the only way I could know for sure. I will go with you, but you must take another person with us," I say.

"Sam, would it really be fair to ask Ebb to go with you?"

"How do you know about Ebb?" I ask.

"Like I said, we've been watching from a distance."

"Can I at least say goodbye?"

Carter groans in pain as he slowly stands up.

"It would make things harder for you, and it would make things harder for them. I don't suggest it."

I look back at everyone. Mast and Helm, standing still, not knowing what to do. Flot, confused. Ebb...

I place my right fist over my heart and slide it downward. The hunters drop their weapons to the ground and return my salute. With tears in my eyes I turn away from them, and walk with Carter back to the dragon.

In the wind I hear something that sounds like my name, but I cannot make out the words that are being said. It sounds like Ebb's voice, but it is so far away that I cannot tell.

As we near the dragon, its mouth opens again. I follow Carter inside, as the dragon swallows us whole.

# Acknowledgements

I would like to personally thank the following people for helping in the development of this story. They provided feedback that made *Sky Child* a much stronger book. I owe them a huge debt of gratitude.

Nicole Vesper

Tess Watson

Lisa Sauerwein

Renee Moore

Jennie Hulgaarde

James Thomas

Brandy Kribbs

Zak Kribbs

Michael Kinney

# Special Thanks

I would also like to thank the people who backed the
Kickstarter project and spread the word about this story.
You are my Sky Children.

Nicole Vesper

Renee, Tom and Riley Moore

Jordan Bennett

Tess Watson

Patty McCalister

Brandy and Zak Kribbs

Michael Kinney

Mandy McCalister

Chrystal Clifton

Elizabeth Betts McCarty

Jessica Warren

Holli Rapp

Brandon and Robin Reese

Dawn Angela Martin

Deborah Brenner

Donita Brenner

Lisa Sauerwein

Jennie Hulegaard

Brittany Thompson

Amy Church

James Thomas

Moses Stickney

James Scharmann

Dan Heinig

Rolla Selbak

Blake Eckhoff

Jenna and Jona Sagapolutele

Chris Batchelor

Kirby McCauley

Josephine

Cherie Huber

Jessica Vaupotic

Heather Beam

Jonathan Bisbee

Gary Powers

Erica and Lee Potter

Mckenzie Fritch

Fabio Pigagnelli

Ana Imelda Yerkes

Alyssa JoJo Barger

Natasha Welch

Asta Staal

Steve Gayler

Chloe Jacques

Marie-Christin Holler

Rocio Carter

Rosie McFaul

Ashley Zema

Varity Schwartz

thatraja

David McCready

Christi Bruce

Carolyn Wolfram

Nicole Hall

Kelly Marie McLeod

J. R. Wagner

Melissa and Nick Nelson

Michael Newlyn Blake

Ashley Oswald

Francis Waltz

Brittni Evans

Katie McFarlin

Calum Webb

Jonathan Stevens

The Riggs Family

The Brenners

Andrea Munson

Jane Meade Glanville

Jason Anderson

Lani Ambitious Brownett

Shepherd

Cosmic Lovegood Love

Christopher Glover

Gloria Minor Fridley

Adilia Stiles-Megara

Kathy Houston Ziglar

Stephanie Giusti

Isabel Castruita

Kathryn Jacoby

Sif Hagelskær Jensen

Karen Sawaya

Amy Sawaya

Marie Cherie

Patrick Chan

Felicia Fitterer

Brandy Neuleib

Shane Anderson

Janet Armetani

Sara Abbott

Courtney S.

Casey Fox

Jenice Powell

Amy C. Smith

J. S. Elliot

Stephanie Bujjoni

And anyone else who may have
backed at the last minute but
didn't make this list.

# About the Author

T. M Brenner lives in California with his editor/wife Nicole. He spends most of his free time feeding his writing addiction. When not typing away feverishly on his laptop, he enjoys visiting the coast, watching re-runs of Psych, and spending time with his family.

To find out more about T. M. Brenner's current projects, visit: www.tmbrenner.com